SEVEN

Tracie M. Brown

Seven

ISBN-13: 978-1729693308

ISBN-10: 172969330X

It's All About Him Media & Publishing

P.O. Box 850

Paw Creek, NC 28130

www.aahmp.com

980-522-8096

Chief Editor: Delisa Rodgers-Fields

Editor: James Ancrum

Cover Design: Todd Brown

Assistant Cover Design: Delisa Rodgers-Fields

Illustrator: Sade Brown

CONTENTS

ACKNOWLEDGMENTS

To my loving family: my husband, Allen; my children: Sade, Todd, and Antinea; and my granddaughter, Antinea. Thank you for your support and love through all of my struggles and growth in our Lord Jesus Christ.

Tracie M. Brown

1

LITTLE GIRL

As the sky began to turn gray, the two women sat on the porch, Karen, a beautiful deep brown skin, strong-willed woman who at times can be stubborn, and Michelle, a light skin toned woman. The two women were the best of friends, sitting on opposite sides of Michelle's small porch watching as people walked their dogs up and down the street and others rode their bikes. Their watching was interrupted with, "Looks like it's going to rain," Karen said with the hoarseness in her voice that she had since the day she learned to speak.

Michelle responded jokingly as she glanced at the sky, "Looks can be deceiving," smiling and laughing at the same time.

Karen thought to herself while laughing with Michelle, *I like Michelle. She loves to laugh, is always talking about her Lord Jesus, and is always trying to get me to come to her church!*

"Hey, Karen!" Michelle speaks with a low tone in her voice. "Do you think I'm too old to start a career?" she asks, occasionally glancing at the sky.

"Michelle why are you asking me that?" Karen answered with a puzzled look on her face.

"You know, Karen, sometimes I think I've gotten too old to go back to school and start a career!"

"Michelle, if you want to go back to school, then go! Didn't you tell me you can do all things through your Christ Jesus?"

"What is wrong with you today?" Michelle spoke with sternness in her voice while rubbing her belly in a hungry motion.

Karen, looking at Michelle's hand, shrugged her shoulders. "I don't know Michelle. I'm feeling some kind of way, not necessarily bad or you know, just in my feelings!"

"Look, Karen! Let's go into the house and get something to drink then maybe you can explain to me what these feelings are you are feeling."

Karen threw her hand up in the air. "I can feel the wind picking up anyway." The sound of thunder (BOOM BOOM), ripped through the sky in the middle of Karen's sentence followed by a strike of lighting. Both women jumped to their feet at once, making a beeline into the house.

"Wow! We got in just in time," Karen laughed.

In the kitchen, they began looking for fruit and water, anything healthy to drink. Both women believed in eating healthy, well, except for an occasional red meat eaten by Karen or Michelle's daily milkshake that she's so desperately trying to detox from, going from large to medium and now two.

"May I please have a small strawberry milkshake?" Michelle started placing the fruit both women were able to collect in the kitchen in her juicer to make their smoothies.

"Michelle," Karen said while sitting on the kitchen counter looking at her newly polished toenails and deciding she did not like the color she let the lady at the nail place pick. "I don't want to talk about you and a career, girl, because you know as well as I do, you can always go back to school. Shoot, everybody is going back these days! Soon, fast food places are going to start asking for an associate degree to flip burgers and drop fries in grease!"

Both women let out a loud giggle as Michelle handed Karen a glass of fruit smoothie. Karen decided to ask Michelle a question that she had been wondering about for a while but just kept putting it off.

"Michelle, let me ask you something! Why are you always talking and praying to Jesus?"

"Karen, girl, you just don't know! I love my Lord Jesus because everything and anything is possible through the Father in heaven. Karen, all these years we have known each other, I'd say about ten, eleven, right?"

"Think so," Karen answered in the middle of sipping on her smoothie. As Michelle continued to speak, Karen started looking in cabinets and the refrigerator for something to satisfy her hunger. Michelle kept on talking while looking at her friend ramble through her kitchen. Karen is a trip, but I love her, Jesus! She whispered to herself.

"There was this girl who everyone called, Little Girl! KAREN!" Michelle raised her voice, "Are you listening to me? I'm trying to tell you something!"

"Yeah! I'm listening," Karen spoke. "Dag, you ain't got nothing in here to eat!"

"It's not ain't, Karen! It's you don't have!" Michelle responded.

Karen responded back with, "Whatever! I'm hungry, and I feel like a hamburger, cheeseburger, something with lettuce, tomato, and a pickle on it! Look, Michelle. I'll buy you a small strawberry shake if we run to the drive-thru!"

"You always do that, Karen!"

"Do what, Michelle?"

"You know exactly what I am talking about, Karen. When you feel like eating your red meat, you tempt me with buying me a shake!"

"Okay, then let's go!" Karen laughed while Michelle searched for her umbrella. "Whose car are we taking?"

Jumping into Karen's car, the women headed to the drive-thru.

"So, what about this little girl you started talking about?" Karen asked while feeling a little guilty for putting her hunger in front of what her friend started to talk about.

"Well, Little Girl," and just as Michelle began to speak,

"May I take your order?" A voice came from the speaker drive-thru.

"Wait, wait, wait a minute," Karen whispered to Michelle. "Yes, ma'am! May I please have a cheeseburger with pickles, ketchup, and oh, a small strawberry shake, please! Thank you!"

After Karen gave her food order, she turned to Michelle, "Sorry about that!"

"Oh, that's okay, "Karen," Michelle said with a smile. "I should know by now nothing comes between you and your hunger!"

"Ha Ha!" Karen snarled playfully, "Okay, so what's going on with this little girl you were beginning to tell me about?" Karen spoke.

"You know what Karen? Why don't we just wait till we get back home? I'm not going to keep starting something when you have food on your mind. It seems like I can't compete with your red meat. What happened to us eating healthy?"

"Oh, come on Michelle! I got you a shake plus, a little red meat every now and then won't kill us!"

"Us? You mean you?" replied Michelle laughing at Karen.

"Look, Michelle! Over there! What the.. ..?"

"You dare, Karen? Thought you are were trying to stop cursing!"

"Whatever!" Karen laughed. "Look at that woman. What in the world is she wearing? Doesn't she know it's raining?"

Both women could not help themselves and busted out laughing.

"Now who told her it was alright to walk out of her house wearing bright yellow leggings and a least four missing tracks of hair from her head? And look at her shoes! They are yellow with an orange strip!"

"Karen, girl, you need to stop talking about people!"

"Michelle, come on, girl! You have to be honest! You know that looks funny!"

"Yeah, you're right? It is kind of weird looking!"

The two friends received their food and headed back to Michelle's house. On the drive back, both women rode in silence, each one in their own thoughts. Finally arriving back to the house and exiting the car, Karen turns to Michelle, "Michelle, what happened to the little girl?" she asks as they walk in the house and settle on the couch.

"Little Girl." Michelle begins to talk in a low tone.

~LITTLE GIRL~

"Hello, little girl, we are your new parents!" Standing in front of the voice was this little skinny light, skinned girl. She watched the woman's lips part to speak, each word coming out like in slow motion. The social worker held the little girl's hand and moved her closer to the strangers who would now become parents number four.

She spoke to Little Girl, "This nice lady is Mrs. Johnson. She and her husband wanted another girl and have decided to become foster parents to you. So, I expect you to be well behaved and listen to what Mrs. Johnson tells you. Okay?"

Little Girl just stood there, not saying a word and looking at her new parent's face. *Ugh!* She thought to herself. *This woman is ugly, and she smells old.*

"Is she shy?" Mrs. Johnson asked the social worker.

The social worker moved up closer to Mrs. Johnson and whispered in her ear. "This one is a quiet one and is always claiming someone has done something to her. You know how children are; they have a big imagination if you know what I mean. I'm sure you all will get along just fine." As the social worker continued to speak, a very tall man walked into the room.

"Well, well! What have we here? Hello, I'm Mr. Johnson!" extending his arm to shake the social worker's hand.

"Hello, Mr. Johnson! It's a pleasure to meet you," responded the social worker. "This here is Little Girl; she is your new daughter!"

"Well, Little Girl, I'm happy to meet you!"

Once again, Little Girl just stood feeling like she just stepped into the twilight zone. Without speaking a word, Little Girl moved closer to the social worker. "Now, now," spoke the social worker, "everything is going to be fine," while pushing Little Girl towards her new daddy, Mr. Johnson. "Well it's time for me to go," the social worker spoke again. "Here are her belongings and my number if you need to contact me for any reason."

"Well, that won't be necessary! We just thank you so much for everything!" Mrs. and Mr. Johnson told the social worker.

Mr. Johnson then turned to Little Girl, "Little Girl, what's your name?"

"Everyone calls her Little Girl as a nickname since she's so skinny," answered the worker. "She won't answer to any other name, and that is a puzzle to me, but anyway, you all have my number. I have to run. Goodbye Little Girl," the social worker said while reaching over to hug Little Girl, but Little Girl just nudged her little body away.

After closing the front door behind the social worker, Mr. Johnson headed back upstairs. "Come with me, honey," spoke Mrs. Johnson to Little Girl. "You must be hungry. Let's see if I can find you something to fill that tiny belly of yours!"

Little Girl followed her new mother into the kitchen. "What's that smell? Yuck!" Little Girl whispered thinking Mrs. Johnson didn't hear her and didn't see the frown that came across Mrs. Johnson's face.

"Here we are," pulling out some stale bologna and placing it between two slices of white bread. Mrs. Johnson placed the dry sandwich on a saucer then filled a glass with water and handed it to Little Girl. "There you are.

This should hold you till dinner. When you finish, I will show you where everything's located in the house."

Little Girl looked at the sandwich on her plate but as hungry as she was, she would not touch it, so she just drank the glass of water. Fifteen minutes passed by when Mrs. Johnson returned. Mrs. Johnson, seeing that the sandwich was not eaten, just simply picked the saucer and sandwich up and placed it in the refrigerator. "We don't waste food in this house, so you can have this for lunch tomorrow, okay?" she said while looking straight into Little Girl's brown eyes, "And by the way, when are you going to speak? Any normal eight-year-old talks. What's wrong with your tongue? You haven't said a word since you got here; well, other than that nasty remark I heard you make about the smell in my kitchen."

Little Girl, looking straight at Mrs. Johnson said in a tiny whisper, "I don't like bologna; your water is nasty. Yuck!"

"WELL!" Mrs. Johnson said in a shocking voice, her eyes bulging out of her face. "Come," grabbing Little Girl's arm, "and let's get you settled in then."

Little Girl followed the woman up a flight of stairs and then up another set of stairs stopping at the top.

"This is our attic but as you see it's been fixed up. Here's your room and look, it has a toilet and sink. Now over there is our daughter's room."

Little Girl, looking surprised, asked, "You have a daughter?"

"Yes, she is thirteen years old and should be coming in pretty soon. She's been playing over at her friend's house down the street. I want you to be nice to her. She is my flesh and blood."

Just as Mrs. Johnson finished her sentence, a very sad and lonely feeling engulfed Little Girl. "Now you go and unpack your suitcase. You can put your things in the dresser over there." Mrs. Johnson pointed her finger to a very small dresser sitting in the left corner of the room. "Now, I'm going downstairs to start preparing dinner. If you need anything, come down and let me know. Oh, also I will explain your chores to you and, according to the papers that the social worker left, I see you have a therapist you see once a week. We will talk about all this later." Mrs. Johnson closed the door behind herself as she left the room.

Little Girl looked around the room and began to cry as she proceeded to put her things away in the small dresser. As she pushed the drawer closed, something caught the corner of her eye. There, next to the mirror, was the most beautiful doll sitting on the floor she ever saw. Little Girl walked over, picked up the doll, and held it like it was her very best friend. For some reason, she found comfort in the doll, so she and the doll laid down across the bed. Without realizing it, Little Girl fell off to sleep.

"Knock knock! Hey, are you okay?" came a voice from the other side of Little Girl's bedroom.

"Hey," Little Girl opened her eyes and answered the voice. "Yes, come in." Opening the door, there stood in the doorway a girl.

"Hi, my name is Betty! What's yours?"

"I'm Little Girl!"

"Why do people call you that? Don't you have a real name?"

"Everybody always called me Little Girl. All the foster daddies I had called me that. My first foster daddy named me that, so that's my name."

All of a sudden, Little Girl found herself talking away to this girl named Betty.

"Do you want to come into my room and play with my dolls with me?" Betty asked with a smile. "I'm thirteen but I still like to play with my dolls. My daddy is always buying me new things if I'm a good girl."

The two girls walked into Betty's room. Little Girl's eyes popped out her head. "You have a lot of toys," she said to Betty. Betty just smiled back.

The two girls began to play with the dolls and other toys Betty's father gives her for being a good girl. A few hours went by, and both girls heard Mrs. Johnson yelling from the bottom of the stairs. "D I N N E R T I M E! You two up there!"

"Okay, mommy! Here we come," Betty yelled back. "We'd better hurry up, Little Girl! Mommy hates when we aren't on time for dinner."

Both girls ran down the stairs sounding like a herd of cattle straight into the kitchen, plopping down in the chairs at the table. Looking down at her plate, Little Girl was shocked to see what laid on her plate: fried chicken, mashed potatoes, and corn on the cob. *Yum! Better than a nasty bologna sandwich*, Little Girl thought to herself.

Mrs. Johnson looked at the two girls, "Where's your daddy?" asking Betty while looking at Little Girl shrugging her shoulders.

Betty responded with a, "I don't know, mommy!"

"Well, you two girls start eating while I go and get him."

The girls proceeded to eat their dinner. "YUCK!" Little Girl let out a scream. "This taste nasty! YUCK!"

"What's wrong?" Betty asked, looking bewildered.

"I don't like this food," Little Girl answered.

"You'd better eat it all! Mommy doesn't like it when we throw food away!"

"Don't like what?" came a voice. Mr. Johnson was standing in the kitchen with his wife.

"Nothing!" Betty said quickly.

"Well then, let's eat," Mr. Johnson said while he and his wife sat at the table. "So, tell me Little Girl, do you like your room?" he asked while swallowing his food without chewing.

Little Girl shrugged her shoulders, "I don't know," she whispered.

"Well," Mr. Johnson said, "I'll come up and see that everything is good. Did you find the doll I put in there for you?"

"Yes," whispered Little Girl.

Mrs. Johnson interrupted her husband and turned to Little Girl. "Now young lady, after dinner you will help Betty wash the dishes, and then I want you and Betty to get ready for bed. Betty will show you where everything is you need."

After dinner was through, both girls finished washing dishes then Betty showed Little Girl where the bathroom was.

"Mommy and daddy use another bathroom," Betty told Little Girl. "Mommy says she doesn't like using the same bathroom I use, but daddy, he always uses this bathroom, sometimes even when I'm taking my bath. But daddy is nice. He says it's important that a daughter and her father get close. He just sits on the toilet and talks to me or while he's peeing. Then the next day, I find a new toy in my room.

"Mommy and daddy always say I'm thirteen, but my brain is small. I'm going to my room now," Betty said to Little Girl. "See you upstairs!"

"Okay," said Little Girl. Little Girl stood at the sink afraid to undress after what she just heard Betty tell her, so she just put on her PJ's and headed upstairs straight to her room for she did not want to talk to anymore to Betty or listen to any more stories. She crawled under the covers with the beautiful doll that she found in her room earlier. As her head rested on her pillow, a small tear rolled down her cheek.

"Hey," came a deep voice standing over her. "Just checking to see if everything is okay with you. I see you have the doll in the bed with you."

Little Girl moved to the other side of the bed, frightened like a small kitten left out in the cold alone. He had that same odor her two other foster fathers always had. He had been drinking.

"Come over here," Mr. Johnson whispered to her, his speech slurred. "Come give your new daddy a kiss goodnight! COME HERE, I SAID!" raising his voice a little. Little Girl just laid there, not moving a muscle. "Never mind, daddy will come to his Little Girl." Mr. Johnson reached out, grabbed Little Girl, and pulled her close to him. Little Girl in her heart knew what was going to happen next but hoped it wouldn't. Mr. Johnson reached under her nightshirt with his big ugly rough hand and began moving and exploring then the big ugly hand proceeded to move down. Little Girl laid there in a small voice whimpering how much it hurts. When the big ugly hand was finally through, it stumbled to its feet and walked out of the room, closing the door behind it. Little Girl laid there half clothed as each lonely tear fell from her tiny eyes.

~Karen and Michelle~

Karen sat there with a half-eaten red meat hamburger and a pickle hanging out the side, eyes wide open as if she was stoned on some kind of drug. She noticed Michelle's face had no expression on it. "Are you okay, Michelle?"

"Yeah, girl." Michelle jumped like she was being woken from a dream.

"So, what happened next?" Karen anxiously asked like she was waiting for her next fix. Karen was no longer hungry. Her thoughts were on every word that was flowing from Michelle's mouth. I wonder who Michelle is talking about? Could the Little Girl be Michelle? If it was, Karen was not going to ask. Not now anyway.

"Michelle, can we get something to drink? My mouth is dry, and I am feeling; I can't even explain what I'm feeling."

"Sure," answered Michelle. "What do you want to drink, or do you want another cheeseburger," laughed Michelle. Karen was not in the mood for a funny and did not understand how or why Michelle could make any kind of a joke. (Karen just didn't know the faith Michelle had in God.)

"Just get me a bottle of water from the fridge!"

"Okie, dokie! Coming right up!"

"So, what happened to Little Girl, Michelle?"

"Well, Little Girl told the social worker when she came for her next visit what Mr. Johnson had done to her, and she was removed from that foster home."

"Did Mr. Johnson go to jail?"

"Nope, Karen, he did not because the social worker did not report it. She lied and said Little Girl was just unhappy and being disorderly. You know, Karen, so many people don't listen to what children have to say. They just believe the adults. Children have voices. God blessed us all with a voice, and I believe that children need to be heard."

"Yeah, you're right, Michelle. So, what happened after they took her from that home?"

"She was placed in another. In this new place, Little Girl lived there about seven years. This was the longest time she ever stayed in one foster home, but the scars from the Little Girl's childhood would remain with her for many, many years."

~Little Girl~

By now, Little Girl was around thirteen years old. As Little Girl walked home from junior high school, she smiled at the boy and girl who were holding hands walking in front of her. *I wonder if their parents know they hold hands*, she thought to herself. *Oh well, let me hurry home before I get into trouble for being late; plus, I have to pee.* As her steps became faster almost running, she busted into the door, making a beeline straight to the bathroom.

"Little Girl is that you?"

"Yes, mommy! I'm in the bathroom." As Little Girl exited the bathroom and entered the kitchen, she looked at her foster mother. "Hi, mommy!"

"How was school, Little Girl? Do you have homework?"

"Yes, mommy. I'm going to do it right now." As she sat down at the kitchen table, she proceeded to do her studies.

"Mommy?" looking up to watch her mother, Mrs. Williams, who is a widow in her 40's and a very compassionate woman yet very strict and set in her ways. "Mommy, what's for dinner?"

"Let's see, Little Girl!" Mrs. Williams turned and smiled at her. "What about red beans, rice, spinach, and fried chicken? How does that sound?"

"Sounds good to me, mommy!"

"Well, you finish up your homework so that you can set the table."

"Okay, I'm almost finished." Little Girl quickly finished her studies, picked up her books, and headed to her bedroom. As she came closer to her room, her steps became slow. She didn't like bedrooms or being alone in one. Little Girl entered her room, throwing her books on her bed. She noticed a beautiful yellow dress lying across her bed. "WOW!" she yelled out loud as she picked up the dress and pressed it against her body. "Mommy, thanks! Thanks, mommy," yelling and running down the hallway into the kitchen.

"You're welcome, honey," Mrs. Williams responded with a laugh. "Where's the box, Little Girl?"

"What box, mom?"

"The box on the floor near your bed."

"You got me shoes, mommy? You bought me the shoes I wanted?"

"Yes, honey. Now go try them on and see if they fit. If not, we have to take them back and exchange them."

"No, they'll fit!" yelled Little Girl. "I know they'll fit!"

"Girl! Go get the shoes," laughed Mrs. Williams.

"Okay, I'm going!" Off she raced back to her room, returning with the prettiest yellow shoes to match her dress. "Can I wear my new dress and shoes to school tomorrow? Please, please!"

"Yes, you can! Please, Little Girl, don't tear the dress or get the shoes dirty from fighting!"

"Okay!" Little Girl said with a sly smile, knowing to herself if someone hit her she would punch their lights out.

That night, Little Girl laid in her bed unable to sleep, so she walked into her mommy's room (Mrs. Williams'). "Mommy, can I sleep with you?"

"Yes, child! Come on, but don't you dare kick me!" answered Mrs. Williams. Little girl crawled into the bed and fell off to sleep.

Putting on her new dress and shoes and after eating breakfast, Little Girl headed out for school.

"Hey, Little Girl!" came a yell from the end of the street.

"Hi, Suzy!" Little Girl yelled back. "Come on hurry up!" Suzy was Little Girl's best friend.

"I like your dress and shoes!" Suzy spoke loudly.

"Thank you! My mommy bought it yesterday. She surprised me. It was on my bed when I went into my room." Both girls walked to school giggling and laughing.

Mrs. Williams cleaned the breakfast dishes and sat down in her favorite chair in her living room. Not feeling too well and knowing she needed to make it to her doctor's appointment, but not wanting to drive, she decided she would call a cab. Content with her decision, she walked into her bedroom and began getting ready for her day. Two hours later, Mrs. Williams sat waiting to be seen by her doctor.

"Mrs. Williams, the doctor will see you now," the nurse called.

"Hello, Mrs. Williams! How are you feeling today?" spoke her doctor.

"Not too good, Dr. Jones."

"Mrs. Williams, your blood pressure is up again. Are you taking your medications and I mean all of them, Mrs. Williams?"

"Yes, Dr. Jones, but the pain in my legs just seems not to want to go away."

"Mrs. Williams, I want to check you into the hospital for a few days just to run a few tests."

"Oh, no!" Mrs. Williams fussed. "I have to take care of my Little Girl, doctor, "and I refuse to leave her with anyone."

"Okay then, Mrs. Williams. I'll set up a few tests I can run here. I want you to make an appointment at the desk for the next few weeks."

"Thanks, Doctor."

After the visit with the doctor, Mrs. Williams arrived home and just laid across her bed to take a nap before Little Girl came from school, wondering to herself, I have got to take better care of myself for Little Girl. That child needs me so much, as she drifted off to sleep.

~Michelle and Karen~

Michelle suddenly stopped talking. "Hey, Michelle!" Karen screamed, "What's wrong?"

"I'm tired, Karen and I am hungry again but for something sweet. I want some junk food. Let's walk to the store; I don't feel like driving." Karen did not want to walk, but for some reason, she did not feel like saying so.

"Okay, Michelle! Let's cheat on our healthy food diet!" Karen could always make Michelle laugh.

"Come on, girl. Let's walk!"

The women put on their shoes, exited the house, and began walking up the street.

"Hey, Michelle!" Karen was hesitating to ask but asked anyway. "So, what happened next with Little Girl?"

"Karen, do you mind if we talk about something else for a minute?"

"Michelle! Really! You're going to do this to me, just leave me in the water to drown!"

"Oh, girl, please!" Michelle laughed. "You are so dramatic, Karen! I don't feel like talking about Little Girl right now."

"Michelle, look at me! I'm going under! Glup! Glup!" Karen said, imitating the sounds of someone drowning. "Can you at least tell me what happened with Mrs. Williams? Please, pretty please! It's my treat at the store!"

"You think you can always buy your way, Karen. Karen, I don't need you to pay for anything for me. My Jesus paid the one price for me a very long time ago.

Anyway, when are you coming to church with me? You said one day you were coming, and you have yet to show your face!"

"I'm coming, Michelle! I promise!"

"Whatever, Karen!" Michelle said as they both entered the store.

The two women browsed through the aisles of the convenient store as Michelle continued to tell the story of Little Girl.

~Little Girl~

Little Girl sat in the waiting room alone. It was just yesterday when she and the woman she called mommy, her foster mother, Mrs. Williams, celebrated Little Girl's sixteenth birthday. Both went out to dinner, to the movies, and Mrs. Williams had a surprise party for Little Girl with all of her friends. Now today, Little Girl sits, waiting to hear what the doctors are going to tell her about the one person who ever cared about her. Little Girl knew the woman whom she called mommy had a bad heart. She knew her mommy would try to hide her pain at times. As Little Girl sat and watched the clock, her mind began to wonder, and as she began to think hard, she realized her mommy was very nice, showed her compassion, and would always smile and laugh with her, but Little Girl could not remember one time when her mommy said, "I love you, Little Girl." Little Girl pushed that thought to the back of her mind where she stored everything else in her life.

"Excuse me, Miss!" Little Girl looked up to find the doctor and another lady standing in front of her. "I'm so sorry," the doctor whispered, "but we were unable to save your mother. Is there anyone here with you?"

"No!" yelled Little Girl, feeling empty, angry, and sad. "Well, this nice lady will help you. She's from child welfare."

Little Girl looked at the doctor, then at the lady, and started running straight out the hospital door onto unfamiliar streets. There was no way anyone was going to put her in anyone else's home. Little Girl ran and ran until she could run no more.

When she finally came to a stop, she found herself in an unfamiliar area. *What do I do?* She thought to herself. *Maybe if I go back to the house, I could stay there.*

But she knew the social workers would come there plus her mommy's (Mrs. Williams') family would be there, and she knew they would not take her in. They liked her, but that didn't mean they wanted her to live with them.

Little Girl walked on scared and hungry until she found herself a small spot under a stairway and crawled into it. As she curled herself into a little ball, she slowly began to weep. Once again, she's alone, and as she wept, all she could ask herself was, *Whose Little Girl am I?*

~Karen and Michelle~

"How much?" Karen spoke with a crackling voice to the cashier.

"$10.65, Miss," spoke the cashier as she noticed the tears running down Karen's face. "Are you okay, Miss?"

"Yes," Karen whispered back. Michelle grabbed Karen's arm, and they both walked out of the store.

"Karen, look at me. We are going to give the story of Little Girl a rest for now."

"Michelle, let me ask you a question. Who is Jesus, really? I know He's God's Son, but that's all I know. I mean, I know about Easter, Christmas, and those holidays we celebrate."

"Karen, those holidays you mentioned are pagan holidays. They are not the holy days. Listen, Karen, when you come over tomorrow, you are coming after you get off from work?"

"Yeah, I'll be by. Where else am I going? I mean, my husband left me for that young girl. I don't have any children. I'm tired of going out to the clubs. Man, my life sucks!"

"Don't say that! You don't know what God's will is for you!"

"See, that's what I'm talking about, Michelle! I don't know any of that stuff! You know when you were telling the story of Little Girl, it got me to thinking about all the stupid stuff I think is so important and the way I talk about people who are homeless. You know what I also say, "Why don't they just get a job? Why can't they wash up somewhere; all they have to do is go into a restroom somewhere and clean themselves! Or, where's their family? I mean Michelle, where's my compassion for people less fortunate than me? I feel bad. I'm always shopping, buying the latest fashion." Karen spoke looking straight into Michelle's eyes.

"Michelle, you are a stubborn woman, but you are stubborn in the way that no one can turn you away from your Jesus."

"Karen don't beat yourself up. If you want to know Jesus and I mean truly want Jesus in your life, just ask. Scripture says, "If you seek, you shall find, knock, and the door shall open, ask, and it shall be given." Look, Karen, are you ready to accept Jesus Christ as your personal savior?"

"What does that mean, Michelle? You ask me questions that I don't understand. Why would Jesus want me? Look at the things I've done and said and let's not forget the year I helped my husband write those bad checks just, so we could take a trip! Why would God or Jesus want anything to do with me? If you weren't my friend...wait a minute, why are you, my friend?"

At that moment, Karen just broke down and wept like a baby. "Why Michelle? Why? What's happening to me? I'm strong! Why do I feel so small right now?"

"Karen, we all fall short of our Lord's glory for we were all born into sin. We are not perfect, but our Lord has mercy and grace and is a forgiving God. Karen, our Lord has a way of humbling us. Lets' pray!"

"Right here, Michelle? In the middle of the sidewalk, Michelle? What will people think? What will they say?"

"Yes sweetie, right here. Never be ashamed of our Lord for if you are ashamed of Him, then He will be ashamed of you. Give me your hands, close your eyes, and open your heart.

"Lord, God, we praise You. We honor You and give You the highest reverence. Lord, we magnify Your name. My Lord, I ask You to touch Karen.

"Show her that You love her, too. Show her if it were not for You, she would not have been able to wake up today for You breathed life in her this morning. Cover her Lord with Your glory for it is through You dying on the cross that our sins are forgiven. Only through You, all and everything is possible for You are the beginning and the end, the Alpha and Omega in Jesus' name we pray, amen.

"How do you feel, Karen?"

"I don't know! I felt calm and filled with a lot of questions."

Michelle smiled at her friend and with a low voice said, "Thank You, my Lord."

"So, what happens now Michelle?"

"Well, I want you to get in your car and drive home. When you get there, find a place in your house where you can call your closet. That will be a place where you go all the time and spend the time to pray and talk with Jesus. You see, you need to have a personal relationship with Him, just you and Him, but first, I need to ask you this. Do you believe that Jesus Christ died on the cross and rose on the third day so that our sins can be forgiven, and we can have eternal life?"

"Michelle, this is a lot for me."

"Okay, Karen! Go home, open your Bible, and read. First, pray. Get on your knees, or you can lay face down, arms stretched, and humble yourself at God's feet. Just talk to Him from your heart because that's where He lives, okay. Now, hug me and get going."

"I love you, Michelle!"

"I love you too, Karen!

Karen retrieved her purse from Michelle's house, got into her car, and drove away. Michelle sat down on her couch and began to thank her Lord for where she is today. Well, let me go take my shower and do my studying.

The sound of keys in the door alerted Michelle. "Hey, Hon!"

"Hello!" Michelle's husband of 35 years came in from work. "Hon, I'm tired! What did you cook for dinner?"

"Sweetie, I'm so sorry! Karen was over here and..."

"Never mind, I'll grab a sandwich."

"No sweetie, I'll bake some chicken and steam some veggies. It won't take long!"

"Alright then! I'm going to wash this dirt off."

Michelle headed into the kitchen to start cooking dinner for her husband. "I'm blessed, and I give You all the glory my Lord." When dinner was done, Michelle and her husband, Joe, sat down and ate. "So, how was your day, Joe?"

"Busy! Michelle, come here!"

"Oh no, not tonight Joe!" Michelle said laughing. "I am exhausted too!"

"Well, tell me what did you and Karen do today? Did you get a strawberry milkshake?"

"Ha Ha! You got jokes, Joe! Go to sleep!"

Joe reached over to give Michelle a kiss. "Good night, hon!"

Michelle laid there in the dark, not wanting to disturb her husband with turning on the light. She began to turn back time to when Little Girl was homeless.

~Little Girl~

Little Girl woke up from under the stairs cold and scared.

"Hey, girl! What are you doing under my stairway?"

Little Girl jumped to her feet and took off running. She stopped in front of a small grocery store. Entering it, she walked down the aisles placing small items of food in her jacket and pockets. She then picked up a soda and went to the front of the store and paid for it. *Wow, that was easy*, she thought to herself.

Little Girl began walking up the street not having any idea where she would go so she hopped on the train and just rode from one end to the other. She noticed a boy who also was riding from one end to the other and who also was watching her.

"What are you looking at?" Little Girl asked. The boy got up from where he was sitting and came and plopped himself next to her.

"Hi, I'm Steve! Who are you?"

"I'm Little Girl!"

"Who?"

"I said, I'm Little Girl!"

"I don't like that! You don't look like a little girl! I'm going to call you, Sunshine! You like that nickname?"

"I don't care what you call me! I don't know you!"

"Sunshine!" the boy Steve said. "I can tell you are homeless, too."

"I am not!" yelled Little Girl.

"Yes, you are! I watched you take food out of your pockets and plus your face is dirty, and your clothes are wrinkled, and you smell!"

"Shut up!" Little Girl yelled again.

"Can I have some of your food, please! I'm hungry, Sunshine! Please!"

"Here!" Little Girl handed him a pack of cookies for it was not in her heart to see someone hungry.

"So, are you going to ride the train all night?"

"I guess so," Little Girl responded.

"Come with me; I have a place I go to when I get tired of riding. It's just two more stops from here."

"Alright then. I'll come with you, but if you touch me, Imma punch you in your face!"

Steve laughed. "Come on, Sunshine! We need to look out for each other!"

Both kids got off two stops away, and Little Girl followed him on a long walk into a park then into a small cave made from a huge rock. "How old are you Steve?"

"Oh, I'm sixteen, will be seventeen soon though."

Little Girl looked around the inside of the cave. She could tell he was living here. There were dirty blankets and trash from stolen food. "Here, you can lay down here!" he pointed to the opposite side of the cave. "Thanks," whispered Little Girl.

"Why are you homeless, Steve? Don't you have anyone who likes you?"

"Nah," Steve replied, "well I do have one sister. My folks died a year ago, and the state put my sister and me in foster care. I didn't like it. I kept getting in trouble in school. Plus, I don't like living with strangers."

"I'm a stranger!" laughed Little Girl.

"That's different; you aren't a grownup."

"You're funny!" laughed Little Girl.

"Sunshine why are you homeless?"

"My foster mother, the only person who cared about me, died. And me too! I didn't want to belong to the state anymore."

"Sunshine, we have a lot in common."

"Yeah, I guess! Let's go to sleep. Good night, Steve."

"Good night, Sunshine."

~Michelle~

Michelle turned over and started to cry. She did not want her husband, Joe, to hear her.

"Lord, I'm emptying my pitcher, so that I can be filled up." It's good to cry; not every cry is a sad cry. "Lord," Michelle continued to talk to the Lord, "I'm happy. You truly have given me all I need. Sometimes, Lord, I get to feeling that my flesh feels like picking up a cigarette and smoking. I know You delivered me from that. I know I can't allow my flesh to rise above my spirit man, so I pray to You for strength. Also, my Lord, guide me and give me the words to speak to Karen for whatever Your will is for me, it will be done. I know it will be done for the good in Jesus' name I pray, amen."

~Little Girl and Steve~

As the sun rose, both kids awoke to voices surrounding them in the park. "Sunshine," the nickname Steve calls Little Girl, "we are going to have to move until night. Let's go."

"Why and where are we going, Steve?"

"Anywhere we can get some money and food. Follow me!" Little Girl walked next to Steve down a long street. There were women wearing shirt skirts and waving at cars. "Sunshine, I want you to wait here. Don't move until I get back. I'm going to get us some money for food."

Little Girl didn't know what to think, so she did what Steve asked her and waited. She watched Steve walk a little way off and wave a car down. The car stopped, and Steve got in it.

"Hey, girl! What are you doing here? This is my corner!" a very tall woman spoke.

Little Girl turned to look at who was talking to her. "I'm waiting on my friend," Little Girl said nervously.

"Well, wait somewhere else! You're messing with my money!"

"I'm sorry! I didn't mean to, but my friend asked me not to move."

"Girl!" the woman spoke harshly. "Move now, or you're going to wear my foot up your you know what!"

So, Little Girl walked down to the next street block and stood for what seemed to be forever and just as she was thinking about leaving, she saw a hand waving at her.

"Sunshine! Sunshine!" It was Steve calling her and running towards her. "Why didn't you stay where I asked you to?"

"Steve, some woman told me to move!"

"Oh, that probably was Juicy! She thinks everyone is taking her business away from her if someone stands on her corner. Sorry about that Sunshine."

"Where did you go, Steve? And what business? Steve, who is Juicy?"

"Look, Sunshine, I'll explain later. Come on, you hungry? I have some money! Let's go eat!"

"Hey, where did you get money from?"

"Just come on, girl. Hey, you want Micky Dees?"

"Who?"

"McDonald's, Sunshine! Where did you grow up, in a cave?"

"Leave me alone, Steve."

"I'm sorry! I don't want you to be mad with me; you're my Sunshine!"

"Whatever, Steve!"

They both entered McDonald's and walked up to the counter. "So, what do you want, Sunshine?"

"What do you want, Steve?" Steve ordered a strawberry milkshake and a Big Mac with fries. "Give me the same, Steve!"

"Sunshine, I love strawberry milkshakes!" From that day on, Little Girl would always order strawberry milkshakes also.

The young kids sat eating their meal. "Hey, Sunshine! There's a shelter not far from here you could stay at if you want."

"Where will you stay, Steve?"

"Don't worry about me; I'll be fine Sunshine. I just don't want you on the streets. It's crazy out here; things happen. Soon, you may get caught up in that ugly stuff."

"What ugly stuff, Steve? That stuff you were doing when you got in that car? I'm not stupid, Steve. I know you were doing something wrong. I just didn't want you to know I knew, and I knew what your friend, Juicy was doing. Why do that anyway?"

"Sunshine, you have a better way or know a better way to make money?"

"No! I don't, Steve! What's this shelter like?"

"They have it where you have to be under twenty-one, and you have to be in an at a certain time. Also, you can go to school in there."

"It sounds nice, Steve! How come you aren't in there?"

"I kept getting jumped on from some boys because I'm gay!"

"Why are you gay? I've never met a gay person before!"

"Sunshine, I don't know. I just like boys. I could say it's because of the things that happened to me when I was younger, but I think I just like boys. Anyway, let's talk about what we are going to do today? Do you want me to take you to the shelter?"

"Okay, but what if I don't like it? Where are you going to be?"

"I'll go to the Village on West 4th street every day about 4 o'clock and wait awhile. If I don't see you, then I'll know you are still there. Anyway, you should come to let me know how you are doing, okay!"

"Okay, Steve. I'm ready. I just don't want to leave you."

"Ah, I'll be fine. Come on, Sunshine."

So, the two walked for a while. "How much further, Steve?" asked Sunshine.

"We are almost there. We just have to past this park and then maybe another five blocks. You're okay, Sunshine. I'll always take care of you, okay. You are my Sunshine, okay!" Then Steve kissed her on the cheek. "Well, we are here. That's the shelter."

Sunshine looked at the tall ugly brick building. As they approached the front door, Steve looked at his Sunshine (Little Girl) and thought to himself, *Hope she meets me in the village.*

"Well, Sunshine, go in and tell them you don't have anywhere to live. Don't forget! Meet me tomorrow in the Village West 4th Street, okay?"

"Okay, Steve! Bye!"

Little Girl opened the front door and proceeded down a short hallway. She walked up to a window where a lady was sitting, writing on a slip of paper. Looking up from her paper she asked, "Well young lady, how can I help you?"

"I need a place to live," answered Little Girl.

"Well, I think we have room for you. You just take a seat over there in that chair, and I will be right out."

Little Girl sat and started to have second thoughts. She wanted to be with her only friend, Steve, but also didn't want to sleep outside. Plus, she needed a bath and to brush her teeth.

"Hello young lady," the woman was now standing in front of her. "Come with me. My name is Ms. Jones, and I will get you settled in, but first, we have a little paperwork to get through then I will introduce you to some of the other girls and explain the rules. How does that sound?"

As the two walked down the hallway and up some stairs, Ms. Jones opened a door that had the number 8 on the door. "Gloria?" Ms. Jones spoke out. "Gloria, where are you, honey?"

"I'm in the bathroom. What?"

"I have a new roommate for you."

The bathroom door opened, and a tall skinny light skinned girl walked out. "Gloria this is? Oh, my goodness.

I'm so sorry, young lady. I did not ask you your name. I don't know what's wrong with me today. I'm so fixed on what numbers to send in." Little Girl had no idea what Ms. Jones was talking about numbers. "Well anyway, what is your name?"

"Little Girl, but my friend, Steve, calls me Sunshine."

"Well, Sunshine it is. Gloria, meet Sunshine, your new roommate."

"Hello Sunshine, you can have that bed next to the window."

"Ladies, I'm going to leave you two for now and Sunshine, we will do your paperwork a little later," Ms. Jones said with a smile as she left the room.

Gloria sat on her bed and pointed to Sunshine to sit on her own bed. "So how old are you?" Gloria asked.

Sunshine spoke nervously, "I'm sixteen! What about you? How old are you?"

"Seventeen and been here for two years. It's better than living on the streets. I used to sleep in people's yards and on the subway until this pimp got a hold of me. I had to have sex with all these men."

"How old were you?" asked Sunshine.

"Fourteen, when I ran away from home. Fourteen when I meet Kevin, the pimp. I wasn't in the streets long. I remember I was on the train when this cute guy asked me my name, told me I was pretty and could be a model. All I had to do was come with him, and he would introduce me to a person who worked with models. I was excited. I was only fourteen then, and I believed him."

"So, what happened?" asked Sunshine (Little Girl).

"He took me to an apartment that had three other girls. One of the girls looked like someone punched her in her mouth, her lip was swollen. He told the girls to leave and go to work, so they all left. He went into a closet and handed me a skirt and a shirt that looked too small and told me to put it on. I asked him where the person that was going to help me model was. He just looked at me and yelled, "Shut up you stupid B---! Put on those clothes!" So, I did while he made a phone call. In about thirty minutes, a man came in, and you know what he did next or do you?"

"Yeah, I do," answered Sunshine, not wanting her own mind to reach back in its own storage closet. "How did you get away from him?"

"I had a trick one day who was very nice and felt sorry for me. He brought me here."

"So, you were with that pimp for a year?"

"Yep, a year and months." The girls continued to talk when a loud bell sounded. "It's dinner time. Come on, follow me. You can sit with me."

"Okay," Sunshine responded.

~Karen~

Karen sat at her desk at work unable to focus for her mind was still on the story of Little Girl and how the story affected her. I can't work today. My thoughts are racing on everything except work. So, Karen decided to leave work early. As she started her car, she juggled with the thought of either going home or stopping by

Michelle's, knowing if she went by there, she would want to hear more about Little Girl. *I don't understand why I am so interested in this Little Girl story, she said to herself. Maybe if I just headed home? Nah, I think I'll go by Michelle's. Shit! I'm going to leave now. There isn't anything happening here that I can't catch up on tomorrow.*

Karen cleared her desk, grabbed her jacket, headed towards the door, and straight to her car, not even a wave to the guard standing near the front who was waving and winking his eye at her. Karen proceeded towards Michelle's house but first stopped to buy a few milkshakes, one strawberry, and the other vanilla.

I don't understand Michelle's life, Karen kept thinking to herself. *I have more money than Michelle and her husband put together, and yet I'm the one who is unhappy. Both of them act like money isn't important. In fact, they don't even care if they have only ten dollars in their pocket. I don't get it. They smile and just are happy. What am I missing? Oh, well. Hopefully, Michelle will give me a book to read on how she gets to be so happy.*

"Hey, Joe!" Karen yelled as she pulled into their driveway.

"Hello, Karen!" Joe yelled back. "Michelle is in the kitchen."

"Thanks, Joe."

Joe pulled off in his car laughing to himself, *That Karen is a trip.*

"Michelle! Michelle! Where are you?" Karen screamed when she saw Michelle wasn't in the kitchen like Joe claimed she was.

"I'm in my bedroom, Karen, and why are you yelling like that? People in China can hear you and why aren't you at work?"

"Girl, I had a half a day today," Karen responded, knowing she was telling her friend a lie.

"Come in here, Karen. I'm trying to clean up this room. Joe has a habit of leaving his clothes right where he takes them off. Ha! Ha! Here, sit anywhere you find an empty spot."

"Dag, Michelle! Karen laughed. "What in the world happened in here?"

"I told you, Karen. I was cleaning my room."

"Michelle looks like you tore this room apart. Why are you cleaning out the closet? Joe's clothes are in the other closet, Michelle."

"Just felt like cleaning it since I'm in a cleaning mood."

"Girl, Michelle, you need to get a housekeeper as I have. Let her come in once a week and pick up all your handy dandies," Karen said laughing hard.

"Karen, you know Joe and I can't afford that, and even if we could, I don't want anyone going through Joe's and my things. I am capable of cleaning up myself."

"Oh, I forgot, Michelle! I bought us some milkshakes and left them in the car. Guess they are milk by now!"

"Karen, that's okay! I am going to take a break now and grab me a sandwich You want one?"

"Sure do! Hey Michelle, are you in the mood tell me about the girl named, Little Girl?"

"Yeah, I will! Just let me finish making these sandwiches. You know Karen; sometimes I think you just come over to eat!" Michelle giggled her words while placing the plate of sandwiches on the table.

"Really, Michelle, is that how you think of me, a moocher?"

"Get over here and eat this sandwich! I need to start charging you for the food you eat!"

"Girl, please!" Karen laughed. "You will feed anyone who is hungry and give your leftovers to the raccoons and any stray animal that will eat! Why do you do that?"

"I don't know Karen; that's just me. Now, do you want to hear more about Little Girl? If so, put the sandwich in your mouth so you can stop talking!"

Whose Little Girl?

She lives in a world of loneliness

Not a soul to see her through

Not a soul to love her

Not a soul to care for her.

She walks down the street

With a pair of worn out shoes on her feet

No one looks at her

Or tells her what she should be

She has nothing to live or smile for

For living to her is just a bore.

Then a shot rang out

She falls to the ground

Only then do people start to look

And gather around

No one asked why

For no one didn't care

For she was just one less lonely person

In this world to compare

Just another statistic.

Compassion: A feeling of deep sympathy and sorrow for another who is stricken by misfortune, accompanied by a strong desire to alleviate the suffering. Mercy, Tenderness.

What does our Lord Jesus say about compassion? Matthews 9:36, "When he saw the crowds, he had compassion for them, because they were harassed and helpless."

2 Corinthians 1:3, "Praise be to the God and Father of our Lord Jesus Christ, the Father of compassion and the God of all comfort."

1 Peter 3:8, "Finally, be ye all of one mind, having compassion one of another as brethren, love as brethren, be pitiful, be courteous."

From the Author:

Reach out and wipe away the tear from someone's eyes. Give hope to someone in need. Feed the homeless. Introduce Jesus to those who do not know Him.

2

WHERE DO I BELONG?

~Little Girl A.K.A. Sunshine~

Both young girls approached the dining area.

"Wow," Sunshine whispered, there's a lot of girls here."

Whispering back Gloria also said, "Wow," in a funny way, "There sure is. Come on Sunshine; we have to get in line." The two grabbed their trays and headed to find a table to sit. "Here, let's sit here," Gloria said. They sat with three other girls.

"Hi," spoke one of the other girls.

"Who are you looking at, Sunshine?"

"You must be new. I haven't seen you before."

"Yeah, I'm new; just got here today," Sunshine spoke back.

Another girl introduced herself, "Hi, I'm Kim. I've been here about a month. Are you a runaway also?"

"Nope," Sunshine A.K.A. Little Girl said in a very harsh voice, "My mother died, so here I am."

"You don't have to sound so nasty. I was just asking!" Kim said in a defensive tone.

"I wasn't being nasty, but I will say sorry."

"Oh, I see. There's a new smartass!" Shirley, the oldest in the shelter, spoke. "So, I hear you are called *Sunshine A.K.A. Little Girl!* Which should we all call you? You sure don't talk like a little girl. You talk like someone who wants to get an ass kicking!"

Little Girl stood up from her chair and without saying a word, started pouring her milk on Shirley's head. Both girls were now pulling hair and punching each other and anyone who got near. Gloria, staring in shock, jumped on Shirley, trying to pull her off Sunshine. Just as one of the house attendants approached, Sunshine and Shirley were sitting in their seats.

"Now listen here," the attendant Bob spoke. "We will not allow any kind of physical contact," looking at Sunshine and Shirley. "Shirley, you know better than that. You already have a few marks against you so don't push it. And for you, you just got here, so the rules need to be explained to you. As soon as Ms. Jones comes back from playing her numbers, I'm gonna tell her about this little incident and make sure she goes over everything you need to know. I don't know why that Ms. Jones has to play those stupid numbers. Every time she dreams a number, there she goes off betting. Well anyway, you girls finish your dinner. Gloria, whose turn is it to wash the dishes?" Bob, the attendant asked.

"I don't know," Gloria said. "All I know is I did them last week. I think it's that girl who wears those weird looking dresses."

"Gloria, her name is Donna," snickered Bob.

"Well, what is Sunshine's chores for this week?"

Bob said, "I don't know. Haven't given her one yet." Bob looked at Gloria and then back at Sunshine. He parted his lips and spoke, "Sunshine, you will wash this week!"

"But Bob," yelled Gloria, "new people don't get those chores just yet. They get to sweep the floor and stack all the forks and spoons!"

"Well, my dear," answered Bob, "since our new friend has come in thinking she's in the Wild Wild West, she can wash and dry the dishes for this week!"

"Ah man," Gloria sighed. "That's okay," Sunshine spoke, "I'll do the dishes."

"Good, it's settled now. Shirley, you will help her. You will dry, and both of you will put all utensils away!" Bob snared.

When Bob exited the dining hall, Shirley took a hard look at Sunshine. "You're gonna get your a.. kicked! Just wait! You think you can pour milk on me and get away with it?"

"Shirley, let it go! Dag," Kim yelled. "You're just mad someone stood up to you. Leave her alone. Anyway, you started it with your smart mouth. Didn't you hear her when she told me she was sorry and wasn't trying to talk nasty. Anyway, it wasn't any of your business! Okay?

"Okay!" screamed Shirley. "I guess I'm sorry, too."

"It's okay," Sunshine said to her.

"Hey!" Gloria spoke out, "Why don't we help those two wash and dry? This way, they will get finished quicker, and we all can go hang out before curfew!"

"That's cool by me," Kim said. "Let's first introduce Sunshine to our little group. Sunshine, you already know Shirley," Kim pointing to Shirley. The girls bust out laughing. "The quiet one here is Pam. (Pam was a very tiny and meek girl.) She's only fourteen; we all protect her. Her father beat her so bad and gave her drugs. She has nightmares sometimes, and she doesn't know where her mother is." Sunshine started thinking to herself about how all these girls had sad stories like hers. She thought to herself, *One day, I'm going to help all the sad people.*

Sunshine, Gloria, Shirley, Kim, and Pam. All five girls rushed to finish kitchen duties.

"Hey!" Kim shouted out, "Why don't we all go to the park? We got about three hours before it gets dark!"

"Let's go then," Sunshine said with a smile. "Oh, but I forgot! Doesn't Ms. Jones still have to do some paperwork on me?"

"Aww, don't worry about Ms. Jones!" Gloria spoke out, "She's probably playing her numbers, and if she hit, she's somewhere sitting and sneaking a drink! She thinks we all don't know, but she's a nice lady!"

Pam interrupted Gloria with a rushed voice, "Are we all finished? Then let's go!"

All five girls headed out the front door of the shelter and walked about five blocks arriving at the park. It was a large park with a large lake. Some people were fishing, others riding bikes, and others just hanging out doing their own thing.

"This is nice," Pam whispered.

"You like it here?" Sunshine asked Pam.

"Yes, I do! It looks happy! I like happy! I always wanted to be happy! That's all I ever wish for!"

Out of nowhere, came a voice, "SUNSHINE! SUNSHINE! OVER HERE! OVER HERE!" Sunshine looked, and there was her friend, Steve. She took off like a little girl who just saw her mother. Both teens hugged and smiled. "How are you, my Sunshine?"

"Steve, I'm happy to see you!"

"Who are those girls you are with Sunshine?"

"I met them at the shelter, Steve. So, where have you been?"

"All over my, Sunshine, trying to make money so I can give you some."

"Steve, I miss you! Why can't I come with you?" Just as Steve was about to answer her, Shirley and the rest of the girls walked up.

"Hello!" Gloria spoke first. "Are you Steve? Sunshine told me about her friend, Steve."

"Yeah, I'm Steve! Who are you?"

"We all live at the shelter with Sunshine."

"I'm glad Sunshine has some friends now," Steve replied. "I won't have to worry so much now. So, what are you all doing in the park?"

"We wanted just to walk around and hang out," Sunshine answered. "What are you doing here, Steve?"

"I'm waiting on a friend. He was supposed to meet me here an hour ago." As the two continued to talk, no one noticed a man wearing a brimmed hat and a gray suit approaching them until he was upon them, standing next to Shirley.

"Hey, Shirley!" The Man whispered as he grabbed her arm.

"Ouch!" hollered Shirley, until she looked and saw who the hand belonged to that grabbed her.

"Where's my money, girl? You owe me fifty dollars!"

"Okay, okay," answered Shirley.

Steve took one look at The Man and knew exactly who he was.

"Are you okay, Shirley?" Steven said in a firm voice.

"She's fine!" The Man answered back, giving Steve a look of *mind your business*. Shirley took The Man's arm and started to walk a distance away.

"Who is that, Steve? Kim asked.

"He sells drugs and women."

"Well, how does Shirley know him?"

"I don't know, Kim! He either owns her or she is on drugs."

Sunshine stood there not saying a word until Pam started crying. "Come here, Pam." Sunshine reached and pulled Pam to her, "Don't be scared. We aren't going to let anyone bother you." As the group of girls watched Shirley and The Man talking, out of nowhere, The Man hit Shirley across the face and then threw a white bag on the ground. "There! You stupid girl! Pick it up! I want my money by Thursday, you hear me?" Shirley bent and picked up the bag with a low yes. Then The Man walked off. The whole group of youngsters ran over to Shirley.

"SHIRLEY! SHIRLEY! Are you okay?"

Shirley just looked at them all and yelled, "MIND YOUR BUSINESS!" They all saw the blood running from her mouth.

"Here," Gloria handed Shirley a tissue, "your mouth is bleeding. What is that bag you picked up, Shirley? Is that drugs?"

"YES!" Shirley said. "I need it to do the things he wants me to do."

"Come on girls, maybe we need to go back to the shelter," suggested Kim. All agreed.

Steve gave Sunshine a hug and whispered, "Please be careful and trust no one." Then he looked at Shirley and gave her a huge hug, kissed her on the cheek, and whispered something in her ear. Sunshine looked at both of them with a puzzled look on her face then smiled at Steve and walked away with the rest of the girls.

As they all entered the front door of the shelter, Mrs. Jones was there to meet them. "Where have you been? Do you know it's ten minutes after curfew?"

"Sorry Ms. Jones," they all spoke.

"Now Sunshine, I need you in my office so follow me."

"See you in the room," Gloria yelled back as Ms. Jones and Sunshine proceeded down the hallway towards the office.

"Have a seat right there, young lady while I get the paperwork from my desk." Sunshine sat in the chair closest to the desk. "Here we are! I need to ask you a few questions. First, your age."

Sunshine responded, "Sixteen."

"Next, male or female?"

Sunshine looked at Ms. Jones like the woman had just lost her mind. "Ms. Jones? I'm a girl!"

"Well honey, you never know these days. I've had some of the most beautiful girls, delightful and also very respectful in here and come to find out; they were boys so that question has to be asked. Now the big question Sunshine, why are you on the streets?"

Sunshine (Little Girl) answered, "My foster mother died, and I did not want to go back into foster care."

"Okay, we are almost finished. Now here are the rules. You are to attend school here. We have in-house school. You are to keep your room clean at all times. Absolutely no boys in your room. We provide an allowance each week. You can also earn money by doing extra things around the shelter. We also provide all medical care that is in our budget. Well, young lady that is all for now. You can go to your room, and I will see you in the morning. Oh, we have staff that patrols the halls all night, so if you are having a problem, you find one and they will help you out. Goodnight."

Sunshine agreed, smiled, and headed to her room.

~Michelle and Karen~

Karen asked Michelle, "What are you doing this weekend?"

"Girl, I have no idea! Why?"

"Well, I thought maybe you and I, that is if Joe doesn't have any plans for him and me, I thought maybe you and I could go shopping for a new Bible for me and some shoes."

Karen put her sandwich down and just looked with a smile. "Girl, yes, yes, yes, and yes! Let's go shoe shopping. I need a pair also."

"Okay then! I'll call you and let you know if Joe has plans."

"Michelle, may I ask you a question about Jesus?"

"Sure, what is it you want to know?"

"What does it mean when I hear people say *He was the ultimate sacrifice, or He is the lamb?*"

Michelle looked at her friend with such a smile, compassion, and joy in her heart for her friend, Karen, was beginning to ask questions. She was becoming hungry for the Word of God. "Well Karen, in the Old Testament, people would sacrifice the lamb and animals as an offering to

God. Jesus, who took human form and came from heaven to earth to be the perfect sacrifice, He was the lamb. His entire dwelling on earth was a sacrifice to mankind. Karen, read in your Bible. Do you have a Bible?"

"Yes, Michelle, I have a Bible."

"Good, then read John 15:13, *Greater love has no one than this: to lay down one's life for one's friend.* Do you understand what I'm saying, Karen?"

"I'm not sure about any of this Michelle, but what I can tell you is this, for some reason which I cannot explain, I just want what you have concerning all this Jesus stuff. When I look at you or listen to you, you seem to get happiness or peace when you pray and a glow when you speak about Jesus."

"Karen, I give God all the glory for that. I wasn't always this way Karen, but someone introduced me to Jesus, and now, I just can't see not having Him in my life. It's as if He's not there; then I am not living."

"Look, Michelle, can you like start from the beginning?"

"Okay, Karen. Let me ask you first. What is it all that you know about the Bible?"

"Michelle, I know there's a God! I know about Adam and Eve. I know the story of David and Goliath, Mary and Joseph, Cain and Abel, and a few more, but I don't feel like I really know anything!"

Michelle started to laugh. "What's so funny, Michelle?"

"It's just that Karen, I was where you are not too long ago, so I understand exactly how you feel. This is what I want you to do Karen when you go home. Start reading the book of Matthew. Now, I just want you to read about maybe two verses then we will talk about what you read. When you read it, first I want you to pray and ask our Father God to give you an understanding of the reading of His Word. Karen, God, is such an awesome God that He gives us His mercy and grace no matter what and forgives us more times than we sin in a day."

"See Michelle, that's what I'm talking about. You know so much about God that it makes me feel like I've been missing out on something very important. I want so bad now to have what you have, and I don't really know why. Michelle, I'm tired of living the way I am living. There's no fulfillment within me. It's like something is missing now."

"Karen, I don't know a lot about the Bible. I just know to study God's Word every day and stay prayed up. I know that no matter what I am going through, I must keep faith in God and His Son, Jesus, and know that everything will work out for good.

"Karen, my life is not perfect. Joe and I don't agree on everything, in fact, I get on his nerves a lot of times, and he gets on me some of the time. Nothing in this world is perfect."

"Michelle, do you mind if I ask you to finish telling me about Little Girl!"

Michelle looked with amazement at Karen and spoke to her friend. "Karen, are you kidding me? We are talking about God, and you want to change to talking about Little Girl?

"I know! I know but come on, Michelle," Karen responded.

~Sunshine~

As Sunshine entered her room, she found Gloria sitting up in her bed reading. "Hey Girl!" Gloria said with a smile. "So, what happened with Ms. Jones? Did you finish all the paperwork?"

"Sure did," Sunshine responded with a yawn as she sat on the bed. She asked Gloria, "What is going on with Shirley and that man? I mean he hit her right in her face!"

"I know, I was shocked to see that myself. She owes him money, too. Tomorrow, we are going to talk to her and really find out what is going on.

I'm going to sleep now. We have to be up early if we want to eat breakfast."

Sunshine laid in her bed with all her clothes on, still not trusting in undressing. As she laid there, the door to her thoughts began to open up allowing some of her past to come in to haunt her night. Finally, she drifted off to sleep.

"Sunshine, Sunshine, wake up! We have to eat breakfast!" It seemed like Sunshine had just fallen asleep.

"I'm getting up, Gloria. Where's the bathroom?"

"The door next to our room. Did Ms. Jones give you your supplies?"

"Yeah, she did. I'll hurry up out the bathroom Gloria, and we can go to breakfast."

"Wait Sunshine, here's an extra pair of pants you can have and a shirt!"

"Thanks, Gloria."

Both girls got their breakfast and looked around for Shirley, Kim, and Pam. They spotted them at the back table. All the girls sat and proceeded to eat their breakfast. Kim was the first to ask, "Shirley, are you going to tell us what is going on with you or not?"

Shirley took one look at Kim and answered with a, "NOT!"

"Why Shirley? Maybe we can help you! You know that guy I know named, Kevin? I can tell him to beat him up if you want!"

"Are you crazy! The Man will shoot him dead or have one of his friends do it and then hurt me," Shirley said yelling back at Kim. "Just leave it alone, all of you! You can't help me! Anyway," Shirley said looking at Sunshine, "Do you really know your friend, Steve and what he does?"

"Yes, I do, and I don't need you telling me anything about Steve."

"Fine," Shirley answered with a smirk on her face.

The girls continued to finish their breakfast. As Ms. Jones entered the cafeteria, she walked straight up to the girls' table where Shirley and the girls were sitting. "Good morning, ladies," as Ms. Jones began to speak,

Sunshine leaned over and whispered to Gloria, "Does she ever go home?"

"No!" Gloria whispered back.

"Girls," Ms. Jones spoke, "I want all of you to complete your assigned chores and to stay out of the park today! Oh yes, girls! I have eyes everywhere, and Shirley, you are to report to my office this evening after dinner. Do you understand Shirley?"

"Yes, Ms. Jones," Shirley responded.

"Good then," Ms. Jones whispered as she exited the cafeteria.

"Who told on me?" Shirley hollered at the rest of the girls. "It was you!" pointing at Pam.

"What's wrong with you, Shirley? Leave Pam alone!" yelled Kim.

Just then Pam spoke out, "I didn't tell on you, Shirley! I promise I didn't."

"Come on you'lll! Let's start our chores and go find something to do!" Sunshine said.

After breakfast and chores, all the girls headed back to the park, ignoring every word Ms. Jones said to them.

"Hey Sunshine, do you think we will see your friend, Steve again?" Kim asked. Shirley looked at Sunshine waiting for a reply. No one had any idea that Shirley knew more about Steve than Sunshine.

"I don't know, Kim," replied Sunshine. The girls continued to walk around the park talking, laughing, and just enjoying the day.

Each day was like clockwork. It became their routine to finish their chores and head to the park except for times when Shirley would disappear. The girls stopped asking Shirley what was going on and just accepted her just as she was. They would bump into Steve at times, and Steve would treat them all to milkshakes, and he and Sunshine would have their strawberry milkshakes together. Steve would talk about what was going on in the streets and about "Juicy" the streetwalker whom Sunshine met when she first met Steve.

Months passed, and the girls became closer to one another. Sunshine was enjoying her life at the shelter. She began feeling like she finally belonged.

"Gloria! Gloria! Gloria!" Kim was yelling as she ran down the hallway of the shelter to Gloria's room.

Both Sunshine and Gloria jumped from their beds and raced into the hallway to see what was happening with Kim. As soon as Kim saw them, she yelled, "Come here! Come here! Hurry up!" The girls followed Kim into her room. Sunshine and Gloria stood there for a few seconds unable to move or even think.

"What's wrong with her?" Sunshine yelled as she walked towards Shirley who was spread out on the floor unconscious.

"I don't know!" yelled Kim. "She was like this when I came in."

"What do you think happened Gloria? Gloria?" yelled Kim. Both girls turned around to find Gloria gone. Gloria had run from the room to find Ms. Jones. All the yelling had now caused the other girls who lived in the shelter to gather around Kim's room.

Some of the girls whispered, "Told you she did drugs!" Others whispered, "Is she dead?"

Sunshine heard them and hollered, "MIND YOUR BUSINESS!"

Just as she was about to go and look for one of the attendants, Ms. Jones appeared. "Oh, my Lord," and ran over to Shirley. She put her hand on Shirley and checked for a pulse; there was none. Ms. Jones then proceeded to run out of the room to call the 911. She told all the girls to go back to their rooms, but that was like talking to a brick wall. No one moved an inch.

Gloria, who had come back with Ms. Jones, tried putting a wet cloth on Shirley with still no response. As the girls stood over Shirley, not knowing what to do, a small figure pushed pass them. It was Pam.

"What's wrong with Shirley?" she asked. Pam walked over, picked up Shirley's arm, and started looking and searching.

"What are you doing, Pam?" Sunshine asked.

"I'm looking for track marks, Sunshine!"

Kim squeaked out her mouth, "How do you know about that, Pam?"

Just then, Pam pulled up her sleeve and started to cry. "My daddy used to put needles with drugs in me, and I have these marks now. My dad used to tell me I overdosed a lot, a few times. He would carry me into the bathtub and put me in water."

Gloria, Kim, and Sunshine all looked at Pam and felt so sorry for her. "Look!" Pam screamed, and there on Shirley's arms were needle holes.

"Everyone back to your rooms this minute!" Ms. Jones was back with the paramedics. "I mean now, back to your rooms!" Everyone headed back to their rooms except for the four girls: Kim, Sunshine, Pam, and Gloria who were not about to leave regardless of what anything Ms. Jones had to say.

"Is she going to be okay, Ms. Jones?" asked the paramedics.

"I'm sorry ma'am, but she's not responding, and her pulse is very weak. Looks like an overdose," one of the paramedics told Ms. Jones. The paramedics then carried Shirley onto a stretcher and rode off with the sirens on. The girls stood at the door of the shelter looking until they could no longer see the lights of the sirens.

"Well!" came a voice out of nowhere. There stood Bob the attendant, "So tell me young ladies, is this what you all are doing now? Drugs?" Everyone looked at Bob, and if looks could kill, he would have dropped dead right there where he was standing.

~Michelle and Karen~

Michelle continued to tell Karen the story about Little Girl. As more words of Little Girl flowed from Michelle's lips, Karen noticed a saddened look on Michelle's face. She didn't ask why her friend looked sad but just continued to listen to the story. She still pondered with the thought if the girl Michelle was talking about was indeed Michelle, herself.

~Sunshine, Gloria, Kim, and Pam~

Months had passed since the death of Shirley. Sunshine was now seventeen and rest of the girls were also maturing. They no longer took walks in the park together. Gloria, who was eighteen, was working and about to graduate high school. She was dating a young man who was in college and majoring in business. Kim was about to enroll in college in another state and Pam was entering high school. Sunshine noticed the change in all the girls since Shirley died.

One day, Sunshine and the girls sat together in the cafeteria.

"Hey! Why don't we all take a walk in the park like we used to do?" Pam suggested.

"Yeah, that's a good idea!" Gloria spoke. They all agreed.

Sunshine wondered to herself if she might see Steve. She had not seen him since the day before the death of Shirley. Sunshine would take walks to the park without the other girls hoping she would bump into Steve, but he never seemed to be there. *Maybe*, she said to herself; she might get lucky.

So, the girls went walking in the park, chatting, and laughing like old times. They all sat on a bench and talked about their future. Gloria talked about her boyfriend. Pam talked about how nervous she was entering into high school. Kim asked the girls to keep in contact with her when she leaves for college in another state. Sunshine listened and was happy for all her friends.

"Hey, Sunshine! We all were talking about you the other night. We want to know how come you dropped out of school and won't go back!"

"I don't know," Sunshine responded, but the truth that Sunshine was withholding from her friends was that she didn't not feel smart. In fact, Sunshine felt stupid. That's what some of her foster parents would always tell her growing up when she was a little girl, and now she has come to believe that about herself, that she was stupid and dumb.

Sunshine wanted to change the subject, so she started talking about getting a job, but Gloria would not allow her to change the subject. "Come on, Sunshine," Gloria said, "why don't you try for your GED?"

"Okay," Sunshine agreed, only in hopes that it would shut Gloria up.

"Look over there," yelled Pam, "isn't that Steve laying on that bench?"

Sunshine jumped to her feet before any of the other girls could respond and ran over to the bench where the male figure was laying.

"Steve! Steve! Wake up!" Steve opened his eyes to see Sunshine looking down at him. A smile appeared on his face.

"Oh wow! Look at my Sunshine!" he said as he began to sit up. Sunshine noticed Steve's appearance was not looking good. One thing she always knew about her friend Steve is that even though he lived on the streets, he would always try to keep up his appearance and hygiene.

"Where have you been, Steve? I've been looking for you for months! Why haven't you even come to the shelter to check on me?"

Steve motioned for Sunshine to sit next to him. "Sunshine, I'm so sorry! I went to jail. I got caught stealing from the store."

"I'm so sorry, Steve! Did you know Shirley died?"

"Yeah, Sunshine! I do! It tore me up when she died. Sunshine, I want to tell you something."

"Okay, what is it?" By now, the rest of the girls were standing over Steve and Sunshine, listening to every word that was being said between them both.

"Shirley was my sister. Remember the first day we met, and I told you I had one sister? Well Shirley was her! It hurts me so bad that she is dead. I brought her to the shelter also even though she was older than me. I tried to look out for her, but *The Man* had control over her with drugs.

"Sunshine, I'm on drugs too, just like my sister. I didn't want you to know. I haven't had a fix though in about two weeks now, and I've been sick and lonely without Shirley. I'm also hungry."

Pam spoke up instantly, "Come on, you'll! Let's go get Steve something to eat! Sunshine, we will be right back."

"Okay, I'll be right here with Steve." The figures of the girls disappeared in the distance. "Come on Steve, let's go!"

"Where are we going, Sunshine?"

"I don't know Steve, but I don't want to stay at the shelter anymore. I'm going to look after you, Steve. Come on before they come back."

Sunshine had begun feeling that feeling she was so familiar with for a while now, the feeling of loneliness. Her friends were moving on with their lives and had plans for their future. She wanted so bad to have that same confidence in herself like the rest of the girls. Why couldn't she? What was wrong with her? Maybe because she was so stupid, and she no longer belonged with them. She was not smart enough or good enough for her friends now, she thought to herself.

So, the two young people walked off. Sunshine never returned to the shelter after that day. She never said bye to the only true friends she loved like sisters.

Seven

~Michelle and Karen~

By now, Karen noticed that this time Michelle's eyes were watery, and tears began to fall from them.

"Sweetie, what's wrong?" Karen whispered as she began to hold her friend.

Michelle replied with a, "I'm good."

"Hello ladies," Joe appeared out of nowhere and startled both women. "What's going on? Why are you crying, Michelle? What happened, Karen?"

"Nothing Joe," Karen answered, "she was just telling me about someone she once knew, and I guess it got to her."

"Here, I bought both of you something to eat. I kind of knew you would still be here," Joe said looking at Karen.

"Look, Michelle, your husband bought us both a milkshake! Should we hug him?" Karen asked, trying to put a smile on Michelle's face.

Michelle glanced at her best friend and laughed. "Thanks, sweetie," Michelle told her husband, Joe.

Joe spoke to his wife with love in his voice and compassion for her, "I have a job to do. Do you want me to bring you anything back home?"

"No, I'm good, Joe," Michelle replied.

"Oh, before I forget. Do you have any doctors' appointments tomorrow?" he asked his wife again.

"No," once again Michelle replied to her husband.

Karen looked at her friend, "What doctor's appointment is he talking about Michelle? Michelle, what doctor's appointment is he talking about? What's wrong with you?"

"Dag Karen, can you wait a minute 'till I get the straw from my strawberry shake out of my mouth? Now! I went to get my mammogram, and they found a lump again in my breast, and now they want to do another biopsy."

"Oh my God," Karen whispered. "Are you okay?"

"Karen, what did I tell you about calling the Lord's name in vain?"

"Oops, I'm sorry. Promise I won't do it again."

"And yes Karen, I'm okay. I don't claim anything, nor will I speak anything into existence."

"Listen, Michelle; I want to know why you were crying when you were talking about Little Girl? Why did it get to you so bad? And what's up with that friend of hers, Steve?"

~Sunshine and Steve~

Sunshine and Steve sat on the train, riding it to the end of the line and back to the other for hours. "Sunshine, we have to get off and start finding someplace to sleep. It starts getting really bad and dangerous the later it gets."

"Okay Steve, we can get off at West 4th. How about that? Plus, we have to get something to eat."

When their train stopped arrived at West 4th Street, the two got off the train and headed out to the streets trying to find a store that maybe they both could find something Sunshine could afford for both. *It looks like McDonald's is what it's going to have to be.* As they entered, people could not help but notice the body odor that came from Steve. "Hey," someone hollered out, "take a bath!"

"Come on Steve, ignore them!" Sunshine said. After their order was taken, they left with their food and started the journey of finding a place to rest their tired bodies.

"Want to try the park?" Sunshine asked.

"Nah, it's gotten pretty dangerous, my Sunshine," Steve answered while chewing his burger. "I know a place, Sunshine. Come on! It's not far, just a few more blocks."

Sunshine turned and looked at her friend, "This reminds me of when we first met!"

"Yeah, it kind of does, my Sunshine."

After about thirty minutes of walking, Steve stopped in front of an apartment building then proceeded into the building and up two flights of stairs. Stopping in front of a door with the number 3 on it, Steve knocked hard on the door and then waited.

"Steve," whispered Sunshine, "who lives here?" Steve did not answer her. Suddenly the door swung open. There in front of Sunshine stood *The Man*. The same man who hit Shirley in the park and supplied her with drugs.

"Come in," The Man spoke, looking past Steven and straight at Sunshine.

"Come on Sunshine; it's safe."

"No Steve, I don't want to go in there."

"Look, I don't want to stand at this door all night. Are you coming in or not?" spoke The Man. Steve grabbed her arm and pulled her into the apartment. Looking around, Sunshine saw how nice it looked. "Here beautiful, you can sit in my chair," The Man said, pointing to Sunshine.

Steve grabbed her hand and said, "That's okay, she will sit with me," he told The Man.

"Very well, you two can sit on the couch. Now, what's up, Steve? What do you need?"

"I don't need no stuff, that's one thing. What I need is a place for us to sleep for the night or maybe a few days."

"That's fine! You both can crash here, but it will cost you."

"How much?" Steve answered with anger in his voice.

"Well, my good friend, how much do you have right now?"

"Come on man," Steve spoke, "you know I won't have any money until tomorrow."

"Alright then. Tomorrow, you will pay me fifty dollars a day Steve, but do not run out on me. You know I will find you and your pretty friend. She looks familiar Steve, where do I know her from?"

The whole time Sunshine listened to them both, not understanding what was going on in Steve's head. Why would he want to stay with the person who gave his sister drugs?

"You don't!" Steve said to The Man, getting angry every minute. "Just tell me where we can sleep."

"Take the room far in the back," said The Man to Steve. Steve took Sunshine's hand and led her to the back of the apartment. Looking in the rooms where the doors were open, Sunshine noticed about two girls in two rooms. When she glanced, she also noticed the girls looked very young.

"Steve, who are those girls?"

"Sunshine, I'm going to school you on a few things. Please don't ask any questions about anything that goes on in here and trust no one with anything."

"Okay. Okay, Steve! But how come you want to stay with The Man that gave your sister drugs and she died from it?"

"Sunshine, we need a place to stay out from the cold. It's called surviving the best way I know how. I hate him and want him dead."

"Lock the door, Steve, please."

"Alright, my Sunshine." "Sunshine got under the covers said good night to Steve and drifted off to sleep.

Seven

~Michelle and Karen~

"Why did you stop talking, Michelle? Is telling the story getting to you again?"

"No Karen, I just want to go into prayer right now. Come on; I want you to come pray with me."

Karen, without saying another word, followed her friend into a room. Watching her friend fall to her knees, she did the same. "Karen, bow your head," Michelle spoke in a very soft low voice, "and talk to God. You can talk openly or silently. First, thank our Father in heaven for allowing you to wake up and see another day. Ask for forgiveness for your sins and just talk to him, Karen. Talk from your heart."

~Sunshine and Steve~

Two weeks have come and gone, and Sunshine and Steve were still living with The Man and having no problems as long as Steve continued to pay. Sunshine stayed most of the time in the room or only went into the kitchen when Steve came back from doing whatever in the streets to earn the money they needed to live on. She also found herself getting tired of staying there and wanted to leave, but she didn't have anywhere to go. She did not want to be separated from her friend, Steve, so she just watched TV, read books, or played cards with Steve when he was there.

Knock! Knock! A knock came from the opposite side of the bedroom door. "Who is it?" Sunshine answered the knock.

A tiny whisper came through, "Excuse me miss, but can I talk to you please?"

It was one of the girls from one of the side rooms. Sunshine got up and headed to the door, but just before she opened it she heard The Man's voice say, "Girl, what did I tell you about knocking on that door?" Then Sunshine heard the slap and then a cry of words saying, "I'm sorry! Please don't hit me!" followed by another hard slap.

Right then, Sunshine began to get frightened. Then came a hard knock on her door, "OPEN THIS DOOR!" once again, it was The Man's voice.

Sunshine opened the door and stepped back. "Look, let me tell you," said The Man looking very angry, "you don't talk to any of my girls! None of them! You hear me?"

"Yes, I hear you," Sunshine said. As The Man turned to walk out of the room, he swiftly turned back around and slapped Sunshine so hard she fell across the bed, and the blood just started flowing from her lips and mouth.

"Now _ _ _ _ _, that will remind you of what I just said every time you look in the mirror!"

Sunshine curled herself into a ball in the corner of the room like she was a child again and wept like a child. She cried for the girls at the shelter who were like sisters to her and Shirley who passed away. Sunshine cried for just being who she was, feeling like a nobody.

"Hey, Sunshine! What happened?" It was Steve grabbing Sunshine and just holding her until she stopped crying. "Come with me, my Sunshine, and clean this blood off of you."

"Steve, I want to leave here!"

"We are, as soon as we clean your face we are leaving, okay! I'm sorry, my Sunshine, I wasn't here!"

"Can we leave now?" Sunshine begged as Steve proceeded to clean up all the blood from her.

"Come get our stuff together. I'll be right back. I'm going to talk to *The Man*."

"No Steve! Let's just go, please!"

"I'll be right back," Steve said and walked out of the room. Sunshine hurried and gathered the few items they had, walked out of the room, and headed up the hallway. As she entered the living room, she found Steve up against the wall with The Man's hand around his neck.

"Stop! Please don't hurt him! Please!" shouted Sunshine.

The Man took his hand from around Steve's neck and turned to Sunshine and said, "If I don't get my money, you and your friend will pay with your _ _ _! Don't think about leaving until I get paid from both of you!"

After Steve was able to catch his breath, he managed to speak the words, "We don't owe you anything! I worked for our stay for you!"

The Man started laughing, "You stupid boy! You worked for the food I gave you so you and your little friend could eat, and I let you keep some money so you could buy your dope!" Sunshine looked at Steve who now could not look at her. "That's right girl! Didn't he tell you?" The Man was now yelling at Sunshine, "Your friend here is back on dope! Why do you think he came here?

"This is what you are going to do, Steve! Get your _ _ _ out on the streets now and get me my money! All of it! Tell your friend how much you owe!"

Steve looked at Sunshine and answered with a, "Eight hundred dollars. I'm sorry, my Sunshine!"

The Man turned to Sunshine without a word, slapped her, yanked her back into the back room, and began to tear her clothes off. After he was through, he made a phone call and told Sunshine to clean herself up. She was going to have some company.

After The Man left the room, Steve came in. "My Sunshine, I'm sorry! Please, I'm so sorry!"

Sunshine just looked at Steve and said without a tear from her eyes, "Let's just make money so we can leave." Steve looked at her. She did not look like his Sunshine but a blank person with no emotion, just a body sitting on a bed. He then walked out of the room.

Sunshine went into the bathroom and looked at herself in the mirror. Her lips and eyes were swollen and busted. She stood there and stared at all the marks on her face. She did not cry; she did not moan. All she did was part her lips and speak the words ... *Where do I belong?*

~Karen~

Karen rose from her knees and opened her eyes after praying to God, to find Michelle had left the room. Karen felt her face and noticed she had tears coming down, so she sat in one of the chairs at the corner of the room. *Wow! What is happening to me? I feel light inside.* She continued to sit there because, for some strange reason, she thought it was strange enjoying the peace that seemed to engulf her. She had not yet realized that everything she was feeling was not strange. It was the power of God she was beginning to feel. It was the peace from God.

Karen sat and without noticing, had begun to talk out loud to God. "God, I don't know much about You but will You help me to know You better. You see, I like this feeling I'm feeling, and I'm also scared."

Michelle came into the room and heard Karen. Taking Karen's hand, Michelle said very softly to her friend, "God does not give us the spirit of fear but the power of love and a sound mind, sweetie," and turned and walked back out the room.

Where Do I Belong?

In the very depths of the night
They approach

Watching.. Waiting...

Striking at any given moment.

Who are they?

They are whoever they please

For they are wolves in sheep's clothing.

Where do I go?

Where do I hide

with this heavy chain on my side.

Their eyes

Hungry... Thirsting...

empty inside.

Who do I run to?

Where do I hide?

How do I break

this chain on my side?

Pain: Physical, mental or emotional distress, torment, misery.

What does our Father in heaven say about pain?

Psalms 12:5, "For the oppressed of the poor, for the sighing of needy, now will I arise, saith the LORD; I will set him in safety from him that puffeth at him."

Matthew 5:4, "Blessed are they that mourn: For they shall be comforted."

Revelation 21:4, "And God shall wipe away all tears from their eyes; and there shall be no more death, neither sorrow; nor crying, neither shall there be any more pain; for the former things are passed away."

Author's Own Thoughts:

Healing from emotional and physical pain is a process. It doesn't happen overnight. Allow God to work in your life.

3

WHO AM I?

~Little Girl A.K.A. Sunshine A.K.A. Bambi~

Sunshine walked towards the window and stood there looking down at the people in the streets. It was now a year, and she was still in the apartment with The Man. As she stood there, her thoughts raced back to the day when The Man came into her room, sat on her bed, told her she no longer had to work for him, and did not want any other man touching her.

"Can I leave then?" she asked.

"No," replied The Man, "I want you for myself! I'll take care of you! I'll buy you whatever you need or want!"

"What about my friend, Steve?" she asked.

The Man laughed and said to her, "Steve can stay or go. It's up to you, darling," while running his hands across her face. Sunshine felt nothing for The Man and felt nothing every time he would touch her.

"I'm not going to call you, Sunshine! I don't want to call you anything that people have called you. You are my Bambi! You remind me of a little deer. Now come here and thank me."

Sunshine's A.K.A. Bambi's thoughts were interrupted by, "Bambi, come out here and collect the money from the ladies," The Man called down the hallway. Sunshine A.K.A. Bambi turned from the window she was looking out of at the people in the streets and headed up the hallway to obey what The Man told her to do. As she proceeded up the hallway, Sunshine A.K.A. Bambi walked like a mechanical robot. No feeling, no emotion, just existing.

She walked into the working ladies' room and did what was told of her. After collecting all the money, she then walked into the living room where The Man and Steve were. Standing and looking at her friend Steve, she wanted so bad to feel sorry for him but the sight of him pushing a needle in his arm, watching him nod in and out of consciousness, and the memory of how he put her in this situation, left her feeling nothing for him.

"Here's the money you asked for," she said to The Man.

"Thanks, Bambi! Here's a couple of hundred! Go buy yourself something pretty. Remember to keep the receipt just in case I don't like it."

"Thank you, Man!" Bambi replied. Bambi took another look at Steve and decided to kick him. After kicking him hard, The Man watching her let out a loud laugh. She then walked off back to her room to get dressed and go shopping.

~Michelle and Karen~

Karen got up from her chair and headed to where Michelle was in the house. Michelle smiled at her friend Karen, not saying a word. She walked towards Karen and just gave her a hug. "Karen, you don't have to say anything." Michelle had so much compassion for her friend. She loved her like a sister.

"Michelle," Karen opened her mouth and spoke, "I think I'm going to go on home now."

"Why Karen? Why don't we go shoe shopping and also I want to buy a new Bible."

Karen said, "Very well, Michelle! I'll stay."

"Great, let me just go find something to change into really quick then we can leave. And I'll tell you more about Little Girl while I'm getting dressed."

Both women went into Michelle's room. Karen sat on the bed and Michelle started getting dressed and telling more about Little Girl's life.

~Little Girl A.K.A. Sunshine A.K.A. Bambi~

Returning from her shopping, Bambi entered the apartment to find Steve throwing up on the living room floor. When he saw her, he reached out his arm to her and whispered the words, "My Sunshine, please help me. I'm sick!"

Bambi looked at her friend and started walking towards him. "Come on, Steve," she said to him, "let me help you to the bathroom." She helped him up and walked into the bathroom down the hall.

"My Sunshine is here to help me now," Steve smiled

"Don't call me *Sunshine*. You know everyone calls me Bambi now. Isn't this what you wanted anyway, for your friend, The Man to use me so you can get your drugs?"

"Please don't be mad at me, my Sunshine. I really want to kick this drug habit. Will you help me, Sunshine? Please help me."

"Steve, I'm going to help you to the bathroom and then back into the living room. I just don't want you throwing up anymore in the living room. It stinks in there now. I thought you were my friend, but you lied and used me for your drugs and let The Man use me for whatever he wanted from me."

Steve started crying and saying, "Please, my Sunshine, forgive me, please. I want us to be friends again. Please help me get off these drugs!"

Sunshine's heart started feeling something for her only, used to be, friend. She cared for him still and wanted so desperately to have someone in her life she could love and love her back as a person, not for their own gain.

"Okay Steve, I'm going to lock you in my room. I'll be back. Don't try to get out and when you start feeling chilly from you being sick. Get under the covers. I'm going to buy some soup and other things that might help."

Bambi walked over again to her friend Steve, gave him a hug and said, "Steve, you will always be my friend no matter what." Then helped him to the bed, walked out of the room, and locked the door with a key. She then headed out the front door and out of the building to gather the things she would need for her friend.

Bambi walked into the drug store and asked the cashier what she could buy to help someone off of heroin. "Honey," the cashier said, "he will need to go to the methadone program."

"What's that?" Bambi asked.

"It's a program, honey, that gives out medicine to people to help them detox off that stuff."

"Where is it?" Bambi asked.

"There's one about two blocks from here, but you need to get there. They will be closing in about one hour."

"Thank you," Bambi said to the cashier and raced outside only to turn around and run back in and ask for the address.

When Bambi approached the tall brick building, she saw a lot of people lined up. She walked past them, headed straight in, and up to the front desk. "Excuse me!" she said to the lady at the desk.

"Yes," the woman said. "How can I help you, young lady?"

Bambi asked the questions she needed to ask, then turned around and headed outside.

"Hey, girl! Did they turn you down?" a voice spoke.

Bambi turned to see where the voice came from. "What?" she answered.

"Did they turn you down, I said!"

"How do you know that?" Bambi responded to the voice, "And yes, they did."

The voice then said to her, "You wanted the methadone for someone else, right?"

"Yeah! Why?"

The voice then said, "Girl, anybody can see you don't shoot up. If you give me some money, I'll sell you mine."

"How much?" Bambi asked.

"Just give me twenty-five dollars!"

So, Bambi gave the voice the money, not knowing if the methadone was real or even what it was supposed to look like and headed back to the apartment. As she entered, The Man was sitting in the kitchen with two other men.

"Hey, Bambi, where you been girl?" The Man asked. "Come and meet my investors."

Bambi already knew who his investors were. They were the men who spent money to be with the ladies whom The Man sold to them.

"Men, this is Bambi! She belongs to me!"

One investor looked and winked at Bambi. "She's a cutie!" he spoke.

The Man stood up, walked over to the investor, stood over him, and put his arm on the investor's shoulder, then said, "If I hear you put your dirty hands on her, I will put a bullet in your _ _ _ _ _ _ _ heart! You understand me? She's mine; all mine so put the word out to all your hungry friends. Nobody touches or approaches her!"

"Okay, man! Okay! I was just joking!

The Man then told Bambi, "Baby, go to the room."

Bambi unlocked her room door, and Steve was lying in bed shaking. The withdrawal from the drug was really starting to get to him. Bambi walked over to him and handed him the methadone. Steve looked at it and already knew what it was. He quickly drank it and, in a while, he was feeling somewhat better.

"Thanks, my Sunshine."

"Steve, I told you don't call me that at least not while we are still living here. The Man will get mad."

"Okay then, I'll call you, Bambi. Ugh! I hate that name!" Steve answered.

~Bambi, Steve, and The Man~

"How are you feeling Steve?" Bambi asked.

"I'm feeling better than I was a while ago."

"Steve, do you owe The Man any money?"

"Yep, I owe him over two hundred dollars. That's why I'm still here and because I refuse to leave you no matter how mad you are at me. You are my Sunshine, no matter what."

"Awe Steve, that's why I'm still here also. Even though you hurt me in the worst way, I would not leave you here with The Man."

"Bambi, when do you want to leave?"

"I don't know, Steve. I've been saving some money, but I want you off that stuff. I can't trust you when you shoot up."

"I understand," Steve told Bambi.

"Hey, Bambi!" The Man was yelling from the kitchen. "Come here girl and leave that junkie alone!"

Steve heard what The Man said but could not get mad for he knew The Man was right. Steve looked at Bambi and said, "You better go see what he wants."

"Yeah, I'm going," Bambi answered and headed straight up the hallway where The Man was now sitting in the living room.

"Bambi, bring me the receipts from your shopping girl," The Man told her. So, Bambi handed him the receipts and brought him the clothes she bought. "Bambi, I like the clothes! Here, throw away the receipts. Go cook us something to eat. I want fried chicken and pork chops. Make me a drink of whiskey, *straight* first."

Bambi did what she was told and brought the drink to him. "Come on baby, sit next to me before you start cooking." Bambi sat next to The Man who now began running his hands all over her body, stopping to sip on his whiskey. She felt disgusted but never said a word just let him carry on his routine. After she got up and started cooking, Steve came into the kitchen.

"Need any help, Bambi?"

"Sure, Steve." Both of them cooked The Man's food and placed it in front of him.

The Man looked at Steve, "So, my junkie! When are you going to pay your debt?"

"Soon!" Steve answered.

"Well you better or I'll be putting some of my men on you, and you know what I mean!" The Man continued to eat.

"Come here, Steve!" Bambi said. Steve followed her into the bathroom and watched her pull out money from a secret place in the lining of her pants. "Here, this is two hundred and fifty dollars. Go give this to him now. Tell him you were waiting to give it to him."

"Are you sure?" Steve answered her.

"Yes Steve, go now!"

Steve went back to where The Man was sitting and did exactly what was told to him to do. He handed the money to The Man.

"Well! Well!" The Man said grinning, "What have we here?" and started counting all the money. "Well boy, I guess you can go! I'm sick of looking at your junkie _ _ _ ! Go get your stuff and get the _ _ _ _ out of my house!"

Steve practically ran back down the hallway.

"Bambi, we can go! Let's get out of here now!"

Bambi, thinking that she was able to leave also, packed some of her things then walked with Steve to the front door. The Man was asleep from drinking.

"Come on, Bambi hurry up!"

The two exited the building and started running to the train station.

"Come on, Bambi! Hurry up!"

The two exited the building and started running to the train station. Standing on the platform, waiting on the train, the two, Steve and Bambi, felt a brick had been lifted off of them.

"Hey Steve, can I ask you something?"

"Sure Bambi! What's up?"

"Steve, did The Man say I could leave with you?"

"No Bambi, he didn't, but I was not about to leave you with him."

"Steve, you know he will come looking for me or have someone look for me!"

"Don't worry! We are about to go to Brooklyn!"

"Well, what's going to happen when you start getting sick again, Steve?"

"We will look for some more methadone, and I will be fine. Come, here comes the train!"

The two rode the train until their stop came and then transferred onto another.

"Come on Bambi! This is our stop!"

Bambi followed Steve up the stairs from the train onto the streets.

"Steve, where are we going? And don't put me in trouble again!"

"Never would I ever do that again, Bambi."

"You can stop calling me Bambi! I hate that name!"

"I'm glad, my Sunshine," Steve said with a joyous smile.

"So, Steve, where are we going?"

"My Sunshine, we are going to rent a room at a rooming house."

"Steve, I only have a few dollars!"

Sunshine did not want her friend to know the amount of money she had been saving for she still did not trust him yet.

"I have money, my Sunshine. I stole a thousand dollars from The Man. I took the girls' money they made before they could give it to him!"

"Steve, he is going to beat them up! You shouldn't have done that!"

"No, he won't! He isn't stupid! He will know I took it! Stop worrying Sunshine and come on!"

The building they walked into smelled bad and winos were leaning over the stairway. Steve and Sunshine walked into the super's office which was also an apartment.

Steve spoke, "We would like to rent a room. How much?"

The super responded with a, "Fifty dollars a week, and if it's going to be two of you, then seventy dollars a week."

Steve handed the super enough money to pay for three months. "Come," said the super to the both of them, "follow me and here are two keys. Don't lose them."

The three walked up three flights of stairs and the first door on the right, the super stopped at.

"Here is your room." He opened the door and there were two twin beds, a small very small kitchen, and also a small TV.

"Where's the bathroom?" Steve asked.

"It's right down the hall."

"Oh no!" Steve said. "Do you have anything else?"

"Well, I have a small studio apartment on the next floor. That will cost you four hundred a month."

"Fine," Steve said. "I want that."

So, the three went up to the studio apartment and opened the door. Steve took one look and said, "Here's the money for two months." The super took back the other keys and handed them new keys for this place.

"Wow Steve! At least there's a bathroom and kitchen! We don't have to share with anyone else."

The two young people started to clean the place with whatever they could find.

"I'm hungry, Steve! Where is there around here I can go get us something to eat?"

"There's a store right next door, but we don't have anything to cook in Sunshine."

"Don't worry Steve; I'll be right back."

"Sunshine, I don't want you going out by yourself."

"Steve, I'm all grown up. Don't you think after everything I have been through; do you think I can't take of myself? I'll be right back Steve."

Sunshine left the building. She did not want Steve to see her money. Sunshine had over two thousand dollars hidden in different parts of her clothes. She also had been dipping in money from the girls and saving from shopping money over the year she lived with The Man.

Sunshine walked until she found a little store that sold utensils and cooking items. She bought one pot and one fork and spoon. She did not want Steve to ask questions if she bought a lot of things. She returned to the studio with all the items and food.

"Sunshine, how did you get these things?"

"I told you, Steve, I had a few dollars, so I spent it on this. Oh, I also bought us some sheets. They were at the thrift store for seventy-five cents. Does the TV work?"

"Yeah," said Steve.

"Well, I'm not cooking Steve. You can if you feel like it. I'm going to make these beds, lay down, and watch TV."

"Okay, my Sunshine. I'll cook whatever you got here from the store."

Sunshine laid on the bed after fixing the sheets, and before she knew it, she was asleep. Steve finished cooking and eating. He did not want to wake up his friend, his Sunshine. *I have to stay sober*, he said out loud while looking at Sunshine sleep.

Steve felt really bad for putting his friend through the things he put her through. He wanted to make her proud of him. She was his family now, and he had grown to love Sunshine. He also noticed a hardness in her now that was not there before they moved in with The Man. She still seemed to have compassion, but also an anger that wants to surface, but if it did what would happen? Steve did not want to find out. His heartfelt something for her. He could sense her loneliness. Steve thought about himself also and wondered who he was and where did he belong. He was getting tired of the streets and wanted a home, a real home. *Maybe Sunshine and I could get jobs somewhere and live in a nice apartment and go back to school. Yeah, we could do that. I'll ask her what she thinks about that idea when she wakes up.* Steve laid down in the other bed and watched TV with a feeling of peace across his face. He was happy for the first time in a long time.

~Sunshine A.K.A. Little Girl and Steve~

Sunshine awoke to see Steve asleep in the bed next to her. She got up and walked over to him. She noticed a smile on his face like he was at peace. She also noticed he had sweat that had run down his face.

"Steve! Steve!" she shook him, but Steve did not move. "Steve!" she ran into the bathroom, grabbed a wet, cold towel, and placed in on his face, but he did not respond

Sunshine ran down to the super's apartment, and they both ran back to hers. When the super looked, he just said, "He's dead, girl!" Sunshine let out a piercing scream so loud some of the other tenants ran to her door.

"Somebody, call 911!"

After the paramedics pronounced him dead, they waited for the coroner to arrive and move the body. "Did he have any family, young lady?"

"No," Sunshine managed to squeeze the word out between her tears.

"Well, he will be buried in Potter's Field."

When everyone left, Sunshine just sat in the studio apartment not making a sound and looking at the razor that was laying on the sink. She just couldn't find any reason to live.

"Excuse me, miss! Excuse me, miss!" Sunshine heard the voice but just would not answer. "Miss, please open the door!" Sunshine dragged herself to the door and opened it. "I thought that was you! I was watching from the hallway when you and the super ran up from downstairs. Don't you remember me? You're *Little Girl*! Remember the shelter? Me, you, Gloria, Kim, and Shirley? It's Pam, the tiny one!"

Sunshine looked at the person and noticed it was Pam. She grabbed Pam so hard and pulled her into the studio.

"I'm so sorry, Little Girl! I saw Steve weeks ago uptown, and I gave him my address. He said you and he were going to move here. I was happy to hear you were with him. I and the other girls were so worried about you. We looked everywhere for you. Every one of us went our own way. I just got home today! I've been staying at my boyfriend's house. What happened to Steve?"

Sunshine told Pam everything that had happened since the day Steve and Sunshine left the park and the girls at the shelter.

"Oh, my goodness, Little Girl! Are you alright? You want me to stay here with you?"

"Please!" Sunshine said. "Stay with me, Pam!"

Sunshine was nineteen years old now, and Pam was seventeen.

"Pam, why are you calling me, Little Girl?"

"I don't know," Pam answered. "I guess the name brings back happy times for me. Why do you, Little Girl, go by so many names?"

"Pam," Little Girl asked with a tear rolling down her cheek. "Pam, do you mind if I ask you a question?"

"Sure, Little Girl! What is it?"

"Who am I?" Then Little Girl just started rocking back and forth chanting the words, "Who Am I? Who Am I?" over and over and over. This was making Pam nervous, so she went into her own apartment and called 911.

When the paramedics arrived, they walked into the small studio apartment to find Little Girl still rocking back and forth and chanting the words, "Who Am I?" They proceeded to give her a shot. She didn't feel when the needle went into her arm. They spoke with Pam to tell her which hospital they would be taking Little Girl. Pam told them she would be there in about an hour.

Little Girl was being taken to a mental hospital. She was having a nervous breakdown. The events of her life and the loss of her friend, Steve, had finally taken a toll on her, mentally.

At her arrival at the hospital, a woman came up to her and asked, "What is your name, young lady?"

All Little Girl said was, "Who Am I?" and started chanting the words all over again and rocking back and forth. The lady called to one of the nurses, and they both agreed that she might be in shock. They put Little Girl in a room with a window that had bars on it and a bed. They had her change into hospital pants and top, left her alone in the room, and locked the door. Little Girl sat rocking and continued her chanting of the words, "Who Am I?"

~Little Girl A.K.A. Sunshine A.K.A. Bambi~

Pam arrived at the hospital where Little Girl A.K.A. Sunshine A.K.A. Bambi, was admitted. Pam walked up to the front desk and inquired about Little Girl. The nurse explained that she had to be admitted for evaluation and that Pam could visit her for only a few minutes. The nurse escorted Pam to Little Girl's room and unlocked the door. She then turned to Pam, "Only a few minutes young lady, okay?"

"Yes, ma'am!" Pam replied.

"Hi, Little Girl!" Pam whispered as she approached the bed and sat next to Little Girl.

Little Girl looked at Pam and said, "Hello Pam! Pam, please call me Sunshine!"

"Okay, Sunshine! I liked that name anyway," Pam said. "So, Sunshine, how long do they plan on keeping you here?"

"I don't know, Pam, maybe a week, maybe two weeks, maybe a day. I don't know."

"Well, do you mind if I come here every day and visit you?"

"Come, Pam! Come every day!" Then Little Girl A.K.A. Sunshine a.k.a Bambi started rocking back and forth again.

"Sunshine, stop rocking! Why are you doing that?" Pam started crying for it hurt her heart to she Sunshine acting strangely.

Pam kissed her on the cheek, Little Girl A.K.A. Sunshine A.K.A. Bambi flinched. "It's okay," Pam said as she stood up. "I'm going to leave, but I'll be back tomorrow to see you. I'm going to see if they will let me bring you some pajamas. Those things you have on are ugly, and I'll bring you a book to read or something to write on. Goodnight Sunshine."

Seven

~Michelle and Karen~

Michelle and Karen walked into the Christian bookstore and Michelle went right to the aisle of Bibles while Karen started browsing around, opening pages, and reading through different books.

"You see any book that might interest you, Karen?" Michelle asked, surprising Karen.

"Yeah girl, I would like to read this one. Look! It reads, "How to Read the Bible." I think I will buy this, Michelle!"

"I'll buy it for you, Karen. My gift to you. You are always buying me milkshakes!"

"Okay then! Did you find the Bible you came for?" Karen asked.

"Yep, I sure did! Now let's head to the shoe store!"

"That's what I'm talking about!" Karen smiled and said.

After paying for their items, the women headed to a little shoe store that was Karen's favorite place to purchase shoes.

"Michelle," she asked, "would you tell me anything about Jesus. I mean, I just want you to talk about Him."

"Well, what do you want to know and if I don't know, I will find out."

"I don't know, Michelle! Just talk about Him. Say anything about Him."

"Alright then, in John 14:6, Jesus said, "I am the truth and the life. No one comes to the Father but through Me." That means that Jesus is the only truth. His word is the truth. His way is the right way. His way is the path that we all should take. It is only through Him that we have life. He died so that we can have live."

"So, what you're saying Michelle is His way is really the only way? The only way to what?"

"Karen, the only way to eternal life, the only way to the Father in heaven. We can only go through Jesus to get to the Father in Heaven. You see, our Father in Heaven, God, loves us so much that He sent His Son, His "only" Son, down here to be beaten, crucified and die on the cross and was risen in three days for us, Karen. He died so that our sins can be forgiven, but we must know and believe without a doubt"

"Wow Michelle, now that's real love," Karen whispered.

Michelle looked at her friend once again and just smiled, "Yeah girl! That's real love!" she repeated as they drove into a parking place at the shoe store.

"Karen, you like these shoes?"

"Michelle, where in the world are you going in those? You know good and well you cannot walk in six-inch heels!" Karen said laughing.

"Well Karen, my dear, Joe, might think they are sexy!"

"Sure Michelle, if you are wearing them with no clothes on!"

"KAREN!! People can hear you! Lower your voice!"

"Michelle, come on now! You know I saw that pole in the middle of your bedroom!"

"KAREN, if you don't stop your lying!"

"I'm sorry Michelle! I'm just having fun. You are married you know! Girl, please take that starch out of your panties!" Both women busted out laughing.

"Yeah, you're right Karen, but can you at least lower your voice?"

"Whatever Michelle, I'll lower my voice. Can we please find some shoes?" Karen asked. "Here Michelle, you like boots a lot: ankle boots, tall boots, any kind of boot as long as it's a boot!"

"Ha! Ha! Karen, very funny, but yeah, I like those. Let me try them on."

Both women bought their shoes and boots and walked back to the car.

"Girl, let's walk around the mall!"

"Karen, you know I don't do malls!"

"Aww, come on. We can go through the first store we pull in front of."

"Okay Karen, let's go, but I am not buying anything else, I mean it."

"Okay, that's fine, Michelle. We can order a salad at the food court and just watch the people."

"Karen, you are a nut, you know that? You are a certified nut!"

"As long as I'm a nut for Jesus!" Karen heard the words come out of her own mouth and was amazed at herself. She liked hearing what she said. It felt good inside saying, *Jesus*.

Michelle looked and said, "Amen!"

In the food court, the ladies received their salads and drinks, found a spot, and sat.

"So, Karen, we are people watching? May I ask you why we are doing this?"

"I do it all the time, Michelle! I just sit and watch people and get to thinking about different things. I watch how mothers interact with their children and watch the young people act like young people. It's amazing what you see about people. Now I've sat here at times and watched a few people while eating read their Bible. It wasn't often, only a few times. I like watching people smile and laugh that's all Michelle. That's not crazy, now is it?"

"No Karen, it isn't crazy girl! Guess I'll sit here and watch with you."

"Thank You, God! Thank You for my friend, Michelle! Michelle, do you think He heard me?"

"Uh yeah! I do, Karen! What made you want to say that?"

"I don't know! I just wanted to say *Thank You* to God!"

"Okay Karen, now have we finished looking at the people? I know I've finished my salad."

Karen looked at Michelle, "Okay, are you ready to go, Michelle?"

"Yes, I am! I want to go and walk around the lake."

"Well, let's walk on over to the lake then," Karen said.

They walked out of the mall on down the path towards a beautiful lake.

"Michelle let's walk over to the other side and sit."

When they reached the opposite of the lake, the two women sat on the bench in silence staring into the water.

"This is very peaceful, Karen. Isn't it?"

"Michelle is it like the peace you get from loving Jesus?"

"Yeah Karen, for me anyway because when I'm alone, I get to loving on my Jesus, not saying a word but just enjoying the presence of peace within my spirit."

"Yeah Michelle, that's how I felt when you left me in the room. I felt such a peace that engulfed me. It was ineffable, you know! Like, there are no words that can explain what you feel."

"Yep Karen, I know exactly what you are saying."

"Let me ask you something, Michelle. Do you ever lose it? I mean get angry and lose it? You know like you are so mad, you start yelling and cussing and then feel bad later?"

Michelle started to laugh, "Karen, I used to get so angry and cuss just like you said, and even throw things and ready to punch someone's lights out and I was saved, and the guilt that I felt, knowing my Father did not approve of my actions. I asked God to forgive me. You see Karen, our flesh rises, but we have to let our spirit man override our flesh. It's not easy, especially in this world today. We are in this world but not of this world."

"I really like this, Michelle! I like this serenity, this feeling of calmness. I could live like this forever. So, Jesus is peace and love, and that's what He wants us to have. Is that what you are saying, Michelle?"

"Yes, I am, Karen. He wants us to treat one another like that, with unconditional love, even our enemies. God lets the sun shine on good and bad."

Karen decided not to ask Michelle any more questions. She just wanted to sit and meditate on everything Michelle had already talked about to her. As she sat there looking at the lake and just feeling the peace within herself, Michelle was very happy for her friend, but Michelle was thinking about her doctor's appointment. She just did not want to go through the same ordeal she went through a few years ago with the breast cancer. *Should I go, or should I just ignore it?* She thought to herself. *It's not like the doctor is saying it came back; they just want to perform a biopsy.*

"Come on Michelle, let's go home. It's getting chilly, and I want to go to my house and take a nap," Karen said motioning with her hand and pointing to the car.

"All right let's go then, Karen. I'm getting tired myself."

"Michelle, come over to my house and rest for a while."

"Very well, Karen."

As they walked back to the car, each walked in silence, enjoying their own inner peace. They arrived back at Karen's house, kicked off their shoes, and the two women stretched across Karen's big California King sized bed. Both were tired and needed rest.

"Karen, I'm going to doze off for a while."

"Yeah, me too, Michelle."

The women closed their eyes and drifted off to sleep.

Three hours went by, and Karen awoke to see Michelle still sleeping. So, she, not wanting to wake her, went into the kitchen and started dinner. Karen wanted to cook something to show her thanks to Michelle for really introducing her to who really Jesus is. *It's one thing to know His name, but does one really know who the Son of God really is?* Karen thought to herself.

After cooking dinner, Karen went into the room to wake up her friend only to find her on her knees praying in silence. Not disturbing her, she exited the room. A few minutes later, Michelle appeared in the kitchen and sat at the table.

"Girl, you cooked dinner!"

"Yeah," replied Karen, "just wanted to do something nice for you and say thanks for teaching me about Jesus!"

"Aww sweetie, you are so welcome, Karen."

"Michelle, I'm going to go with you to your doctor's appointment. When is it?"

"It's tomorrow, Karen."

"Well let's eat, and I want you to go home and rest some more and let's get dressed up for this appointment."

"Really Karen, it's just a doctor's appointment."

"So, let's have some fun, okay? Come on! I know you aren't worried are you, Michelle?"

"No! I'm not worried just concerned a little, but I know God's will, will always be done."

"That's what I'm talking about! That's my girl," Karen screamed with joy.

Michelle laughed at Karen, "Girl, you are a nut, but okay, I'll dress to the nine's, and put on my makeup."

Karen, with love from her, replied with, "And after we leave your doctor's office, we are coming back over here, and you will finish telling me the story about Little Girl."

~Michelle, Joe and Karen~

Michelle sat in the waiting room with Karen while Joe, her husband, went to park the car. Joe always stood by his wife, Michelle, no matter what.

"Are you nervous?" Karen asked.

"Nah," Michelle replied, "just, well yeah, I am, Karen."

Just as they continued to talk, Joe appeared at sit next to his wife. "You want me to go in there with you," he asked.

"No sweetie, I'm good. You stay out here with Karen and listen to her talk and talk and talk!" Michelle told her husband. All three laughed as the nurse came out and called Michelle's name. *Here goes,* Michelle whispered to herself.

In what seemed like forever, Michelle came back through the doors where Joe and Karen were waiting. "Well!" Joe and Karen said at the same time.

"I have to return tomorrow at seven in the morning for the biopsy," Michelle told her husband, Joe.

"I'll be right here," Karen spoke.

"Girl, you need to take your behind to work, Karen," Michelle spoke back to her.

"Nope," Karen said, "and you can't make me," poking out her lip.

"We will both be here tomorrow Michelle, waiting for you," Joe whispered. "Now, let's get out of here. I'm hungry, and I need to get back to work. So, ladies, where do you want to eat? And please don't say a *milkshake?*" Joe said as he winked and smiled at his wife.

"Your wife is coming over to my house and yes Joe, we want milkshakes!" Both ladies burst out laughing after Karen spoke her demands.

"Very well! Let's go find you ladies a strawberry milkshake since Karen has to be so demanding!"

Joe dropped the ladies off at Karen's house after their short travel to retrieve the milkshakes at one of the fast food places near Karen's house. Both women waved at Joe as he drove off, headed back to work.

"Well, Michelle let's go in and please tell me what is really going on with you and this breast thing." Karen put her key in the door and then turned to Michelle, "Look, honey, if you are scared, please remember I am here for you."

"Karen, please stop being so dramatic! I'll be fine! Now just open the door, so I can sit down, I'm tired!"

"UGH! You are a little grumpy, aren't you?" Karen laughed at her friend. Michelle just laughed back.

"Karen, I'm going to use your restroom."

"Okay, Michelle," Karen answered.

Michelle went into the bathroom, fell to her knees, and started praying, praying in a soft whisper. "Father, my Holy Father, please comfort me in this time of my need. For Father, it is only You who will be able to bring me out of this pain, for no one knows my Lord, the physical pain I endure. You have been there through all my troubles and enjoyments. You have brought me out of so many things. God, I love You so very much and am truly thankful for all You have given me, so I ask whatever Your will is for me, let it be. I'm just tired now, Lord. Please bless me with physical strength for there's so much work to be done for You."

While Michelle continued praying, Karen sat on her couch wondering why Michelle hasn't spoken about her children lately. She was lost in her own thoughts, not noticing Michelle had come back into the room.

"Hey girl, a penny for your thoughts?" Michelle asked.

Karen stretched out her arms and yawned, "I was thinking about your children, Michelle. You haven't mentioned them in a while. How are they doing and your granddaughter?"

"They are all fine. Suzy has the highest paid position on her job. She also has gone back to making up the model's face and hair, so she's pretty busy. Her daughter, Angel, has been playing tennis at her school and has become very good at it!" Michelle said with a giggle. "Karen, you should see her run up and down and across that tennis court with those long pretty legs of hers! She's really good.

"My son, Thomas, has graduated from his third college and is dressing these high-priced models. Also, he is a manager of some jewelry store. And my youngest daughter, Alice, is away in college about to graduate. So there, Karen, that's all of them!" Michelle said laughing.

"Well, when was the last time you spoke to any of them, Michelle?"

"I spoke with my granddaughter just the other day. She wants to come and spend a week with me next month if she doesn't have tennis practice. Now, are we done with talking about my children. Can we talk about something else?" Michelle asked as she sat in another chair across from Karen.

"Yeah, you are going to finish talking about Little Girl or whatever name she goes by."

~Little Girl A.K.A. Sunshine A.K.A. Bambi~

"Young lady, how are you today? I'm Dr. Francis."

Little Girl sat in the chair looking at the doctor wondering what he could possibly do for her. Little Girl had been to a few therapists when she was a child, and so far, none has done anything or said anything to make her feel any better.

Dr. Francis began to talk to Little Girl, but the words coming from the doctor's mouth seemed distant to her. At the end of the hour session, the doctor said, "Well young lady, we will put you on some medication. It looks like you have had a breakdown, but we need to have a few more sessions. I would also like if you would open up more. I understand that your friend has passed away and I am deeply sorry for you. You will stay the rest of the week in which then I will release you with a prescription. I want you to start talking. You will also start outpatient treatment."

Little Girl nodded her head, got up, and walked back to her room. As she sat on her bed, she could not get the question out of her head, "Who

Am I?"

"Medication time!" the words came over the intercom. All patients began to line up at a window next to the nurse's station. Little Girl lined up with the others, received her pill and water, then started to head back to her room again when one of the attendants walked up to her.

"Young lady, would you like to go into the recreation room? We have books, puzzles, board games, and a TV you can watch. Come on with me. I'm Sandy, one of the floor attendants here."

Little Girl walked with Sandy into the rec room. "You can sit where ever you feel," Sandy said in a soft, compassionate voice so, Little Girl found a spot on a small couch. "Now, what is your name?" Sandy asked.

Little Girl replied, "People call me whatever they want to name me."

"Well young lady, what do you want me to call you? I'll call you whatever name you want to be called, not the names that others have given you."

Little Girl liked the sound of that. In fact, it kind of made her feel like she was in charge of herself. She was able to make her own decision.

"I don't know what name I want to call myself," Little Girl said while looking at the nice attendant. "I don't know who I am. I want to be somebody. I don't know how."

Sandy took Little Girl's hand, "Look, sweetie; you are who God created."

"Sandy, I want to be called *Little Girl*."

"Very well, then that is what I will call you. Now, what is it you would like to do? Would you like to put together this puzzle or I could play a board game with you?"

"I want to put together that puzzle," Little Girl responded.

Little Girl and the attendant, Sandy, started working on the puzzle.

Who Am I?

Her mother did what she wanted

Her father's love was for another

Yet in the dark of eve

a little girl was conceived.

Her father would not stay

Her mother plaid too many games

Now, who's gonna tell Little Girl who she is?

Who Am I?

Happy, sad, confused, angry, mad, joyful, beautiful inside, blessed, and
courageous.

What Does Jesus Say About Who I Am?

Romans 8:33, "I am his elect, full of mercy, kindness, humility, and
longsuffering."

Matthew 5:14-16, "You are the light of the world, a city on a hill cannot
be hidden... In the same way, let your light shine before man, That they may
see your good deeds and praise your father in heaven."

Ephesians 2:10, "I am God's workmanship, created in Christ unto good
works."

Author's Own Thoughts:

Help someone find direction in his/her life. Pray, Lord, put a lamp at
my feet and a light in my path. Teach God's Word, and they will find who
they are

4

TRYING TO FIT IN

~Little Girl and Pam~

Little Girl waited in the visitors' room for Pam to show up. This was Little Girl's day to be discharged from the hospital.

Sandy sat with Little Girl. "Now remember, you have my number. If you need to talk, you just call me no matter what time okay?" Sandy said to Little Girl.

Sandy and Little Girl had become friends. Sandy was twenty-two, just three years older than Little Girl. Sandy wondered to herself, *This girl is nineteen, but if you looked straight into her eyes, you would think you can actually see a little girl looking back at you.*

"Gotcha Sandy," Little Girl responded.

"There's your friend, Pam. Come on, let's meet her halfway."

"Hey, Pam." Little Girl gave Pam a hug and said her goodbyes to some of the nurses and gave Sandy a hug.

"Don't forget!" yelled Sandy.

"I won't!" Little Girl yelled back as she and Pam walked on out the building. "Come on Pam; I want to hurry and get back to my studio apartment!"

"Uh, Little Girl, the super rented your place. He refunded your money. Here, he gave it to me to give you."

"Why Pam? Why would he do that?"

"He said he didn't think you would want to go back to a place where your friend died!"

106

"Who the h--- is he to say what I would like or wouldn't?"

"LITTLE GIRL! What's wrong with you? Why are you talking like that? He was just thinking about you!"

"Whatever Pam! Now, where am I going to stay?"

"Little Girl, you can stay with me! I moved from that place. I live in Queens now. I think you will like it."

"Pam, let me ask you something."

"Yes, what is it?"

"Where do you work?"

"I have a part-time job and my student loan money I use for my rent."

Little Girl looked at Pam and blurted out the words, "YOU'RE IN COLLEGE?"

"Yep!" Pam answered.

"But you're only seventeen!"

Little Girl began to feel that familiar feeling rising up in herself, that feeling of not being good enough; inadequate. She quickly pushed it back like she did most of her feelings. "I'm happy for you, Pam."

"Come on Little Girl; we have a train to catch.

Little Girl followed Pam off the train and up to the street where they waited for a bus. After getting off the bus and walking a few blocks, there was a very nice apartment building with a park and a lake across from the building.

"Hurry, Little Girl!"

Little Girl followed Pam into an elevator up to the seventh floor.

"Here we are," Pam said as she took out her keys and opened the door.

Following Pam inside, Little Girl looked, scanning the place with her eyes. "Pam, this is nice! It's really pretty!"

"Thanks, Little Girl! Come, let me show the room you will be staying in as long as you want."

Little Girl's eyes nearly popped out of her head. "Wow! That's a big bed, Pam! Is that where I'm going to be sleeping, in that big bed?"

Pam chuckled at Little Girl's remark, "Yes, you will be sleeping in that bed! I said this room is yours as long as you want!"

Little Girl turned around and gave Pam a huge hug.

"Come on. Let me show you the kitchen, and we can find something to eat. Just throw your things on your bed."

Little Girl tossed the one bag she had on the bed and followed Pam into the kitchen. "Wow, Pam! This is pretty! I like the colors, yellow and green!"

Pam searched around her cabinets to find something for them to eat. "Here we go! How about I make us some sandwiches! Is that okay with you, Little Girl?"

"Sure Pam, whatever you make, I will eat."

Pam made the sandwiches, and both sat down at the table to eat.

"Pam, how much rent do you pay for this place?" Little Girl asked.

"I told you. I use my student loan money, and I work part-time," answered Pam.

"What do you want to do, Little Girl? Do you want to work or go back to school?"

"I think I want to study for my GED!"

"Great!" Pam screamed with happiness. "I know just where you can go and it's not far from here. You saw that building we passed a few blocks back? You know that building with the gate around it, and the flowers in the front? They have evening classes from six to nine in the evening. We can go and get you signed up if you're ready. You know after everything you just been through, you might want to rest for a few days."

"Nope," Little Girl said, "I want to go as soon as possible. When can we go?"

"We will have to go Monday. They aren't open on the weekends, and it's too late to go now. They close early on Friday's," Pam replied, "Plus my boyfriend works there. He's one of the teachers who tutors the ones studying for their GED. He just works part-time too. You'll meet him. He's coming over here tonight to meet you. I told him all about us and the rest of the girls from the shelter."

Little Girl did not like the idea of some stranger knowing all those horrible things about her.

"Come, let me see if I have some clothes you can fit."

Little Girl walked into Pam's room and just could not believe how pretty her room was. *Something ain't right*, Little Girl thought to herself, *how can Pam afford all these nice things on her part-time job*? But as always, Little Girl pushed that thought back in her mind where she stored everything else.

Looking through her closet, Pam pulled out a pair of jeans, a shirt, and a sweater. "Here Little Girl, you can have these. Go try them on and see if they fit you."

So, Little Girl went into the bathroom to try on her clothes and yelled through the door, "Hey Pam, throw me a towel and cloth! Also, do you have an extra toothbrush?"

"Sure do, look under the sink in the cabinet. You'll find everything you want."

After about an hour, Little Girl came out. Her hair was neatly brushed down around her face, the clothes fit perfectly, and she even put on a little of Pam's makeup. Pam looked at her longtime friend. "You look beautiful, Little Girl!"

"Thanks, Pam! Now, what are we going to do now Pam?"

"I know," Pam said, "let's walk around the neighborhood so you can see where exactly you are staying or, I could call some of my friends from school to come over, and we could just hang around here."

"That sounds better. I don't really feel like walking."

So, Pam made a few phone calls, and within the hour, people started knocking on her door. First, a tall, slim, handsome guy came in.

"Hey, girl! What's happening?"

"Hi, Charley! I want you to meet my friend, Little Girl."

Charley extended his hand out, "LITTLE GIRL?" Charley asked. "Why do people call you that? From what I see, you are definitely not a little girl!"

Little Girl shook his hand. For the first time, she felt funny being called that name. Standing there with her hand in his, she responded with, "It's just a nickname someone gave me when I was young, and people who are close to me still call me that."

"Then I, too, shall call you *Little Girl*," Charley answered back.

Then came another knock at the door. Pam opened the door to see her classmates, Greg and Yvette. "Hey, guys! Come on in! You all know Charley, and this is a longtime friend of mine, Little Girl, who now is my new roommate."

"Hello, Little Girl!" Greg and Yvette said with a smile as they walked past her and straight into the kitchen. "Hey Pam," they yelled backed, "who else is coming over? Is Jason, your boyfriend, coming?"

"Yes!" answered Pam and just as she answered, Jason walked right into the apartment grabbing Pam and slamming a big kiss on her mouth.

"Hey, baby! What's new?" he said after removing his lips from her face.

"Jason, I want you to meet someone special to me. Little Girl, come over here," Pam said happily.

Little Girl had taken a seat on the couch across from Charley who was gazing through one of the magazines on the coffee table.

"Little Girl, this is Jason, my boyfriend. Isn't he handsome?"

"Hello, Little Girl!" Jason said. "So, I finally get to meet you! Pam talks about you and the other girls she used to live with a lot."

As Jason continued his conversation with Little Girl and Pam, three other people came into the apartment. "HEY EVERYONE! THE PARTY IS HERE!!!" one of the people hollered as they entered the apartment. Pam screamed with joy and ran over to the three people.

"What's happening, guys!" she yelled. She then pushed them over to Jason and Little Girl. "You all this is Little Girl! Little Girl, this is Ricky, Brenda, and Donna!"

"Glad to meet you, Little Girl," all spoke. "So, Pam, what's the plan? You got us all over here! What's going on?"

"I just wanted us all to hang out, you know, listen to music, eat, and I wanted you all to get to know my friend, Little Girl!"

"Hey, is that a nickname?" Ricky asked looking at Little Girl.

"Yeah, that's what we call her," Charley spoke up, smiling at Little Girl and giving her a wink.

"Come on Pam," Brenda spoke loudly. "Play some music and you guys run out and buy some beer!"

Jason, Charley, Greg, and Ricky left to retrieve some beer while the girls Pam, Little Girl, Yvette, Donna, and Brenda gathered in the living room. All found a place to sit or stretch out across the floor.

"So, Pam, play some music and let's get this party started," Yvette said, "And I know you got the pills!" she whispered to Donna.

"Sure do, but only a small amount. The rest is for Pam to sell."

Little Girl tried not to look at Pam while listening to the girls' conversation.

"Hey, Pam, how much money did you make off the last bundle of pills?" Brenda asked.

"I don't know, maybe about a thousand dollars!" Pam answered.

"You sell pills, Pam?" Little Girl asked loudly.

"It's just a little speed, Little Girl. No harm. I need the money to pay for this place and other things."

"But I thought you said the money comes from your student loan!"

"Hey, where did you find this girl," Donna yelled, talking about Little Girl.

"She's okay," Pam said, "she's just looking out for my best. Now Brenda, go get the bags and let's start bagging some of these pills up."

Brenda got up and returned and dropped on the coffee table some small yellow paper bags. Donna pulled out her purse a huge plastic bag full of pills.

"Okay girls let's start filling the paper bags," Pam suggested. Looking at Little Girl, Pam asked, "Do you want to help us?"

"Sure," Little Girl answered but not really wanting to.

"Well, watch what I do, and you just do the same."

As the girls continued to fill the little yellow paper bags with pills, the boys arrived back from the store.

"Girls look what we got!" yelled Ricky as he and the boys gathered around the girls.

"What Ricky? What did you all get?" answered Pam. Pulling out the large bag the Greg was carrying were three bottles of booze, a bag of herb and a small package with white powder in it. Little Girl knew instantly what the white powder was, either heroin or cocaine. "Where's the beer?" Pam asked.

"Right here, my lovely!" Ricky laughed.

Just as Little Girl was going to ask Pam a question on what was going on, Charley grabbed her arm, pulled her aside, and walked her to the end of the couch. "Here," he spoke to Little Girl, "sit here next to me. You don't seem to fit in in all this stuff."

"Hey Charley," Rick yelled across the room, "Come on and get a beer and give Girl one too. You don't mind me calling you *Girl*? Little Girl is too long for me to say!"

"I don't mind," Little Girl said.

Charley got up, walked over, retrieved two beers, and then walked back to where Little Girl was sitting. "Would you like a beer?" he asked as he stretched out his arm to hand a beer to Little Girl.

"Sure," she responded and took it from his hands.

"Is this a party?" Little Girl turned and asked Charley.

"Yep, this is a bunch of us college students getting together and just hanging out. I don't indulge in the getting high part though, but I do like my beer!"

Little Girl listened to what Charley was saying and also watching Pam. Little Girl would have never thought Pam, the youngest of all the girls at the shelter, would be selling pills.

Brenda, who was a little conniving, got up and walked over to where Charley and Little Girl were sitting. As she approached the two, she handed Little Girl a straw that had been cut in half with some white powder that was made into a straight line on a saucer.

"No thanks," Little Girl," said.

"What do you mean, no?" Brenda said. "You can't be a Miss Goodie Two Shoes? Weren't you homeless once? What college do you attend? Oh, that's right, you haven't graduated high school, right?"

"What does that have to do with me saying no to your stinky drugs?" Little Girl said in an angry voice. "You had better get out of my face with that stuff before I shove it up your *you know what*!"

"Well excuse me," Brenda said back. Then she yelled, "Look, everyone, Miss Uneducated won't party with us! Thinks she's too good. From what Pam has told us, her boyfriend died from drugs! Oh yeah, that wasn't your boyfriend, now was it? That was your gay friend who sold his body so you and he could, what's the word you used Pam? Oh yeah, survive!"

Little Girl sat there listening and debating on whether to knock her out or just keep her mouth shut. And just as Brenda began to speak again, Pam jumped across the room, lifted her arm up, and landed a hard punch across Brenda's mouth. Now both girls were punching and rolling across the floor. Jason ran over and grabbed Pam while Ricky took a hold of Brenda.

"Now girls, please no fighting over me!" Ricky smiled and said with a laugh.

Jason responded with a, "Not now, Ricky!"

"Aww, come on guys! Why is everyone getting fussy?" Ricky said. "Look, Brenda; if *Girl* doesn't want any then she doesn't want it! Leave her alone. Come on you and I will do a line!" So, Ricky took Brenda's hand, and both walked into the kitchen.

Jason and Pam sat on the couch with Charley and Little Girl. "I'm so sorry, Little Girl," Pam said as she tried to ease the tension she could tell that was engulfing Little Girl. "I don't know what's wrong with Brenda!"

"She's high and drunk! That's what's wrong with her?" Jason responded. He looked at Pam's face and ran his hand across her eye. "Baby, your eye is beginning to swell. I think she got a good one in! Also, I think this party should be over. Tell everyone they need to leave, or would you prefer I have the pleasure of escorting everyone out the door?"

"You do it, Jason. I want to sit here with Little Girl."

"Okay baby. I'll go tell them." So, Jason went to talk to the others about leaving.

"Little Girl, are you alright?" Pam asked.

Little Girl turned and just said, "Don't ever call me *Little Girl* again, Pam! You're a liar, and I don't believe anything you said or will say. You sell drugs and take drugs!"

"No, I don't do drugs, Little Girl! And yes, I sell some pills! Everyone in here sells speed except Charley! The money helps us pay our bills!"

"So then, this is your part-time job, Pam?" Little Girl asked.

Pam answered, "No, it is not. I have a part-time job at the college. I work in the bookstore on campus. I just want to live decently and be happy with myself. You remember how we had to live in the shelter and the things we went through? I refuse to live like that again, Little Girl. That's why I'm determined to finish college and get my degree."

Little Girl started feeling that feeling of herself being dumb begin to rise in her. It seemed like when someone mentioned themselves going to school, that feeling always surfaces.

"Don't be upset with me for trying to better myself, Little Girl! I want you to get your GED and get into college too. As I said, Jason will tutor you."

"Alright, then Pam. I'll get my GED and see what happens next."

Pam whispered, "I'm really sorry about Brenda and everything she said. She was drunk and high."

"It's alright," Little Girl spoke. "She didn't say anything that really would have made me slap her."

"Alright," Charley spoke up, "that's enough talk about Brenda! Let's all get something to eat."

Jason had now returned from putting everyone else out of the apartment and returned to his seat next to Pam.

"Hey, didn't you guys buy some pizzas?" Pam asked.

"Oh Yeah, we sure did!" Charley responded. 'Come on, Little Girl. Let's you and I go in the kitchen and heat a few slices up and get some plates."

"Okay, Charley." Little Girl was beginning to like Charley, but she just didn't want to trust him. She couldn't; men were liars and will take whatever they wanted when they wanted it.

"So, Jason," Pam asked, "what do you think about Little Girl?"

"I don't know, Pam. She seems to be in thought most of the time and watches everything around her, She also seems like wanting to be an outsider and yet wanting to also belong, know what I mean?"

"Yeah, I do Jason. She's been through a lot like me. I want you to really tutor her and help her get her GED."

"Anything for you, my princess," Jason responded and smacked a big kiss on Pam's lips.

While in the kitchen, Charley reached for some paper plates while Little Girl grabbed a few slices of pizza. "Hey Little Girl, do you mind if I ask you a personal question?"

"No Charley, go right ahead. I don't have to answer if I choose not to!" Little Girl said with a laugh.

"Little Girl, how come you don't have a boyfriend?"

"Charley, I don't know! I did have a very close friend who passed away from drugs, but I don't know too many guys who I trust. Maybe that's why."

"Little Girl, I want to start dating you."

"Charley, you don't know me, and I don't know you. Come on let's get back in the living room with this pizza."

~Karen~

"Michelle," Karen asked, "what is it about Little Girl that you get sad at times when you tell her story?"

"Karen, I can't tell you that but what I will tell you is that I'm very close to Little Girl."

"Well, where is Little Girl now, Michelle?"

"Karen, you are a nosy person," Michelle giggled. "I'll tell you what I need to tell or want to tell. Got it?"

"UGH!" Karen laughed. "You are a trip, meaning a good trip! So, my lady, are you ready for tomorrow?"

"Yes Karen, I am ready. I've put it all in GOD's hand so, I am going to ask you to drive me home so I can get some rest and prepare myself for tomorrow."

"Then let's go," Karen said.

Both ladies got up, headed out the front door, and walked to the car. On the drive to Michelle's house, Karen began to speak.

'You know something Michelle, can you tell me something about why your children don't come and visit you more?"

"Karen, please leave my children alone! I don't want to talk about them! They have their lives, they are healthy, and I am very happy and BLESSED for them.

"Now, we are here at my house, so I am going to say have a BLESSED evening and be ready about 6 am. Love you my crazy nutty best friend."

"Love you too, Michelle, and I will meet you and Joe there. Goodnight, my friend."

Michelle got out of the car, walked up to her driveway, and disappeared into her house. Karen sat for a minute in Michelle's driveway, once again wondering to herself, *What is Michelle not saying about Little Girl, or about herself? Oh well, time will tell.* Then she drove off, headed not home but to the nearest restaurant, parking her car in the parking space at the restaurant. Karen headed into the place, took a seat at a small table, and waited on the waiter.

"Hello, my name is Keith. I'll be your waiter today. What would you like to drink?"

Karen responded with, "I'll have red wine, a bottle of water, and a tall cup of hot water, please."

"Very well," answered the waiter, Keith. "Here's your menu. I will be back with your drinks."

Karen looked around at the other people seated in the restaurant. While waiting for her drinks, she allowed her mind to race once again back to everything Michelle had told her about Little Girl. Karen continued to wonder, *Why is Michelle so sensitive when it comes to telling the story. Where is this, Little Girl, and what is her real name? Why doesn't Michelle tell me everything? She will tell me all about Jesus and God, but what is it about the girl she calls, Little Girl?*

"Here's your drinks, ma'am," Keith, the waiter, appeared placing Karen's glass of wine, bottled water, and a glass of hot water. "Have you decided on what you would like from the menu, ma'am?"

"Keith, I think I'll have a bowl of vegetable soup and the house salad, thank you."

"Coming right up."

Karen took her utensils and placed them in the glass of hot water to sterilize them and began sipping on her small glass of wine. *I wonder where all these people are today, those who did not die,* Karen thought. Keith, the waiter, returned with her soup and salad.

"Ma'am, are you okay?" he asked Karen.

Karen looked up at the waiter and noticed he was a very attractive man, had to be maybe in his late forties. "I'm good" she answered.

"Excuse me, I don't mean to pry, it's just that you seem to be in deep thought. I don't usually do this, but if you need to talk to someone, I get off in five minutes and can sit here with you and just be an ear for you."

Karen looked at the waiter with a surprised look on her face, then without a second thought, she parted her lips and the word, "Yes," came jumping out.

"Great, give me five, and I'll be right back," said the waiter, Keith.

As he walked away, Karen laughed to herself, *What in the world did I just do? I just invited a stranger to come and sit with me.* Karen started on her soup and salad, taking a sip of wine between the salad and soup.

"Well, beautiful lady, I'm back. May I have the pleasure of sitting here with you?" It was Keith, the waiter dressed in his plain clothes.

"Please," Karen said pointing to the other seat.

"So, let me introduce myself again. My name is Keith, and I am the manager, waiter, host, and owner of this restaurant."

Karen reached out to shake his hand. "I'm Karen, the woman with a lot of thoughts and trying to sort a few things out. First, may I ask a question," as she sipped on her glass of wine. "Why do you wait on tables and host when you own the place?"

"Well Karen, I feel it's important to help out others. Just because I may own this place, doesn't mean I should just sit back and do very little. I get along well with my employees. I believe in respecting all of them, and I believe in receiving respect back. Now that's enough of me for now. Talk to me about your thoughts, Karen."

"Okay, it's like this, Keith, I have a friend whom I love as if she was my own blood sister, but I just feel like there is something going on with her that she isn't saying, and I don't know why. We usually tell one another everything. I have to meet her and Joe, that's her husband, at the hospital early tomorrow morning. She's having a biopsy done and to tell the truth; I'm the one worried. She, her name is Michelle, seems not to worry about it."

Keith began to speak with a very soft and gentle tone in his voice. "Karen, let me say something to you. If you believe in Jesus, all and everything is possible. Is your friend, Michelle, a believer in Jesus and the Father in Heaven, and if she is, that's why she isn't worried because her faith is in Him."

Karen put her glass of wine down and just looked at Keith with her mouth wide open. "Wow, you sound like Michelle! She is always talking like that. So, you are a believer in Jesus, also?" Karen asked.

"Yes, I am, Karen. I found our Lord and Savior many years ago after my mother passed away. I was so depressed and just wanted to give up on life then I watched this program on TV about Jesus and how He can heal everyone and everything. At first, I had my doubts because mother was already dead and what could Jesus do for me? So, I called the prayer line and asked them to pray for me.

They did. They also asked me to join a church and start reading the Bible. I was obedient and did just what was asked of me, and this is what my Lord did for me. I own my own restaurant through hard work and keeping my faith no matter how hard things got. You see, God said, *I know the plans I have for you. Plans for you to prosper and not harm you. Plans to give you hope and a future.* When I read that in the Bible, I believed every word of it. Your friend has faith and knows that whatever God's will is for her, it shall come to pass. She finds her peace in Him, so she doesn't have to worry for the truth is with Jesus. That's where you'll find the answers to everything that you are thinking about, Karen.

"Now, do you mind if I order us a cup of tea and some chocolate cake. I seem to have a sweet tooth, and your meal is on the house, Karen."

"Yes Keith, let's have some tea." Karen felt a calmness inside her, and she liked this stranger.

After the tea and cake arrived at their table, Karen asked, "Are you married? I mean, I don't want to get you into any trouble with your wife. You are a very nice man, and I thank you so much for taking the time to sit and talk with me."

"No Karen, I am not married. I'm waiting on the Lord to send the right woman for me. Are you married, Karen?"

"Oh no! I was, but he ran off with a younger woman so, it's just me; no children."

"Then Karen, would it be to forward of me to ask if I could see you again? I would like to have invited you to breakfast, but since you are going to the hospital to be with your friend and if your friend won't mind me being there, I could meet you at the hospital for moral support."

Karen, without thinking, answered with a, "Yes, I think I would like that Keith. It's the private hospital on Elms Street. I will be there about 6:30 am. Michelle doesn't have to be there until 7 am. It will give us some time to introduce you to everyone."

"Well then, I'm going to call it a night, my lady. I have a lot of paperwork to finish and employees to help get out of here. My number is on this business card. You call me in the morning. You have a wonderful and blessed night."

"Goodnight to you too, Keith, and again thank you."

"No Karen, let's give God the glory for all good things, but you are very welcome, my lady friend."

Karen watched as Keith walked off to attend to his restaurant. *Wow*, she thought to herself, *he seems like a very nice man.*

~Michelle, Joe, Karen and Keith~

Ring!! Ring!! Michelle rose from her bed to reach over to turn off her alarm clock. She then went into her bathroom and fell to her knees to pray as she does every morning. After praying, she then showered, dressed, and went in to wake up Joe.

"Joe! Joe!" she whispered. "It's time to take me to the hospital for the surgery."

Joe jumped up. "Baby, are we late?"

"No Joe, we have plenty of time. I just want to get there early."

"Alright honey, give me a few minutes, and we will be ready to leave. Are you okay, Michelle?"

"Yes Joe, I'm blessed."

Michelle waited on Joe in which it didn't take him long to shower and dress. "Okay honey, let's get in the car." As they rode in the car on the way to the hospital, neither spoke a word. Joe's thoughts were on his wife and hoping everything will turn out good. Michelle's thoughts were on praying and talking to God in her mind.

As they pulled up to the front of the hospital, Joe let her out while he went and parked the car. Michelle stood there waiting for his return when Karen walked up.

"Hey, girl! How are you feeling?" she asked Michelle.

Michelle looked at Karen. Karen looked like Karen, but yet something seemed different. "I am doing good, Karen," Michelle replied. "You, on the other hand, look somewhat different." Karen just smiled. "What Karen, tell me, girl? Don't start hiding something from me!"

Karen still smiled and said, "You will see!"

"Girl, if you don't tell me," Michelle said.

"Okay, okay! Dag, you are a pushy one this morning!" Karen laughed. "Look, I met this guy last night when I went out to eat. He was the waiter at this restaurant I go to sometimes, but anyway, he saw that something was really on my mind."

"So, he saw something written across your mind!"

"Come on Michelle; you know what I mean! Well anyway, he started talking with me and girl, he started talking about Jesus!"

"Get out of here!" Michelle yelled with happiness. "Karen, you found someone who loves Jesus?"

"Sure did girl, and Michelle, we talked for a while. He seems to be such a nice person. Oh, and I found out, not only is he the waiter, but he owns the restaurant. He is also meeting me here to give me moral support for you. He wanted to take me out for breakfast, but I told him I needed to be here with my dearest friend. So he should be here soon."

"Hey ladies," Joe's voice was being heard. "Come on and let's get my wife signed in and prepped for her surgery."

All three walked into the hospital to the location where Michelle needed to be. As she signed and filled out paperwork, a tall, handsome man approached them and walked right over to Karen.

"Good morning, my lady!" It was Keith.

Joe turned around and tapped Michelle on the shoulder and nodded his head in Karen's direction. Joe whispered to Michelle, "Who's that?"

"That's Karen's new friend. She said he is very nice and loves to talk about Jesus."

"That's good then. Maybe this guy might be the one for her!"

"Come on Joe, Karen just met him!"

"Well, you never know. I'm just saying."

"Hey, you two, I want you to meet a very nice friend of mine," Karen spoke as she walked closer to Michelle and Joe. "This is Keith. Keith, this is my dearest friend and only best friend, Michelle and this is her husband, Joe."

Joe extended his hand to Keith. Both men shook, and all four went to find seats until Michelle was called for prepping before her surgery.

"So, Keith," Joe asked, "how did you and Karen meet?"

"Joe, I'll tell you later," Michelle interrupted.

Keith responded with, "I met this beautiful spirit in my restaurant."

"Oh, did she eat and not pay and have to wash the dishes?" Joe asked with a laugh.

"Ha, Ha, Joe!" Karen laughed with him.

Keith laughed as well and said, "Even if she hadn't enough money, I would have just let it slide!"

"Well looks like Karen has an admirer," Joe said. "Listen, when all this is over, why not all four of us get dressed to the nines, hit a movie, and dinner?" Joe said.

"That sounds like a plan!" Keith is agreeing.

"My people," Michelle said, "it's time for me to go into pre-op and prepare for surgery. Everyone grab hands so we can go into prayer."

The four held hands in a small circle and started praying. After prayer, Michelle kissed Joe and turned to Karen and Keith and thanked them both for their support and walked away down a long hallway.

Karen then asked, "Is she going to be okay, Joe?"

Joe just smiled at Karen and said, "Karen, you know Michelle. She has so much faith in her Lord, and she will always tell you whatever His will is, it will be done."

"Amen," responded Keith, "now that's a woman of faith."

"Come on everyone, let's go and find a place to sit and wait," Joe said.

Karen asked, "Joe, I want to ask you a question concerning Michelle."

"Sure Karen, what's up? Fire away! Let's sit first." All three found a place in the waiting room where they were able to sit together. "Okay Karen, what's the question?"

"Joe, has Michelle ever talked about a girl by the name of *Little Girl* to you?"

"Yes, she has, but not much. Why?"

"What did she say about this Little Girl?" Karen asked Joe.

"Karen, she really didn't say too much except she remembers the pain the Little Girl had to endure many years ago. Why are you asking me this, Karen?"

"Joe, she's been telling me the story about Little Girl, and I was just wondering if you knew who this girl was, and sometimes I just wonder if she's talking about herself!"

"Karen, I doubt, she is talking about herself. I think she knew this girl years ago and maybe they were really good friends, or she knew someone that knew the girl. Whatever the case Karen, I want to focus on what's happening now in that operating room and when she will be coming out into recovery."

"Joe," Keith responded, "you know your wife and the faith she carries, so I believe she is going to be just fine. In fact, she already is. In the name of Jesus, I speak healing over Michelle."

"Thanks, Keith, I know she is fine. Sometimes, I wish I had the faith and knew Jesus the way she does. I just tell her to pray for both of us."

"Well," Keith asked, "Do you want to know him, Joe? I can tell you so much about His love for us."

"Wow," Karen spoke up, "Michelle is teaching me about Jesus and how to pray. Joe, Jesus, our Lord, is awesome and amazing. I found myself one day praying straight from my heart and the feeling that engulfed me; I cannot find the words to explain. It was such a peace. Joe, the more Michelle teaches me about our Lord Jesus, I wonder why it has taken me so long to want to give my life over to him. I still don't know anything like Michelle, but what I do know and believe is that He loves me so much and all I have to do is have faith. Michelle told me once to study to show myself approved, stay in His word and don't worry about what others say or think about me. And," Karen says with a little giggle, "she told me to bridle my tongue and stop gossiping about people!

~Little Girl, Pam, Charley and Jason~

"Here, you guys! Here's the pizza. Sorry, it took us a while! We were talking in the kitchen!" Charley explained to Pam and Jason.

Little Girl and Charley found a spot on the floor and sat next to one another. "Jason," Charley began to speak, "don't you think Little Girl and I would make a great couple?"

Little Girl's mouth flew open, and her eyes got wide. "I think you both would!" Pam butted in saying.

"She said that we don't know one another to be a couple yet!" Charley spoke.

"Okay, I'll tell you something about him," Jason said. "What do you want to know about him, Little Girl? Okay, I'll tell you what! I'm just going to talk about him right in front of him.

"Charley is studying at the college with the rest of us. He's majoring in Engineering; gets honors on most of his tests. He has his own place, works at some business office doing what, I haven't a clue!" Jason said with a loud laugh. "What is it you do again?" Jason said laughing and talking to Charley at the same time.

Charley just laughed back and replied with, "I am an intern with the firm, Steve and Steve. I answer phones, schedule appointments, etc., etc. Now go on Jason, finish telling this beautiful girl all about me."

"Now Little Girl, Charley is also a calm person. He loves to play tennis, even though I, myself, think he's playing baseball the way he's always hitting the ball with his tennis racket onto someone else's court!

"Your turn Pam!" Jason says turning to Pam. "Tell Little Girl what you know about Charley!"

"Okay, my turn!" Pam says. "Little Girl, I think you and him would make a good couple because number one, you both are good looking!"

"Really Pam!" Jason says. "I know you can think of something else!"

"I'm not finished, Jason!" Pam laughs. "Charley is really sweet, will give you the shirt off his back if you needed it. He doesn't indulge in drugs of any kind. He loves his beer, though. He drives his own car!"

Jason burst out with a loud laugh, "Is that what you call that thing?"

Charley looked at Jason and responded with a, "Shut up man!" while laughing along with Jason.

"Anyway," Pam continued to talk, "Little Girl, you are nineteen and Charley is twenty-one. Why don't you to just start talking and dating? You know, go out to the movies or shopping or something maybe a walk in the park!"

"Yeah that's what we should do!" yelled out Charley. "Why don't we all four go for a walk in the park tomorrow? What do you think about that, Little Girl? Please, pretty please! I'm begging."

Little Girl smiled and said, "You're crazy Charley, but yeah, I'll go with you guys to the park!"

"Great then! I'm going to say goodbye now and if I go straight to sleep, tomorrow will be here quick!" Charley said with a smile. "But before I go, can I give you a kiss on the cheek, Little Girl?"

Just before Little Girl could answer with a yes, Charley had jumped up, landed a kiss on her cheek, and gave her a wink with his eye.

"Well, it's late. I'm going to leave also Pam, darling. You and Little Girl get some sleep and Charley, and I will see you two tomorrow afternoon."

"Bye baby," Pam said and kissed Jason, and both guys left the apartment. Little Girl stood up and smiled at Pam. "What?" Pam said again, "What?"

"He's so nice, Pam! Is he really like this all the time or is this just an act to get in my pants?"

"No, Little Girl! He's like this all the time!"

"Then why doesn't he have a girlfriend?" asked "Little Girl.

"He did," Pam responded. "She used him and cheated on him. It broke his heart. She lived with him and had sex with some guy while Charley was in class in Charley's apartment!"

Little Girl asked, "How did Charley find out?"

"His class let out early, and he got home and saw them both in bed.

Charley beat him and threw her out."

"How long ago did this happen, Pam?" Little Girl asked.

"Last year, Pam said. "A lot of girls want to date him, but Charley is very picky. He sees something good in you, Little Girl. Give him a chance; I bet you and him will become a couple."

"What a day this has been, Pam. Tell me what is wrong with your friend, Brenda! Why is she so mean? You know who she reminds me of?"

"I know! She reminds me of her too!"

"Shirley!" both girls spoke at the same time.

"Yeah, it kind of hurts still that she's gone."

"Yeah," Little Girl said and started crying.

"What's wrong?" Pam asked. "Are you thinking about Steve?"

"Yes!" Little Girl said in a whisper. "I miss my friend so much!"

Pam put her arm around Little Girl. "It's going to get better. I promise," Pam said. "Look, it's been a very long day. Let's go to bed. We can clean this mess up in the morning."

"Yeah, let's, Pam," Little Girl said. "Thanks for letting me stay with you and giving me a room to lay my head."

"You're welcome. I'm going to bed. You get whatever you want if you get hungry, okay. See you in the morning girl, good night!"

~Karen, Joe, Keith and Michelle~

"How long has it been already?" Joe said out loud.

"About an hour already," Keith responded. "I think the doctor should be coming out soon to let us know that she's in recovery. Let's wait a few more minutes then we will go ask what's going on," Keith said.

"Alright then. I'll wait ten minutes more. So, do you two want to come over and sit with Michelle and me when they release her?" Just as Karen began to answer Joe, the doctor came into the waiting area and asked for the Brown family. "That's me!" Joe yelled jumping to his feet.

The doctor came over to where Joe was standing. "Hello, I'm Doctor Harris," extending his hand to shake Joe's hand. "I have to say we are going to have to keep your wife overnight. We ran into a complication. Her blood pressure dropped to a dangerously low, and we would like to keep an eye on her. Everything else went well. The tumor was removed."

Karen then spoke out, "I thought it was just a biopsy being done!"

"No ma'am! She was having the cancerous tumor removed."

Karen looked at Joe with eyes full of questions. Joe looked at the doctor with the same look Karen showed on her face.

"Doctor Harris," Joe started speaking with a soft voice, "my wife said it was just a biopsy being done."

"I'm sorry sir, but it was a tumor that was removed, and your wife knew that. I'm sorry she didn't explain it to you. She will need to take chemotherapy and some radiation for a few weeks. She's been through this once before, is that correct Mr. Brown?"

"Yes, doctor. When can we see her?"

"Come with me. She's in a room now. We wanted her settled in her room before we came and spoke with you."

"That's fine, doctor," Joe responded.

Karen was speechless. She grabbed Keith's hand without acknowledging what she had done. He held her hand and walked with her, Joe, and the doctor to Michelle's room. As they entered the room, Joe looked at his wife laying there with an oxygen tube hanging from her nose, a blood pressure cup on her arm, and an IV in her arm. He walked towards the bed slowly whispering her name, "Michelle? Michelle, honey are you okay?"

Michelle, feeling extremely groggy from all the anesthesia, whispered, "Joe?"

Joe took her hand and gave her a smile. "Please don't speak, honey. Just lay there. I'm here, okay, and Karen and Keith are right over there," as Joe spoke he motioned his hand for Karen and Keith to come over to the bed.

Karen approached, trying desperately to fight back her tears but was unsuccessful in trying. "Hi Michelle, how are you feeling?" she spoke, fighting through her tears.

Michelle looked at her friend and managed a smile, "Now, I know you are not crying," Michelle softly spoke then dozed back to sleep.

"What's wrong with her doctor?" Joe asked.

"She's going to be fine, Mr. Brown. Let's let her rest now. You all can come back tomorrow. She will be awake by then and feeling a little stronger."

"I'm not leaving," Joe managed to say.

"Neither are we," Keith also spoke.

"Well then, you all may wait in the waiting room. The nurse will show you to the waiting room on this floor."

As the three were shown to the waiting room where there were two long couches and a pullout recliner, Karen turned to Joe and asked, "Why didn't she tell us, Joe? Why didn't she say anything about the cancer?"

"Karen, I don't want to talk about that right now. Let's sit down and gather our thoughts and maybe figure out on eating something. You look like you can eat a little something right?"

"Joe!" Karen spoke loudly. "Joe, I'm not hungry. Answer me, Joe."

"Karen, I don't want to talk about it right now! Please don't ask me again!"

"Come on you, two," Keith spoke. "Let's all see what they have in the cafeteria. I think we all could also use some fresh air and a bite to eat. We need to put something in us to keep up our strength."

"Very well," Karen said. "I'm sorry Joe," Karen said, reaching and giving Joe a tight hug.

"It's okay, Karen! I know you love Michelle also, and you're concerned about what's going on but as Keith said, let's go get a bite and walk around outside for a while."

The three went to the cafeteria, ordered their food, and walked out the hospital doors down a path leading to a little spot where there were a few benches and tables. A cool breeze was blowing across them as they took a spot on the benches. "This breeze feels good out here," Joe spoke.

"Yeah, I agree," Karen also said.

"Well, what shall we do the rest of the day?" asked Keith. "We can sit here 'til the sun goes down then go back into the hospital. Or we can go to my restaurant and eat, eat, eat, and eat some more!" Karen and Joe looked at him with a crazy look. "Come on guys; I'm trying to humor us. Tell me, Joe, what would Michelle want us to do?"

"Keith, she would want us to laugh. She always said to make her laugh. She would rather you make her laugh than buy her something," Joe responded.

"I love Michelle," Karen said with a smile. "You are so right Keith, and you haven't had the chance to really get to know her yet."

"I think I know her spirit," Keith said. "Now come, let's go back into the hospital and sneak into her room!" Keith said.

"Yeah, let's do that!" Off they went smiling and laughing. It was like hearing Michelle laughing with them.

As they approached Michelle's room, they quickly slid in the door of her room. They all looked surprised. Michelle was sitting up watching TV! "Hey," she said in a hoarse and weakened voice. "Where did you guys come from?" Joe rushed over to her side and hugged her. Michelle let out a loud, "OUCH!! Joe, my boob!"

"Oh, I'm so sorry, honey. I'm just happy to see you sitting up."

"Joe, where is your faith?"

"Hi Keith," Michelle said looking in the direction where Keith was standing. "Have these two been driving you up the wall? If I know them, these two were worried."

"NO!!!" Both Joe and Karen said at the same time. "We were concerned! Remember, you taught us that God said not to worry!" Michelle looked at Joe and Karen and chuckled softly.

Keith walked over to Michelle and took her hand, "My sister in Christ," he said. "your faith is beautiful."

"You are a man of God, Keith?"

"Yes, I am a true believer, truly blessed with his love." Just as they were chatting away, the room door opened and a nurse walked in.

"What are you people doing in here? You all will have to leave right now!"

Michelle looked at the nurse and asked, "Please let them stay!"

"Ma'am, I just told a few other people they could not come into your room. Everyone looked at the nurse with a puzzled look.

"Who was here?" Michelle asked.

"Look, I'll go get them this one time and let everyone visit you for only a few minutes. I'll be back with your fan club," said the nurse as she closed the door behind herself.

"Who do you think she's talking about, Joe?" Joe just turned his head and looked at Karen. Karen smiled and turned away. The room door opened and in came Michelle's children.

"Hey mother," Thomas came in with his two sisters, Suzy and Alice and Suzy's daughter, Angel.

"Hi, Nana!"

"Hey, mommy!" Both daughters ran over to the bed and gave a light hug. "How did daddy and Karen get in here."

"Sweetie, you know your dad and Karen! They snuck in!"

"Papa!!" Angel said, "That's my papa. Hey, who's that?" Alice asked pointing to Keith.

"That's a friend of mine," Karen said while holding Keith's hand.

"Wow, aren't you all too old to be holding hands?" Angel said while looking at Keith.

Michelle laughed, "Come over here my little ladybug and give Nana a light hug. So, now this here is truly a blessing from God. Who called you all and told you I was going to the hospital?"

All said at once, "KAREN!!!!"

~Pam and Little Girl~

"Hey sleepy head, it's eleven o'clock! The boys will be here soon!"

Little Girl smiled to Pam while rubbing her eyes and yawning. "Dag, did we sleep this late? Okay, Pam, I'll be ready. Give me thirty minutes." Little Girl jumped in the shower and dressed. She wanted to look extra pretty for Charley but didn't want it to be too noticeable.

"Hey Pam, what time did they say they were coming over?"

"Jason said this afternoon."

"Okay Pam, this afternoon meaning *when they get up* or this afternoon meaning *normal time* twelve o'clock afternoon?"

"I don't know Little Girl!"

"Hey Pam!" came a yell from the living room.

"Well Little Girl, looks like your question was just answered."

"Pam, he has a key?"

"Sure, he does. I wanted him to have one. I feel safe if someone can check on me just in case. Now come on, hurry up. The boys are in there waiting on us."

Little Girl walked into the living room, and to her surprise, only Jason was standing there. "Where's Charley?" Pam asked.

"He'll be here. He's in traffic, I guess."

"Traffic? he lives three blocks away, Jason" Pam yelled.

Little Girl started feeling stupid when "SURPRISE!" Charley jumped out from behind the door. "Charley Smith, I'm going to kill you! "Don't you ever do that again!" Little Girl found herself saying.

"Well, looks like someone does like me, maybe just a little! Ah? Come here, Little Girl. I'm sorry, but it was funny to see your face." Charley than gave Little Girl a hug in which she pulled away quickly. "What's wrong? I just wanted to hug you, baby!"

"I'm sorry Charley. It's okay."

"Come on you girls! Ready to head to the park?"

So, they all left the building for their walk in the park. Jason and Pam walked in front holding hands, laughing, and stopping a few times to share a kiss. Charley and Little Girl walked behind. Charley was talking about what he wants for his future while Little Girl listened with no thoughts for her future and wishing he would change the subject before he started to ask her about her future. Too late...

"So Little Girl, what plans do you have for your future?"

Little Girl didn't know what to say so she began to make something up. "Well Charley, you know by now I want to get my GED and then, I want to enroll in college and study to be a teacher for younger children."

"That's great Little Girl! I love a girl with a plan and who wants something for her future."

"Yeah, that's what I want to do Charley! Be a teacher, and if that doesn't work out, I want to be able to help the homeless or people who are in need."

"Wow! That's nice! You have a good heart, Little Girl. Look over there?

134

Let's buy some ice cream. Come on; I'll race you over there." Charley had no idea Little Girl was used to running and that she did. She ran so fast; she was at the ice cream stand about four seconds before Charley. "Dag girl, you can run!" Both laughed, ordered the ice cream, then started looking for Pam and Jason.

As they walked, someone called from behind them. "Charley! Charley!" It was a woman's voice. Both turned around to see who the voice belonged to. It was Brenda.

"Hey, Bren! How's it going?" Charley asked.

"I'm doing fine," she answered without even a hello to Little Girl. "What are you doing out in the park?"

"Little Girl and I decided to take a walk together."

"OOhh!" Brenda said sarcastically. "Hi Little Girl, did Jason start tutoring you for your, oh yeah, GED!" she spoke loudly.

Little Girl answered in a low voice, "No, not yet!"

"Can I ask you a question?" Brenda continued to talk.

"Sure," Little Girl said not really wanting to hear what the question was.

"Can you count? I hear you don't know how to add! Let me tutor you. Let's see, what's one plus one?"

"That's enough!" Charley grabbed Brenda's arm. "If you ever talk to my girlfriend like that again. I will let her beat the s--- out of you! Do you understand me?" Charley than shook Brenda's arm loose and walked away with Little Girl holding his hand. "I'm so sorry, baby! Please don't let her get to you. Some people can be so cruel."

"I'm alright, Charley. I've been through worse!" But the truth was Little Girl wasn't okay. She knew Brenda was right. She was not good at math and did not know her multiplication or algebra. She did know one plus one.

"Are you sure you are alright?"

"Yeah, I'm fine, Charley! I promise I'm fine." Then Little Girl said, "Let's go find Pam and Jason."

So, the two walked looking for their two friends. While Charley talked, Little Girl didn't hear a word he was saying. Her thoughts were on, *How do I become one of them? How can I fit in with Pam, Jason, and Charley? I'll just have to start pretending that I'm as smart as they like then everyone will really like me, and no one will ever make fun of me or think I'm stupid. Yeah! That's what I will do.* So Little Girl now had a plan on how to fit in with the crowd. She will finally belong with everyone else.

"Hey, there they are Little Girl!" Charley began yelling, "JASON!! JASON!!"

"Hey Charley, we were looking for you two! Where were you and Little Girl?"

"Man, we bumped into Brenda who started her crap with Little Girl."

"Are you okay?" Pam asked Little Girl.

"Yeah, I'm fine. I just want to know why she wants to have something nasty to say to me. This is the second time she has started with me Pam," Little Girl said with anger.

Charley interrupted Little Girl and began to explain to her the reason Brenda might be picking on her. "Little Girl, let me tell you something. I used to date Brenda. I caught her in the bed with some guy when she was living with me."

Little Girl looked straight at Pam with an expression of, *Why didn't you tell me?*

Listening to all that was being said and getting tired of the conversation of Brenda and not giving one hoot about the girl, Jason blurted out, "Let's go find something to eat! I'm tired of listening to all this crap about Brenda. Who cares what she thinks or says?"

"Yeah, let's find something to eat and let all this crap go," Little Girl said in agreement with Jason while feeling a little betrayed by Pam. She was also feeling determined to fit in with everyone no matter what it would take. Little Girl was tired of being different and unloved by anyone and being the black sheep of the crowd.

The four friends changed the subject of Brenda to, "Where do we want to find a place to eat?"

"Hey," Charley said, "there's a restaurant a few blocks away. Let's go there!"

All agreed, so the friends walked on laughing, talking and enjoying themselves. When they reached their destination, they found a little table and sat.

"Guess what Pam," Little Girl said. "After I get my GED, I'm going to study to become a teacher for young children," Pam screamed with excitement. She was so happy her friend wanted a future. "Oh, also Pam, Charley is my boyfriend now!" Pam screamed again with joy.

"PAM!!" Jason yelled, "Please stop screaming! You have people looking at you like you are crazy! Can we now order our food?"

"I can't help it, Jason! I'm just so happy for my friend!"

~Michelle, Joe, Their Children, Karen and Keith~

Michelle just laughed. "What am I going to do with you, Karen? Thanks, sweetie, you are a very special friend!"

"Nana!"

"What is it my darling, granddaughter?"

"Can I come and visit with you when you get home?"

"You sure can, Angel! Just ask your mother, my loving daughter, to bring you. Why don't you all come over and stay a few days with me?" Michelle asked her children. "Thomas, can you take a few days off from the stores?"

Thomas replied with, "I wish mama, but we are doing inventory in all my stores, and I have to be there to make sure my employees know what they are doing and do it right."

"What about you, Suzy? Can you?"

"Momma, I wish, but the job won't let me off!"

"You're the top person on your job, Suzy!" Michelle said.

"I know mother, that's why I can't get off right now."

"Well how about you, Alice? Can you take a few days off from school?"

"Can't mommy. We have finals."

Keith stood there listening to Michelle's children explain why they couldn't take the time to come and stay a few days with their sick mother. He also saw the expression on Michelle's face as each of her children told her no. He noticed how she covered up her hurt with a "That's okay, then. I'm happy to see you all now, and that's a blessing. Now come and give me a kiss before the nurse comes and tells everyone it's time to leave."

So, all three children and granddaughter reached and gave their mother a light hug and a kiss and a promise they would call and check on her.

Joe also gave his wife a kiss and a, "I will see you bright and early when the roosters wake!"

Karen made her way over with Keith and they, too, hugged her and said, "See you in the morning." Then everyone left, leaving Michelle to herself in her lonely hospital bed.

"Thank You, Lord," she began to pray. "Thank You for all Your blessings You have given me." Michelle's hospital room door opened and behold there was Joe. "Joe, what in the world are you doing here? Do you want to get put out the hospital?

"Shush lady! The nurse already told me I could stay, but everyone else had to go."

"Aww Joe, thanks."

"Now I'm going to move that recliner chair over there next to your bed, and we are going to get some sleep." Joe moved the chair next to his wife's bed, found a blanket, and laid next to Michelle's bed.

"Joe!"

"Yes, Michelle! What is it, honey?"

"It's been a lot of years, hasn't it?"

"Yeah, honey! It's been a lot," Joe answered.

"And Joe, so many said we would never stay together, or I wasn't good enough for you or you weren't good enough for me but look at us now Joe! God has kept you and me together. I love you, Joe Brown."

"I love you too, Michelle Brown! Now go to sleep, you need the rest."

Joe and Michelle both fell asleep smiling and feeling a peace between them both.

~Michelle and Karen~

Michelle awoke to find Karen sitting in the chair next to her bed.

"Good morning, beautiful! Karen said to her friend. "How are you feeling this blessed day?"

Michelle smiled and replied, "Girl, I feel like jogging a block, not two now, just one block!" Both ladies laughed.

"Where's Joe?" Michelle asked.

"He and Keith are out at the nurse's desk signing papers so that you can come home. Your doctor is with them. They all will be in here in a minute."

"So, lady," Michelle began to speak but was interrupted by the doctor, Joe and Keith entering the room.

"Look at you," Dr. Harris said, "Looks like my patient is ready to go home. I was told your family all came last night to visit with you and a few snuck in!" he smiled and said while taking a look at Joe. "My lady, everything has been taken care of all. I want you to do is follow up with your chemotherapy and radiation treatments and please rest for a while. Joe, make sure she doesn't do any lifting for a while."

"Gotcha Doc," Joe answered back.

"Well, if there aren't questions lady, I will release you into your family's hands. You all have a wonderful day and Joe, you have a wife with strong faith," as he exited the room.

"Let's hurry and get you dressed so we can leave," Joe told his wife.

Keith and Karen said, "We will wait for you two in the hallway. Please hurry up! I want to get out of this place as quick as possible."

"How are *you* doing?" Keith turned and asked Karen as they both walked out of the room.

"I'm blessed, Keith. I have a friend whom I love closer than a sister and has once again survived breast cancer. And now, I have a nice man in my life who's a man of God and is truly interested in me. I can't complain. I'm beginning to understand the power of God. It's so beautiful." Karen reached and placed her arm into Keith's arm. They stood there talking waiting for Michelle and Joe.

"I'm ready," Michelle said as she and Joe came out of the room.

"Ma'am," a nurse called to Michelle, "you can't leave until we find a wheelchair to take you down. We called for transport. Someone should be coming in a minute. Oh look, here he comes now."

"Thank you, "Michelle said to the nurse, "thank you for everything."

"You're welcome, ma'am."

The four friends headed towards the elevator, and as they entered, all were silent and in their own thoughts. Michelle thought back on when Little Girl had three friends whom she hung out with. Karen's thoughts were on Keith and how nice of a man he was and hope she does nothing to mess this relationship up. Joe's mind was on why his wife didn't tell him about her having cancer again and how happy he was she was coming home.

TRYING TO FIT IN

All gathered together in their "clique".

High heel pumps,

Fancy dresses.

Chatter about who's who in their world of belong.

She sat in the distance

Watching them;

The girls that belonged.

They glance her way,

Whispers are exchanged,

Her thoughts to herself...

If I buy a new dress

If I change my hair

If I give myself...

If I do what they do,

Maybe I'll fit in;

For this is what I long

And maybe I, too, will belong

I Just Want A Friend......

Trying to Fit in: to be accepted in the group you want to be acknowledged.

What does Jesus say about trying to fit in?

1 Peter 2:19, "For God is pleased with you when you do what you know is right and patiently endure unfair treatment."

John 15:19, "If ye were of the world, the world would love his own: but because ye are not of the world, but I have chosen you out of the world, therefore the world hateth you."

2 Corinthians 6:14, "Be ye not unequally yoked together with unbelievers: for what fellowship hath righteousness with unrighteousness? And what communion hath light with darkness?"

Author's Own Thoughts:

We are fearfully and wonderfully made by our Lord. Think about that and believe it each time you look at yourself. And oh, how beautiful you are! Feel it in your spirit. Smile at yourself. See, you are beautiful. God says so.

5

FRIENDSHIP

~Little Girl, Pam, Jason and Charley~

Little Girl and her friends finished eating their meal and headed back to Pam's apartment. As they entered her place, each found a spot to crash on.

"I'm full and sleepy," Charley spoke. "Do you mind if I lay down on your bed Little Girl?"

"No Charley, go right ahead but I'm not coming in there with you."

"Why?" Charley asked. Then Little Girl quickly thought to herself about fitting in with everyone.

"Okay Charley, I'm coming in with you."

"Me and Jason are also going to take lay down," Pam said also. So, the four parted in twos to each girl's room.

"You have a nice room and a huge bed," Charley said as he plopped down on the bed. He patted his hand on the bed in a motion for Little Girl to join him and so she laid next to Charley, reluctantly. Charley put his arm around her and moved her closer, so her head laid on his chest. "Now go to sleep, Little Girl. I will not do anything you don't want me to. I like you very much okay."

Little Girl did not believe Charley with what he said. She knew that the only thing a man wants when he lays next to a girl is sex, but she closed her eyes and started thinking about her friend Steve, whom her heart ached and hurt for. Little Girl also, for the first time in years, thought about her childhood, all the pain she had to endure, and the hurt that has now turned into anger and mistrust.

She also realized now that there will never be a true friend for her, so she has to start fake liking what they like; that's the only way people will accept her. Her mind was made up. She will be whoever they want. *Why not,* she continued to think to herself, *I'm not smart enough to go to school. I'm not really pretty and no one cares so, yes, I will like what they want me to like. If they want me to take pills, I will. If Charley wants to have sex, then I will.* Little girl, after going over her plans and thoughts in her mind, tried to doze off to sleep, but was unable to.

Meanwhile, Pam and Jason laid across Pam's bed talking. "Hey Jason, pass me that bag of pills, I need a pick me upper."

"Yeah, me too," Jason said back. Each took one pill and washed it down with some beer.

"Jason, do you really think Charley likes Little Girl?"

"I don't know, Pam," Jason answered. "Truthfully speaking, she is not in his league. And you and I both know Charley; he falls in love so easily and is always wanting to help the needy. Maybe this time it will work."

"Jason," Pam said, "Little Girl hurts very easily and will fight someone if pushed. So are you really going to tutor her?"

"If that's what you want, babe."

"Thanks, Jason, I really want us to help her. Let's just keep all the other stuff that goes on away from her like the little cocaine we do sometimes or the pills we take. And Jason, please don't ever tell her about the swinging we do for money."

"Okay, Pam! Now, do you mind shutting up and giving it up?" Pam smiled and moved over to Jason.

"Little Girl!! Little Girl!!" Charley whispered, "Where are you?" Charley got up and walked out of the room. "Hey, what are you doing over there near Pam's bedroom door? You aren't peeking in, are you?" Charley laughed as he spoke.

Little Girl had left her room when Charley started snoring. She wanted to ask Pam a question about Jason tutoring her, when he would he be able to start, but as she approached Pam's room, she heard Pam and Jason talking and didn't want to interrupt them, so she decided to wait. Since the door was cracked open, she leaned against the wall and listened to the entire conversation that was being said.

"Little Girl, do you hear me?" Charley whispered so Pam and Jason wouldn't hear him.

"I hear you, Charley. I just wanted to ask Pam a question but they're sleep."

"Come with me," Little Girl said pulling on Charley's arm. "Let's go into the kitchen. I want something to drink." She did not want Charley to know she had been eavesdropping.

Charley and Little Girl went into the kitchen and Little Girl poured herself something to drink while Charley sat at the table looking at her. Turning around to see Charley staring at her, she asked, "What?" in an unfriendly sort of way.

"What's wrong with you, Little Girl? Why do you sound like that?"

"I just asked, What? You were staring at me, so I was wondering what's wrong?"

"Nothing, I just like looking at you. You are very pretty to me and I think you are one of the nicest girls I know; that's all.

"Charley, I need you to be honest with me about something."

"Sure, Little Girl. Ask me anything."

"Charley, how long have you known Pam and Jason?"

"Well, I've known Jason longer than Pam and Pam I've known for about a year. Why do you ask, Little Girl?"

"Just asking, that's all Charley," Little Girl answered as she sat in a chair next to Charley.

"How close are you three, Charley?"

"I don't know, Little Girl. I hang out with them and sometimes I would rather not. It depends on what those two are up to that day. You know, they can do some out of the way things for money that I just don't approve of."

"Really?" Little Girl said, acting like she wasn't aware of anything, not letting on she had heard plenty standing near Pam's bedroom door. "Like what, Charley? What could they do that is so bad?"

"Let me put it this way, Little Girl, I would rather let Pam talk to you if she wants to. I don't want to talk about them. I want to talk about you and me, lady."

"What about you and me?" Little Girl asked.

"Now that we are involved with one another, I want to take you on a date to the movies and dinner tomorrow," Charley asked.

"You can't! You have class tomorrow and I have to start studying for my GED."

"That's my girl," Charley said holding Little Girl's hand. Little Girl did not like Charley saying, *That's my girl.* It made her feel stupid, but she just smiled and pretending like it didn't bother her. Their conversation was interrupted with....

"Well! Well! Look, Jason, at the new couple sitting at the kitchen table." It was Pam walking into the kitchen, looking like she had just been in a wrestling match.

"Dag!" Charley said and busted out laughing. "What happened to you? You look like you've been in a fight!"

"Shut up Charley!" Pam said.

Seven

~Michelle and Karen~

"Feels good to be home doesn't it?" Karen said as she helped Michelle to bed.

"It sure does, Karen! Where are the guys?" Michelle asked.

"Oh, they went over to Keith's restaurant to pick up something to eat for us all. Nobody is in the mood to cook today," Karen told her best friend.

Michelle smiled at her friend and said, looking straight into Karen's eyes, "Now, tell me more about your Keith. I've noticed you smile wide when you talk about him, so wide I can see all your cavities!"

"Michelle, please girl, we are just friends getting to know one another and so far, yes I like him. We are taking it slow and if it's in our Lord's will, then yes, he will be the one. Michelle, stop looking at me like that. I hate when you do that!"

"What Karen? I'm just laying here taking in every word that you are saying and looking at the happiness I can see in you. I'm truly happy for you. My spirit is jumping on a trampoline right now, Karen."

"Michelle, do you want anything to drink?" Karen said, trying to change the subject.

"No sweetie," Michelle replied back, "but what you can do for me is hand me my phone book. I want to call my sisters later tonight."

Karen reached into Michelle's desk and pulled out a little purple phone book. "Michelle," Karen asked, "when was the last time you spoke with your sisters?"

"I spoke with them the day before I went into surgery."

"You did?" Karen asks.

"Yeah, I did. I wanted to tell them what was going on."

Karen then spoke in a gentle tone asking, "Michelle, why didn't you tell

Joe and me what really was going on? I mean you just said it was going to be a biopsy and it was surgery for another cancer tumor."

"Karen look," Michelle spoke gently, "I love you and I know how you can get if something is really wrong with me. I could not afford to be wondering how you are doing when I needed to focus on God and me at the time. Plus girl, if I can remember, anytime I get sick, you act like you have a degree in nursing and it just tickles me to see you acting like that! Karen, I love you more than a sister. You are my spiritual sister now as well as my best friend. I'm going to be fine. In fact, I already am, so let's change the subject back to you and Keith."

"Really Michelle? Are you kidding me.? I don't want to talk about Keith, Michelle. I want us to study more of our Lord's words after you have rested some," Karen asked.

"Karen, I will be happy to. What do you want to study on?

"Michelle, I want to know about the angels, the archangels."

"Well girlfriend, then we shall as soon as I have rested a few days. Karen," Michelle spoke, "can you pray for us now? I'm tired and just want to lay here and feel God's presence while you pray."

Karen was felt honored that her friend asked her to pray. "Yes, for sure Michelle. Now, I can't pray as well as you."

"Karen, what did I tell you about that? "You pray the way Karen prays. It is you, your heart, your spirit talking with God. Pray, my sister."

Michelle held Karen's hand, closed her eyes, as so did Karen.

"Lord, I come to You today giving thanksgiving for blessing my friend, Michelle, to see another day. We thank You, God, for You are a mighty God. There is no other but You. I say thank You for loving us enough to allow us to come together again. Please continue to bless us with Your mercy and grace. Humbly, we thank You for all You have done and will do. We know we are not perfect and You still love us through all our mess. I pray this in Jesus' mighty name, amen."

"Thank you, Karen," Michelle said. "Don't you ever let me hear you don't know how to pray!"

"Gotcha!" Karen said with eyes full of water. "Thank you, Michelle, for introducing me to Jesus."

"LADIES!!! LADIES!!!"

"We're in here, Joe!" Karen yelled back.

"How are our beautiful ladies doing?" Keith asked.

"We just came out of prayer and my beautiful friend prayed for me."

"Amen. Wonderful," Keith said. "It's beautiful when women of God come together and share in our Lord's glory."

Now Joe smiled and said, "Truly, we are all blessed and if someone would be kind enough to say GRACE, we can all eat!"

"It would be my pleasure," Keith responded.

"Wait!!!" Michelle shouted out. "First, tell us, ladies, what did you get us all for dinner?"

"Well, Keith," said Joe answering his wife, "It was going to be a surprise. He went into the kitchen in his restaurant and about an hour later, came out with these two huge bags. I haven't a clue what is in those bags. The only way to find out is to open them."

So the friends set an eating place on Michelle's bed, then Keith began pulling containers out of the bag, placed them in a row with plates and flatware. "I smell fish," Michelle said. "I'm allergic to seafood, Joe. I know you didn't' know."

Keith apologized to Michelle. "I do have a nice chicken breast salad, chocolate cake with a can of whipped cream, also some hot wings, potato salad, beef ribs, broccoli, spinach, a half of gallon of strawberry lemonade, and your favorite, a strawberry milkshake Joe put in the freezer until you're ready for it."

"Wow!" Michelle responded. "That's a lot of food. Thanks, Keith, that was very thoughtful of you!"

"You are so welcome, Michelle. Now let us bless our food saying, Grace." They all said Grace and began to eat.

"So, young lady," Joe began to speak to his wife while munching on a beef rib, "why didn't you tell me about the surgery?"

Michelle looked at her husband and just said, "Joe, eat your food. We will talk about that later. Okay, sweetie?"

"Alright now!" Joe answered back. "I expect an answer later."

Michelle just laughed. "Joe, eat your food!" she said and gave Joe a big kiss on the cheek.

Karen said very little while she ate as Keith and Joe talked like old friends. Michelle dozed off into a peaceful sleep after eating very little of her salad.

~Little Girl and Pam~

After the four spent some time in the kitchen eating and talking, the guys left to prepare for their classes tomorrow. Little Girl was still sitting at the kitchen table waiting for Pam to come back from seeing the guys to the front door and saying her goodnight to Jason.

"So, Little Girl, did you have fun today?" "Little Girl gave Pam a smile and nodded. "Well, I have class tomorrow. What do you want to do Little Girl while I'm in class?"

"Don't know Pam! What do you think I should do?" Little Girl said with sarcasm.

"What's wrong?" Pam asked, noticing the sarcasm in Little Girl's voice.

"Nothing Pam. I'm just tired." Little Girl had to quickly remind herself she is trying to fit in and that's not how to get people to want her in their clique. She decided that there aren't people in this world who can be trusted or that love, like, or feel real. So why not just float along with the crowd? There really wasn't any future for her. And what is love? It sure wasn't like she had seen on TV. Looks to Little Girl like everyone is just trying to please themselves at the cost of whatever is at hand at the time.

"I think we should go to bed," Pam said.

"You go on," Little Girl responded. "I think I'm going to sit here and if you don't mind, drink some of that Vodka you have in the cabinet."

Pam looked at Little Girl surprised. "What did you say?" Pam asked.

"I want some of your Vodka!"

"Little Girl, you don't drink! What's going on?"

"Nothing Pam! May I have some, yes or no?"

"Sure, Little Girl, I'll have a little with you."

Yeah, I figured that, Little Girl thought to herself.

Pam poured them both a small amount of Vodka in two small glasses and they both went to drinking. Little Girl put the glass to her mouth and just gulped it down.

"Wow Pam, that stuff is nasty, but give me just a little more."

"Are you sure?" Pam asked.

"Yep," so Pam poured Little Girl more of the Vodka but this time, she poured more than the first glass. Little Girl gulped that down also. Pam was just finishing her first glass when Little Girl then asked for some water. So, Pam poured her a tall glass of water. Little Girl then got up and went looking through the food cabinets for peanuts. "I know I saw some peanuts in here yesterday! Where are they, Pam?"

"Little Girl, there in the other cabinet. I think you're a little tipsy," Pam said to her.

"Really Pam? I like this feeling." Little Girl found what she was looking for, sat back down, well, wobbled back down in the chair.

"Little Girl, are you alright?" Pam asked again. "Did Charley say something mean or try something you didn't want him to?"

Little Girl was now pouring some more Vodka, but not much this time. "Charley didn't say or do anything wrong. I just wanna drink! You all drink right? Just thought I'd give it a try! Why can't I try it, Pam? What's wrong with me trying, Pam? Ah, Pam! What's wrong with me trying to drink a little Vodka?"

"Okay, Little Girl! You're drunk! You need to go and lay down."

"I don't want to lay down Pam, I want to talk. Talk to me, Pam. Tell me all about your college, your friends, and oh, about your cocaine, and your swingers, Pam!"

Little Girl was now officially drunk. Pam gave Little Girl an angry look.

"You were listening at my door!"

"Yep, I sure was, and I want to do the same things you do, Pam! I mean what harm would it do?"

"Little Girl, you don't know what you are talking about!" Pam responded while drinking her second glass of Vodka now.

"Pam, we are friends, right?" Little Girl asked while she munched on the peanuts and drank her water. See, what Pam didn't realize was that Little Girl, through the people in her life, had seen the best drunks and dope fiends, drug pushers, call girls, con artists, thieves, and etc., so Little Girl knew how to do it all. She just didn't feel it was right to do. See, munching on the peanuts meant putting a lining on the stomach with grease to help with drunkenness. Water helped come down off the drunk slowly. So, while Pam continued to drink Vodka, Little Girl was now drinking water, but still tipsy.

"Yes," Pam responded, "we are friends. We have been friends since I was what, fourteen? We may have lost contact with one another, but we were always friends, Little Girl."

Little Girl got up from her chair and went and poured herself some more water and put a lemon in it while Pam continued to drink.

"Don't you want some more Vodka?" Pam asked.

"Sure," Little Girl reached for the bottle and poured some right into the water and lemon.

"You aren't going to drink it straight?" Pam asked.

"I am drinking it, Pam! Finish talking to me; it's been years. Have you heard from any of the other girls that lived with us at the shelter?"

"It was only four of us left after Shirley died. I think Gloria still lives here in the state. I don't know what ever happened to Kim. Remember, she was going away to college? Oh, that's right, you left with Steve, so you didn't see Kim when she left. Kim went to UNCC in North Carolina. She would write for a while, then her letters just stopped."

Little Girl sat listening to Pam talk while thinking to herself, *We were good friends until everyone became smart*. Little Girl stayed dumb when it came to school. "Hey, Pam, why don't we try finding Kim?" Little Girl" suggested. "If you have any of her letters, we could look at the return address. Think about it, Pam. She was just starting college right, so she was eighteen? You were going to high school. You skipped a grade in high school. You also finished early and attended college at seventeen, so this should be her last year." Little Girl was unaware of herself that she had just added and subtracted and figured out an answer.

"That would be fun to do, Little Girl! Why don't we start today? It is about 2:00 am in the morning now. I don't think I will be going to class today. I know we are going to have a hangover in the morning."

Little Girl laughed to herself for she knew she was not going to have a hangover. She did what she observed people in her past do when they drank.

"Where are Kim's letters, Pam?" Little Girl asked.

'Some, I think are in my old suitcase on the floor of my closet."

"Then that's where we will start. Come on! Let's go on a treasure hunt!"

"Now!" Pam squealed.

"Yes, now." Little Girl said.

So both girls walked into Pam's room and began digging in the closet. "Here it is!" Pam yelled with excitement.

"Open it, Pam!" Pam opened the suitcase and found the letters from Kim.

Little Girl then said, "Read the post date on the right corner of the envelope on each one, find the latest one, then read the letter." Pam began to read the letter. "Well!" Little Girl screamed. "What does it say?"

"It says," Pam began to read,

"Dear Pam,

When you read this letter, I hope it finds you in the best of health. I am doing another year here. I took a year off to give birth to my baby daughter. I live off campus now in a small apartment. The rent here is a lot cheaper than back home. The father of my child wants nothing to do with me or the baby. I'm also working and going to school. Have you heard anything from any of the girls? I miss us all being together. I really miss Little Girl! I know I write this in each letter in hopes you will respond with a yes you have heard from someone. Here's my address to my apartment in Charlotte, NC, and my phone number. Call me soon. Well, I have to go and get the baby ready for daycare. Oh, her name is Kelly. Goodbye for now."

Pam and Little Girl looked at each other while sitting on the floor in Pam's closet. "Pam? This is the first time you are reading this letter? Why?"

"I don't know Little Girl, I just been too busy to read it."

"Pam, what's the post date on the letter."

"April 13."

"Pam, that's just one month ago! I thought you said she hasn't written in a while? Come on, where's the phone?"

"Little Girl, I know you aren't going to call someone this late at night?"

"I sure am, Pam." Little Girl got up from the floor in the closet, went into the living room, and dialed the number that was in the letter. Pam raced in the living room behind her and both girls waited anxiously while it rang on the other end.

Someone picked up and with a sleepy voice and said, "Hello." It was a woman's voice.

"Hello?" she said again.

Little Girl spoke, "Sorry to bother you so late but may I speak to Kim, please?"

"This is Kim," the voice said. "Who is this?"

Little Girl got so excited. "This is Little Girl and Pam is sitting next to me." The voice on the other end of the phone screamed so loud that Little Girl dropped the phone but retrieved it quickly.

"Little Girl?" Kim said. "Is this really you? And where's Pam?"

Pam got on the phone, "Hello Kim! When are you coming up to visit us?"

"How about you two coming down to visit me?"

"I can't right now, Kim. I have class."

"So do I, Pam."

"I know what! What about Little Girl coming down for a week? She can study while she's down there then I'll meet you both after this week's classes. It will be Spring Break anyway."

Little Girl looked at Pam and thought to herself, *Pam, you do not control when or where I go,* but she also wanted to fit in so, "Okay, Pam. I'll pack today and you take me to the train. Kim," Little Girl got on the phone. "I'll be coming by train so please don't forget to pick me up. It's going to be fun seeing you. Goodnight or good morning!"

All the girls hung the phones up. Pam and Little Girl started hugging and smiling like two little school girls. Pam looked Little Girl in her face and spoke these words, "Little Girl, don't you ever let anyone tell you that you are not smart." Little Girl felt a little rise in her gut; it was a strange feeling, but it felt nice. "Well, let's go and get you packed," Pam said, "since we are up anyway. I have some extra suitcases you can use, and you are welcome to use whatever clothes I have in my closet."

Little Girl started feeling bad because of the mean thoughts she had towards Pam earlier. Maybe she really likes me as her friend and that other stuff she is protecting me from because she wants me safe. Little Girl just pushed that into her closet in her mind where she stores most of the things she hasn't dealt with.

The girls started packing and sipping on more Vodka, laughing, and talking about the life in the shelter years ago.

~Michelle~

Michelle awoke to find Karen asleep in her recliner in the bedroom. Not wanting to wake her friend, and not wondering or even interested in where the men left to, she tipped-toed to the bathroom. She ran some bath water, added a little blessed oil, and sank into the warm soothing tub. Michelle loved her private time with her Lord. She just laid in the tub, listening to her soft gospel music and enjoying the serenity. She felt all of God's love. She thought to herself, *One cannot really explain in words. It's ineffable, the power of God's love, and the anointing of the Holy Spirit. One must have a true unwavering relationship with our Lord.*

She thought of herself as a child. She thought about her sisters and brothers and how amazing God is. *Here I am, the one who was the black sheep of everything and now I have a peace within that only God can give.*

Michelle finished her bath, dressed, and went back into her bedroom to find Karen still asleep. She was tickled at her friend who sat there sound asleep in the chair. Karen was the only friend she had ever had in life whom she could count on for anything. She thanked God for such a person in her life. She also thanked God for Karen wanting and starting to be hungry for God's Word and truth. "Glory to the Father in heaven for all His blessings on everyone," she said aloud.

"God," she began to talk to her Lord, "You know me better than I know myself. You knew me before I was formed in my mother's womb. You have been with me through the fire. My Lord, I ask You, Am I wrong for not telling my friend Karen all the things that have happened in my life? I don't know when You will bring me home to You. You also know my friend better than I or she knows herself. Lord, I want her to become so strong in Your Word and to live the life You have planned for her and not get in Your way. She's been a true friend these past years. I know she worries. I'm trying to tell her You don't want her to worry for in Your Word says in Philippians 4:6-7, "Do not be anxious about anything, but in everything by prayer and supplication with thanksgiving let your requests be made known to God. And the peace of God, which surpasses all understanding, will guard your hearts and your minds in Christ Jesus." So, my Father, of whom I humbly bow to, I ask You to continue to watch over her. She's just a babe right now, crawling her way to You. And Father, if and when You bring me home, I ask You to please put someone in her life here on earth who also walks with You. I don't know this man, Keith, she is seeing right now. He loves You and is a man of God. If he is the one for her and that is Your will for her, then Your will must always be done in Jesus' name."

Michelle sat on her bed with tears rolling down her face. Each tear was a tear of peace that at one time were tears of pain that the Lord turned into peace and joy that comes straight from the heart where God lives. Michelle could not stop the tears, nor did she want to, for she loved God more than her life itself.

"Are you okay, Michelle?" Karen spoke. Karen had been awake for a while but did not want to interrupt Michelle when she was communing with God so she kept her eyes closed and talked with God herself.

"I'm blessed," Michelle responded to Karen while beginning to wipe her eyes.

"I was listening to you talk with our Lord, Michelle," Karen spoke, "and I have a question. How come Jesus' own people didn't believe He was the Son of God who is God? Wasn't it prophesied by the early prophets and then John the Baptist?"

"Karen, some believed that He was the coming Messiah, but the Jewish high priests didn't believe and believed the Messiah had not come yet, as well as many other Jews. They accused Jesus of blasphemy. You see Karen, our Lord's will must always be done. It was the will of God. When Jesus went into the Garden of Gethsemane (Mount of Olives) to pray, He asked the Father .. *My Father, if it is possible let this cup pass from me. Yet not as I will, but as You will.* See, our Lord loves us so He gave us His son to die a criminal's death on the cross and shed His blood for us so our sins may be forgiven and we can repent.

"Can you imagine giving your only son to die, Karen? That's our Father's love for us. To watch His Son being beat into minced meat, thorns on His head, nails in His hands and feet, sword in the side, vinegar to drink, that breaks my own heart and so many people today will not give our Father in heaven any thanks or even acknowledge Him. All He asks is to love Him as He loves us. He's such an awesome Father. He gives us a choice and wants us to choose His love, and study and know His word. He is talking to us through His word which is the truth, light and the way to

Him. Some people make it sound so complicated. His word is so simple even a child could understand it. We should study and meditate on His word every day. Watch and pray, clothe ourselves in the armor of God."

Karen sat listening to every word that flowed out of Michelle's mouth. She could taste the words and the taste was good. Karen's spirit wanted more of what Michelle was saying.

"Michelle," "Karen asked again, "Let me ask another question. What happened to you that made you seek and want to know God?"

Michelle just smiled a soft smile and replied with, "That's a question for another time, Karen."

"Then answer this, did Little Girl know Jesus?"

~Little Girl and Kim~

The train pulled into the station. Little Girl sat anxiously, longing to see her friend from years ago. The ticket man announced the stop, "Charlotte, NC!" Little Girl jumped to her feet and headed straight to the door. As she got off the train, she looked around for Kim.

"Little Girl! Little Girl!" a screaming voice came with a running body pushing a stroller.

"Kim, is that you?" yelled Little Girl as she ran towards Kim. Both girls ran into one another's arms. "Kim, I'm so happy to see you!"

"Me too, Little Girl!"

"Is this your baby girl?" Little Girl asked.

"Yep!" answered Kim. "Isn't she just a beauty? Come on! Let's hurry and get your luggage so I can drive us back to my place."

The girls retrieved Little Girl's suitcases, loaded them into Kim's car, and was off to Kim's apartment. "Do you like living down south, Kim?" Little Girl asked.

"Yeah, I do! It's not so much hustle and bustle. Things are a lot cheaper and I am almost finished with school. Plus, I don't want to raise my daughter back home. Here we are," Kim said cutting the conversation off while pulling up into a very nice apartment complex.

"Is this where you live?" Little Girl asked.

"Yep!" answered Kim.

The girls carried the suitcases and the baby into the apartment from the car. Little Girl looked around. "You have a nice apartment, Kim!"

"Thanks!" Kim answered back. "Now, let's get you settled so we can talk and catch up," Kim said. "Also, I need to put Kelly to bed. Here follow me." Little Girl followed Kim down a small hallway. "This will be your room while you visit," Kim said as she walked into a room with a twin bed, baby's crib, and a dresser with a small lamp sitting on it. "This is my baby, Kelly's room, but I let her sleep with me. "Oh, I took a week off from my job so we can spend a lot of time doing things and just hanging. I'm going to put Kelly to sleep. You unpack. I'll be right back. I'm happy you're here, Little Girl. Really, I am. I miss us all, especially you."

"Me too, Kim!" Little Girl said back.

Little Girl sat on the bed and looked around. She began thinking how two of her friends from the shelter have their own place and are in school. Little Girl started asking herself, *What is wrong with me? Why can't I have this too?* She packed those thoughts up and stored them with the other feelings she stored deep down into the back of her mind and heart. She started to unpack her suitcases and turned on the little TV that sat on a small TV stand against the wall. Little Girl watched the news and noticed the crime here was as much as back home. She finished putting away her clothes, then laid across the bed. She felt comfortable, something she wasn't used to feeling so she closed her eyes and fell fast asleep. She slept not worrying who would come in her room while she slept and take her body like it was theirs for the taking. Peacefully, she slept not having to listen to girls being sold for money or even herself. Her sleep was nice, not having to hear drugs being sold and arguing about who owes and who's going to get beat up for not having the money. Little Girl did not dream, she just slept for she was comfortable and had a little peace.

Kim peeked into the room and saw Little Girl asleep. Kim thought to herself, *She looks like a little girl, wow!* She also saw that in Little Girl's eyes every time she looked into them. Her eyes seemed empty and sad. Kim's heart always liked Little Girl but was cautious. There seemed something about Little Girl that if she got very angry, she would hurt someone really bad.

Kim headed to the kitchen to find something to cook for dinner for the both of them. While looking through her cabinets, her telephone rang. Picking it up she answered with a, "God bless, this is Kim, with whom am I speaking?"

"It's Pam! Kim, did you just say, God bless?"

"I sure did, Pam."

Pam responded with a, "Oh! Okay! How's Little Girl doing?"

"She's sleeping right now. She must be tired from the train ride," Kim told Pam.

Pam hurried to get off the phone. "Just tell her that Charley wants to know if it's okay if he calls her there or if she calls him."

"I sure will, Pam," Kim answered back. "Goodbye."

Now Little Girl was standing in the kitchen, listening to them both talking on the phone. Kim turned around, "Oh, Little Girl, I didn't know you were standing there. I could have given you the phone. It was Pam. She wanted to let you know that Charley wants to call you or you call him if it's okay."

Little Girl smiled at Kim and said, "No Kim, right now, I just want us to visit. Kim, that was the first time in my life I slept so comfortable. It must be the mattress."

"I don't think it was the mattress, Little Girl! I had my house anointed and blessed," Kim said.

"You what? What's all that? I don't know what all that means, but okay!"

"So, what are we going to eat, Kim?"

"Well, I could make some burgers and shakes."

"You know how to make milkshakes, Kim?"

"I sure do. I have a milkshake maker. Is that what you want?"

"Sure do!"

"I like the idea of burgers and a shake! Can we make strawberry?" Little Girl asked.

"Yep, we can!" Kim answered. "You watch the baby while I run up to the store. I'll be back in a few minutes, need some meat to make the burgers. Be back!"

Kim left, and Little Girl stood in the kitchen looking around for a minute then went to Pam's room to check on baby Kelly. After that, she walked into the living room, sat on the couch, and turned on the TV. She changed channel after channel but could not get her mind off of Kim saying about the apartment being blessed but like everything that bothered her, she stored in the back of her mind or her heart and left it.

Little Girl sat there gazing at the TV when she heard the baby crying. She walked into Pam's room and picked baby Kelly up in her arms. She felt so soft and gentle. This was the first time Little Girl had ever been this close to a baby in her arms. She felt good about it. She walked with baby Kelly back into the living room and sat on the couch holding baby Kelly and just smiling at her. She just held the baby like it was her own. Baby Kelly stopped crying and fell back to sleep in Little Girl's arms just as Kim was coming in the front door.

"Did she wake up?" Kim asked.

"Yeah, she did, but I rocked her back to sleep, Kim." Little Girl spoke, "She is so pretty and gentle. I think I just want to stay in your apartment for a day or two before we see the town. You don't mind, do you? Your place is so quiet and comfortable. Plus, I like your baby and you are different from years ago."

"Let's go put Kelly back to bed and you and I can cook our food," Kim suggested.

"Can I lay her on the bed, Kim?" Little Girl asked.

"Sure go on, just place her in the middle and put those pillows around her." Little Girl felt such real joy from just laying the precious baby Kelly down on the bed. "Let's hurry out of here before she wakes up," Kim said.

Back in the kitchen, the girls started making burgers and strawberry milkshakes for Little Girl. "Let's take the food in the living room and we can eat in there and talk or watch TV, whatever you wish, Little Girl."

"Kim, I feel so comfortable here in your place. I know I said it earlier, but I do."

"Little Girl," Kim asked, "what have you been doing since the last time I saw you and Steve in the park? How is he anyway?" Little Girl looked down at her strawberry milkshake and started crying. Kim moved over to her and put her arm around Little Girl.

"What's wrong?"

"Steve died, Kim!" Little Girl answered while weeping for her dead friend.

"Aww, I'm so sorry! We don't have to talk about it, Little Girl. Let's talk about you and what you have been doing. How did you meet up with Pam?"

Little Girl sat back on the couch and began to tell Kim everything that happened and what was going on now all the way up to how she met Charley. Kim sat there and listened to every word that was spoken feeling so sad for Little Girl. Kim started to pray. Little Girl suddenly stopped talking and watched and listened to Kim for Little Girl had no idea what was going on. When Kim was finished, Little Girl said to her, "What were you doing, Kim?"

"I was praying for God to watch over you always."

"Oh," Little Girl said. "Kim, let's watch a movie." Little Girl changed the subject. She had no idea what Kim was talking about and didn't want Kim to think she was stupid for not knowing.

~Michelle and Karen~

Karen sat waiting for Michelle to answer her question about, "Did Little Girl know Jesus?"

Michelle answered with, "I will tell you another time, Karen, about that too."

Karen looked at Michelle with a smile and responded with, "Girl, you are a trip! Why can't you just answer at least one of the two questions I asked?"

"So tell me! How's everything with you and Keith coming along?" Michelle said changing the subject.

"Everything is going great!" Karen said. "We are taking it slow. Michelle, girl he is a good man, and I mean a really, good man. He hasn't been married, no children and Michelle, he loves God! I'm really happy with him." Karen stood up from her chair and began walking around the room.

"What's wrong, Karen?" Michelle asked. "Why are you pacing the room?"

"I don't know Michelle. I'm just happy right now thinking and talking about him. I can't keep still!"

Michelle let out a gentle laugh. "Karen," she asked, "why don't we all go to the beach this summer? When you take your vacation from work."

"Michelle, I'm thinking about finding employment elsewhere. I didn't want to tell you, but I quit my job. I'm tired of sitting behind that desk day in and day out."

"YOU DID WHAT!" Michelle yelled, raising her arms in the air.

"I quit my job!" Karen yelled back.

"What are you going to live on, Karen? You know you have bills and you love to shop!"

"Michelle, I have enough money saved that I can live on for at least two years!"

Michelle's mouth flew open. "Really, Karen! You have saved that much?"

"Yep, I sure have. Plus, I think this will teach me how to budget. Also, I'm putting my home up for sale," Karen said lowing her voice.

"Karen, what is going on with you? Why these changes so suddenly?"

"Michelle," Karen answered her in a calm voice, "I've been thinking about doing this for a least a year now. It's not a sudden decision. I'm thinking about moving closer to you and I'm looking for a smaller house. Wouldn't that be nice? You and me closer instead of me across town?"

"Karen, let me ask you this. Are you concerned about me so much that you want to sell your house that you love and put so much money into?"

"Michelle, girl, I can't lie to my best friend. Yes, I am concerned. I'm concerned about your health and the things you aren't telling anyone because you don't want anyone to worry. I know worrying is a sin, but you and I are like sisters so again I will say, yes, I'm concerned and there is nothing you can do about it. I can move anywhere I want," Karen said and stuck her tongue out like a small child. "Now, what do you have to say about that? Ha!"

Michelle busted out laughing so hard she had to grab her stomach. "Girl, I promise you, you can make me laugh! Fine, just make sure you have prayed about everything you just told me before you go forth."

Karen laughed also with her friend Michelle and responded with, "Already did! So again, ha!"

"Get out of my bedroom!" Michelle said, teasing her friend, Karen.

Both ladies laughed and talked about Karen's decisions she had made. Michelle got up to go get something to drink from the kitchen. "Where do you think you are going, lady?" Karen snarled at her friend playfully.

"To get something to drink ma'am, if you don't mind," Michelle snarled back also playfully.

"I'll get it for you! What do you want?" Karen said.

"I want my strawberry milkshake!" Michelle replied.

~Little Girl and Kim~

The girls went through Kim's collection of DVD's and agreed on a movie.

"Let's pop some popcorn or would you prefer some other kind of junk food?" Kim asked Little Girl.

"Popcorn is good," Little Girl answered back. Kim went into the kitchen to put the popcorn in the microwave while Little Girl popped in the DVD. When the popcorn was ready, Kim came back into the living room with a large bowl and some soft drinks. The girls sat and began watching the movie which was a comedy.

After hours of movie watching and stuffing themselves with popcorn, Little Girl and Kim sat just talking and laughing and enjoying the rest of the evening. Little Girl was enjoying herself so much that didn't think about anything negative or her past. She felt good and didn't care about anything else but enjoying her visit with Kim. She didn't even want to call Charley.

"How late do you stay up, Kim?" Little Girl asked.

"Not too late. Remember, baby Kelly gets up early!" Kim answered.

"Well then, I'm going to bed, so I can get up with you and baby Kelly," Little Girl said.

"Okay then. I'll see you in the morning. If you get hungry or want something to drink, make yourself at home," Kim said. "Good night, Little Girl."

"Goodnight Kim."

The two girls went into their rooms for the night. Little Girl turned on the small TV and laid herself down in the bed. She noticed a smile on her face, a real genuine smile. She could almost feel the smile from inside of herself. The only times that she smiled like that was when Mrs. Williams, one of her of foster mothers, surprised her with a brand-new dress and shoes and when her friend, Steve, who is dead now, would make her laugh while they drank their strawberry milkshakes.

Little Girl watched TV and during a commercial, Little Girl noticed a book with a leather cover sitting on the table next to the lamp. She got up, walked over, and picked up the book. The cover read "HOLY BIBLE." Little Girl remembered a lot of her foster parents having the book in their house and also sending her to church but never understood anything that had been taught in Sunday School. Her thoughts were always on how unhappy she was and how could she run away from the home.

Little Girl opened the Bible and looked at the first page. She noticed the one book had a lot of books in the one book. Also, the names of a lot of these books were too hard to pronounce so she started to read the first book which was the book of Genesis. *In the beginning, God created the heavens and the earth.* Little Girl read some more though she didn't understand a lot, she was reading. She still read. After a chapter, she put the book back on the table. *I wonder why God let's all these bad things happen to little girls and little boys?* she asked herself. *Why does God let mean people live? Why does God let men hurt girls?* With her thoughts on, *Why God?* Little Girl fell off to sleep.

~Joe and Keith~

Joe and Keith sat at a table in Keith's restaurant talking about the two women in their life. "Keith man, why do you think my wife didn't want me to know about her surgery that she had cancer again?"

"Joe," Keith began to say, "I think your wife, from what I've come to know, was more concerned for you and Karen. I think she knows you two so well and knew how you both would have reacted if she would have said anything before. That's just my opinion, Joe."

"Yeah, I guess you're right."

"That's it, Joe," Keith said.

"So, man, tell me what's up with you and Karen? You know she's like a sister to me and she and my wife are closer than any sister. They talk about everything, things I don't even know about!" Joe said laughing.

"Joe, I like Karen. I like Karen a lot. I find myself thinking about her when I'm not with her and when I'm with her, I don't want to leave her."

Joe smiled and said, "Man, are you falling in love with her?"

"I don't know, Joe! What I can tell you is I hope she feels for me the way I do for her."

Joe laughed again and said, "Keith, you sound like you are in high school again!"

"It feels right, Joe! It feels right!" Keith said repeating himself.

"Well, I'm happy for you then Keith. Karen is a good woman. So, tell me about this restaurant you got here? I would like to make some extra cash. Need any help here?"

"Can always use some good help, Joe! What can you do or what would you like to do?"

"Keith, I don't have a clue about running a restaurant or what do in one. I know how to tell a waiter or waitress what my order is!"

"Joe, let me think about it and see what I come up with and you and I will talk, okay," Keith said. "You think we should maybe go back to your house and check on the ladies?"

"Nah!" Joe said, "If I know those two, they are either talking about the Lord or talking about something Michelle or Karen said to the other and laughing about it. Or now that you're in the picture, I think you are probably the subject!"

Keith started laughing. "You know Joe, you three are very nice people. I'm glad you three are in my life now. I feel blessed to have good friends. Joe, are you a man of God?"

"Yes, I am, Keith. I'm not at the place my wife Michelle is but I believe and pray. You know with a wife like Michelle, one gets to know God and start believing in Him."

FRIEND (THE LITTLE BOX)

Humbly she walks.
She walks for Him and only Him does she walk.
She humbly walks carrying her little box,
Kneeling at night to give Him praise
and thank Him for another day.
I watch her
For in her heart holds love for many.

Who are you, lady that carries this box?

She parts her lips to speak His truth

And when she does, my spirit just can't move.

What is in your little box, I ask?

One day, she came to me

and handed me a key.

Opening the box with amazement, I did see.

For in her box,

Came out the notes of music plaid by the harp of an angel.

Also, so many colors of a rainbow.

Butterflies flew with such bright colors.

Scriptures of His word, His truth, danced around one another.

They filled my spirit, don't you see?

For I, too, wanted a little box just for me.

She handed me a book,

Told me to read, also pray.

Then she explained His truth is the only way.

Ask Him to plant His words in your heart

Then I, too, can have a little box.

So, I read, knelt, and prayed, opened my heart

and that is where His words were placed.

Today, the lady and I are friends.

We open our book, read His word, and pray.

And when we cry, we look at our little box and start to smile.

You, too, can have a little box.

All you have to do is open your heart

For His truth is in the book... THE BIBLE.

Friendship: having a bond with someone you know.

What Does Jesus Say About Friendship?

Proverbs 22:24-25, "Do not make friends with a hot-tempered man, do not associate with one easily angered, or you may learn his ways and get yourself ensnared."

John 15:12-15, "My command is this: love each other as I have loved you. Greater love has no one than this, that he lay down his life for friends. you are my friends if you do what I commend. I no longer call you servants, because a servant does not know his master's business, instead, I have called you friends, for everything that I learned from my father I have made known to you."

Proverbs 27:17, "As iron sharpens iron, so one man sharpens another."

Author's Own Thoughts:

True and loyal friendship is a blessing. Cherish it; hold on to it. Jesus is a friend who will never leave or forsake you.

6

HIDDEN SECRETS

~Little Girl and Kim~

Little Girl woke up feeling well rested, excited to see what the day would be like. She walked out of the bedroom, headed towards the bathroom, and took a quick glance into Kim's room. She noticed Kim was on her knees with her eyes closed so she continued to the bathroom to get herself dressed for the day.

I wonder why Kim was on her knees? Little Girl asked herself. As soon as she was finished in the bathroom, Little Girl headed back into Kim's room. Seeing Kim sitting on the bed now feeding baby Kelly, Little Girl asked, "How's baby Kelly doing?"

"Good morning, Little Girl!" Kim said. "How did you sleep? Did you sleep well?"

"Kim, I slept great! It was the best I can remember."

"I'm happy, Little Girl!" Kim said back. "What do you want to eat for breakfast?"

"Whatever you have," Little Girl replied. "If you want, I can cook," Little Girl suggested.

"If that's what you want," Kim answered back. "You just find anything in there that will make a breakfast and I will eat it!" Kim laughed at her friend Little Girl.

"Can I hold the baby for a minute?" Little Girl asked.

"Sure!" Kim handed baby Kelly to over to her. Little Girl reached out with gentle hands and took hold of the baby.

"She's so beautiful, Kim!" Little Girl whispered. "Can I change about cooking breakfast and just sit in the living room and hold her?"

"Sure!" Kim replied back. "But first, I have to change her."

"Oh, let me!" Little Girl asked anxiously. "Just show me how! I've never changed a diaper before!"

Kim guided Little Girl on how to change a baby diaper and afterward proceeded towards the kitchen to cook breakfast for them while Little Girl sat rocking baby Kelly on the living room couch. In the middle of scrambling eggs, Kim's house phone rang. At the other end of it was a male's voice. It was Charley.

"Can I speak to Little Girl, please?"

Kim went into the living room to hand the phone to Little Girl. Little Girl just shook her head back and forth in a *no* motion. Kim then put the phone back to her mouth and began speaking to Charley. "I'm sorry but she doesn't want to talk at this time. Please call back a little later. Thank you," and hung the phone up. "Why didn't you want to talk to him, Little Girl?" Kim asked.

"I don't know! I just don't want anything from back home here with me. I feel relaxed here, I guess."

"Okay," answered Kim. "I'm going to go back into the kitchen and finish breakfast while you continue to rock baby Kelly in your arms."

Once breakfast was done and the two girls ate and cleaned the kitchen, Little Girl asked Kim if maybe they could take baby Kelly for a walk in the stroller.

"I thought you wanted to just stay in for a few days," Kim answered.

"I did, but I want to go outside now," Little Girl said with a smile.

"Well, come on. Just let me get my keys so we can drive to the park and we can walk around there." So, the girls loaded baby Kelly into her car seat and then headed to the park.

~Michelle and Karen~

The men arrived at Michelle's house, laughing like they were friends for many years.

"What's so funny?" Michelle asked as both Joe and Keith entered her room.

Joe, between laughs, pointed to Keith and responded with, "I like Keith! He's alright with me!" Then Joe looked at Karen and said, "Lady, you have a good man right here! If you mess it up, I personally will take a switch to you! You understand?" Karen smiled at Joe with a grin so big, one could see her cavities. "Dag lady, I haven't seen you smile that big in a while!"

Keith walked over to Karen and placed his hands in hers, giving her a short and gentle kiss on the forehead. He proceeded to whisper in her ear, "Darling, what is your favorite color?"

Karen looked at Joe with the look curiosity on her face. She then whispered back in his ear, "I like the color red. Why do you ask?" she said.

"Just want to know for the future," Joe answered back.

"Hey, you two," Michelle spoke, "what's up with all the whispering back and forth?"

"Stop being so nosy!" Joe said back to his wife, Michelle, with a grin of love on his face.

"Alright Joe, it's not for me to know!" Michelle said as she gave Karen a wink of the eye that meant *tell me later.* Karen returned the wink with a wink of her own that Keith and Joe saw.

"So, my beautiful wife, how are you feeling?"

"I'm feeling great, Joe!" Nothing for you to worry about. I'm just sitting here with Karen sipping on my strawberry milkshake."

Karen sat in a chair listening to Michelle while Keith stood beside her. Karen started wondering once again what hidden secrets Michelle was hiding about her relationship with Little Girl for Little Girl enjoyed strawberry milkshakes also. *Why doesn't Michelle open up more about how she met Little Girl? And where is Little Girl now?* Karen opened her mouth and asked Michelle, "Where is Little Girl now?"

Michelle gave Karen a look of shock and of, *Have you lost your senses asking me something like that in front of Joe and Keith?* Michelle answered Karen, "Why do you ask me that, sweetie?" with a stern tone in her voice between taking sips from her strawberry milkshake.

"Yeah," Joe said looking at his wife, "who actually is this Little Girl, Karen asked me questions about?" And again, Michelle looked at her best friend with a, *Ohhhh, I'm going to get you when no one is here.* Karen saw the expression on her friend's face and quickly looked at Joe for help.

Joe continued to ask his wife Michelle. "Well, who is she, Michelle? I remember you telling me about her a few times."

Michelle looked at everyone and smiled. "You all are too nosey. She is someone I knew many years ago and I am going to leave it at that for now. And for you, missy," Michelle said looking in Karen's direction, "you just wait 'til you and I are alone."

"Joe, don't leave me here with her!" Karen said laughing, "She might hurt me or even make me drink her strawberry milkshake!"

Keith looked at his new friends and laughed, "You people are so funny. I see and can feel so much love in this room."

Joe agreed with Keith and said, "My friend, welcome to the family!"

Karen's, upon hearing those words from Joe's mouth, spirit jumped on its trampoline. She was so happy. Michelle noticed the joy in her friend and that joy made her feel extra happy. She knew Karen had been through a rough divorce. Karen's ex-husband left her for a younger woman. When he walked out on Karen, she was so devastated. She cried for days and was unable to work. It took a toll her physically and mentally. Michelle remembered how Karen would lay in bed for days only getting up to use the bathroom and shower, then back to bed she would go. Michelle was there with her friend through it all, giving her friend whatever was needed and telling her that if it is in God's will, God will send her someone who will be so awesome because anything that comes from God that is a blessing is good. She would tell her friend, "Just wait on God."

~Little Girl and Kim~

The two girls, Little Girl and Kim, walked, pushing baby Kelly in her stroller in the park enjoying the small breeze that filled the air and the smell of the flowers around the edge of the path. Little Girl walked over to the lake where the geese were swimming in the water while some ate the bread people were feeding them.

"This is really nice," Little Girl said to Kim.

"I know it is nice, Little Girl. I like coming here a lot when I want to enjoy the beauty of God's creation," spoke Kim, smiling and glad her friend was happy. "Let's go over and get a hot dog from the food stand over there," Kim suggested. So, the two walked over, ordered some food, and found a picnic table, and sat down.

"Is baby Kelly hungry?" spoke Little Girl. "If she is, can I feed her?"

"Sure, you can," Kim said.

Opening the baby bag, Kim reached and got a bottle of milk and handed it to Little Girl. Little Girl took baby Kelly in her arms and proceeded to feed her. Kim got up and walked over towards the lake. Little Girl watched her walk and wondered how, after everything Kim went through in her life, did she manage to be happy and not worry about anything. What Little Girl didn't know was that even though Kim loved God, Kim had her hidden secrets. Kim prayed every day for God to hear her and to help her for she was too ashamed to tell anyone, and she only trusted her Lord.

Little Girl finished feeding baby Kelly then rocked her back to sleep and placed her back in her stroller. Little Girl sat watching and looking at all the people walking, jogging, and fishing in the park. She wondered to herself what each one's life was like. She got up and pushed the stroller over near the lake and sat on the grass. She closed her eyes and felt a soft breeze against her skin. The feeling was cooling and relaxing for her. She could have stayed like that forever. It was like she was the only one in the world. Little Girl didn't hear Kim walk up and sit down next to her.

Kim noticed Little Girl looked relaxed and peaceful and did not want to disturb her, so she picked baby Kelly up out the stroller and held her in her lap. Little Girl opened her eyes, saw Kim sitting next to her, and gave her a smile.

"You ready to walk some more, Little Girl?" Kim asked.

"No, I think I'm ready to go somewhere else. I want to see more of the place you live."

"Well, let's go over to the petting zoo. It's just right down the street."

The girls got in the car with baby Kelly and headed towards their next destination. Arriving at the petting zoo, they bought some food to feed the animals. Little Girl reached her hands out to feed the animals.

"Wow!" she said. "This is amazing!" Little Girl had never been to a zoo or even fed any animal. She was so overwhelmed with joy. Little Girl felt something on her face. As she touched her skin, she noticed tears flowing down. She did not understand why she was crying. She felt happy. Little Girl did not know that someone could experience happy tears, so like everything she didn't understand or could not handle, she stored it in her hiding closet deep down in heart or way back in her mind. She wiped away the tears and continued to enjoy feeding the animals. She was like a kid; it was a world she never knew.

"Hello," a voice came from the left side of where she was standing. She turned to look to see who had spoken to her. There stood a young man, a very handsome young man. "Hello again," the man said.

"Hello!" Little Girl said back.

"My name is Pete."

"Everyone calls me Little Girl," she answered.

"I see you came here with Kim," Pete, the young man said. "Kim comes here a lot with her baby, Kelly." Little Girl was so busy feeding the animals she had not noticed Kim had walked away to another part of the animal park.

"I work here at the park. I keep the stalls cleaned and sometimes hose the animals down." Little Girl listened to Pete while still feeding the animals. She politely excused herself from listening to Pete and walked over to where Kim was.

"Hey, I saw Pete talking to you over there! What did he want?" Kim asked Little Girl.

"Nothing! He was just telling me that he knew you and that you come here a lot."

Kim and Little Girl walked and talked and fed the animals.

~Michelle, Karen, Joe and Keith~

The four friends arrived at the church and were escorted to their seats. Michelle sat next to her husband, Joe, and Keith, next to Karen. The pastor of the church began to preach. He spoke on Philippians 4:9, "Those things, which ye have both learned, and received, and heard, and seen in me, do: and the God of peace shall be with you."

As Michelle listened to God's words being spoken by the pastor, she thanked her Lord for His love for her. Karen sat there listening and enjoying being fed all this wisdom from the words of God. She was so hungry for more and more. Joe listened and felt good about all that was being said. Keith closed his eyes and went into a silent prayer.

After service, the four went up to the pastor and Michelle introduced Karen and Keith.

"I'm very happy you visited our church today. We hope you will make it again." He then turned to Joe and said, "Joe, I want to see you more in here. Put some of those jobs on hold and give our Lord some time." Then he shook Joe's hand, turned to Michelle and asked how she was feeling.

"I can't complain, won't complain, pastor," she said back. Then the pastor walked with them to the front of the church and outside.

"I want to see all four of you next Sunday!" he said once again and headed back into the church.

"That was a good sermon," Keith said.

"Amen," said Karen. Everyone turned and looked at her. "WHAT!" she said.

Then they all said in agreement, "Amen! Karen, we are happy for you; that's all. You are growing in the Lord, that's why we looked at you. We looked at you with joy in our hearts."

"Come on everyone!" Keith yelled. "Let's go to the restaurant and grab something to eat, and maybe if we are all in agreement, we can go see a movie."

"Sounds good to me," Joe replied.

As Keith and Karen headed for his car and Michelle and Joe to theirs, a shout in the distance stopped them in their tracks.

"JOE! JOE! JJOOOOEEE!!!!!" They all turned around to see who was yelling so loud for Joe. Joe looked into the distance and could see a man running up to him still shouting his name. As the man approached closer, he was now yelling. "Joe, get to your house quick! Someone broke in!"

Joe turned to Karen and yelled, "Take Michelle with you! Come on Keith!"

Keith and Joe raced away in Joe's car while Michelle and Karen were still standing, unable to move for a few seconds.

"Is everything alright?" one of the other church members said to Michelle. Some of the church members that had gathered together to talk after church witnessed the man calling Joe.

"I'm fine!" Michelle responded back. "Joe left to see what is going on."

"Well, if you need us, Sister Michelle, you just call, okay!"

"I sure will, Sister Rose," Michelle said and gave Sister Rose a hug, then went to Karen's car where Karen was waiting behind the driver's seat.

"Karen, did I hear right? Did that man just say my house was just broken into?"

"Yeah girl, you heard right!"

"Oh, Jesus!" Michelle said and then went to pray.

As the ladies drove up to Michelle's house, there were two police cars and two policemen who were talking with Joe and Keith while two more were looking at the lock on the front door. As Michelle walked up to Joe and the policemen, she heard Joe say, "My two guns are missing!"

Michelle looked at Joe and anger rose up in her. "JOE BROWN! How could you? I told you never to bring guns into this house! What else have you brought in our home?"

"Michelle, this is not the time, honey, okay?" Joe said back to his wife.

Michelle didn't hear a word Joe said. "Why Joe? Now someone out there has two guns to do harm with? I've told you we needed to move. This neighborhood was getting bad but no, who listens to me? And who was that man anyway, yelling for you at the church? I've never seen him before. How did he know where you were Joe?" Michelle was so outraged with her

180

husband, she forgot the police and everyone else who was standing around.

"Michelle, I thought I had them hidden in a place no one could find them," Joe tried to explain to his wife.

Michelle looked at her husband shook her head and said, "JOE! What other hidden secrets do you have?" Then she stormed off, heated like a firecracker on the Fourth of July, ready to explode. Karen hadn't seen her friend this angry in a long time. She knew that Michelle was tired from the surgery even if Michelle wasn't telling anyone something was going on with her, Karen felt it in her spirit.

Keith calmly walked over to Karen, touched her hand, and pointed to Michelle without saying a word. Karen understood what Keith was saying, then proceeded over to her friend. "Come on, sweetie," she said in a very calm voice. "Let's go inside and see what's going on."

Michelle was crying by now. She felt betrayed by her husband. "Why Karen?" she asked. "Why did Joe keep that from me? I tell him everything concerning our home. I mean, I don't tell him the things you and I talk about, at least not everything, you know. It's girl talk."

"Michelle, calm down. It's going to be fine. Let's just be thankful to God you weren't here alone."

"Karen, I love Joe so much. Karen, I'm tired now. I want to lie down."

"Okay, Michelle. Come on. Let's go inside."

As the two women walked into the house, they found the house a mess. So much was thrown around.

"My safe!" Michelle yelled and ran into her room then under her bed. It was still there. "Thank You, Jesus!" Michelle moaned.

The police entered her room and asked if anything in there was taken. "No," Michelle said. "Things in here are still in order."

"Okay," said the officer, "we will go and talk with your husband."

"Karen? Do you think I was a little too hard on Joe? I didn't mean to snap at him like that, but he and I discussed having guns in this house and we both agreed on *NO*, we will not!" Michelle said.

"Yeah Michelle, I do think you were a tad bit hard on him, but I also understand you have a lot going on right now."

"Really Karen? What do I have going on right now, other than I just had surgery on my breast? And come to think of it, why did you mention Little Girl to Joe?"

"MICHELLE!!!" Karen whispered. "Why are you jumping on me, sweetie?"

"I'm sorry Karen! You're right. I do have a lot going on. I'm tired and want to get into my bed and let the men do whatever they need to do to resolve all this."

Michelle went into her bathroom, changed into something comfortable, then laid across her bed. Karen got on the bed next to Michelle.

"Michelle! Talk to me. You and I have been friends for years. What's eating at you? You used to tell me everything and me, you."

Michelle began to talk to her friend Karen. "Karen, I am just feeling like my children don't appreciate me or even care if I live or die. They haven't called me since I returned home from the hospital to even say, *How are you feeling? Is there anything you want or need?* It hurts Karen. Joe works so much and when he's home, I feel like he's not really interested in me. I kind of feel like I'm losing him to what, I don't know. I know I'm being emotional, but I love them more than they could ever imagine. I just want us to come together as a family when a crisis arises to be supportive when I need support. Maybe I'm being too whiney. I'm going to pray to my Lord to please help me to see and do what His will is for this situation."

Karen listened to her friend talk. She wanted so eagerly to ask Michelle about what connection Michelle had with Little Girl, but she knew this was not the time for that.

Seven

~Little Girl and Kim~

After a long and enjoyable day and putting the baby in her crib, Little Girl and Kim relaxed with a pizza and a bottle of Coca-Cola on the living room sofa.

"I'm tired from walking today," Little Girl said between bites of her slice of pizza. "I had so much fun feeding the animals. That was something I've never done before."

"I had fun, also I'm tired too," Kim said back. "Let me ask you something, Little Girl. What are you going to do when you get back home?"

"I don't know, Kim. I still want to study for my GED, but I don't think I want to live with Pam, but I have no choice. I have nowhere else to stay."

"Why?" Kim asked. "What's wrong with Pam? I thought you like her as a friend."

"I do!" answered Little Girl. "It's just they do some things I don't want to do."

"Like what?" Kim asked.

"I would rather not talk about them, Kim. I just want to talk about anything else. Let's talk about you, Kim. What are you going to do when you finish college?"

"I want to further my education. I would like to maybe go for my Master's in Education, then become a science teacher for a while and go back for my Ph.D.," Kim said with excitement just thinking about her goals for herself.

"That's great, Kim!" Little Girl said and with that, Little Girl changed her mind about living with Pam. She decided she wants to live with Pam. Maybe Pam's boyfriend, Jason, will help her really help her get her GED.

"Kim," Little Girl said, "I think I'm going to go back home early. I want

183

to get started on studying for my GED."

"Little Girl," Kim interrupted what Little Girl was saying. "I'll help you while you are here so when you go back you will know a little more."

Little Girl thought about it for a few minutes. "Okay," she managed to say.

"That's great!" Kim smiled. "Tomorrow, we can start with math!"

"Now let's not talk about school anymore."

"Little Girl, I want to tell you something that I haven't told anyone but God, who already knew. Please don't tell anyone. I just know I can trust you. After we let the shelter and everyone went their separate ways, before I left for college, I met this guy. He was very nice and really good looking. He always had a lot of money. First, I thought maybe he was selling drugs, you know the hard stuff.

"One day, he invited me to his place. I went, and we were sitting and talking and eating when someone rang his doorbell. When he went to answer it, he first went into the kitchen and came out with a gun, then he went to the door and opened it. There were two guys, and both had guns, but he knew them, so they came in. They all went into the kitchen for a while. I stayed in the living room watching TV. After about an hour, my guy friend told me to come with them. They were going for a drive, so I went. Little Girl, they drove for a while then stopped. My friend asked me if I was hungry, so I said yes. He also asked me if I wanted to drive back. I was excited about driving so yeah. I said yes again. I told him what I wanted to eat and all three went into this restaurant to get some food. I waited for about five minutes when they came out, jumped in the car, and yelled at me to drive. I hesitated for a minute and a man came running out of the restaurant with a gun and started shooting at us. So, I slammed on the gas and drove so fast. I was really scared Little Girl.

"We didn't go back to my friend's house. We went to one of the other guys' house and when we went inside, my friend turned and slapped me so hard and called me a stupid "you know what!" He said I could have gotten all of them shot. They dumped a lot of money on a table then handed me some of it. I told them I didn't want it. My friend told me the next time, to leave the car running and watch out. I told him no and said I wanted to leave. He cursed at me, opened the door, and said if I told anyone, he was going to cut my throat. Little Girl, I'm so ashamed of what I did. I don't like hidden secrets. No one can hide anything from God."

Little Girl listened to Kim's story and said, "Kim, none of that is any of your fault. You didn't know what your friend was planning so don't feel bad anymore, please."

"Thanks for listening to me, Little Girl. I've been carrying that for years, even when I prayed about it. I felt like I needed to tell someone."

Just as Little Girl began to say something, Kim jumped up. "I'll be right back," Kim said as she got up. "It's time to feed baby Kelly. I want to hug her right now."

"Go ahead!" said Little Girl. "I'm going finish this pizza and watch some TV."

Little Girl sat glazing at the television, not really watching just letting her mind think about so much. Little Girl's brain has stored so much stuff. She just didn't know what to do about any of the things she has experienced or knew. She trusted no one. She wanted so bad to trust people. Everyone has something bad to say, she thought to herself. So many people have died, even the streetwalker, Juicy, the streetwalker she met the day after meeting her best friend, Steve, who told her to walk on a corner 'til he got back from doing whatever he did that day for money. Juicy was killed by one of her tricks. Little Girl wondered to herself why is she still alive. For what reason is she still walking around on earth? How long before she winds of dead like so many others?

Little Girl's thoughts were running all over the place. *Where's the mother who gave birth to me? Where are my sisters and brothers? The social worker said I have sisters and brothers. How come no one is looking for me? I guess I don't belong anywhere. I guess no one will ever love me like a person, only Steve did. I like to be nice to people. I like giving and helping people but people only like me when they want something from me.*

"I'm back," Little Girl's thoughts were interrupted by Kim coming back into the room and plopping down on the couch. "You can stay up as long as you like," said Kim. "I think I am going to go to sleep. Goodnight Little Girl."

"Goodnight Kim."

About one minute later, the phone rang. "Get that for me, Little Girl!" Kim yelled from her bedroom. (there were no cell phones back then lol)

Little Girl answered, "Hello!"

There was a man's voice on the other end of the phone. "Is this Little Girl? It's me, Charley!"

"Hi Charley," Little Girl said in a low voice.

"Hey, you don't sound happy to hear from me. Is everything alright down there?"

"I am fine, Charley," she said.

"Little Girl, want me to come there and visit with you? I can stay a few days if you want."

"Let me call you back, Charley," Little Girl said to him. She didn't want him with her. In fact, the more she thought about Charley, she wasn't sure if she wanted to be his girlfriend anymore. She wasn't actually sure what she wanted at that time. *I'll talk with Kim about it*, she said to herself then she cut the TV off and went into the bedroom to get some sleep, hoping she would be able to sleep peacefully like the other night.

Seven

~Michelle, Karen, Joe and Keith~

Joe walked into the bedroom where his wife, Michelle, was laying down with her friend, Karen. Both were engaged in conversation when Joe asked Karen if she didn't mind, he would like to speak with his wife in private.

Karen answered, "Sure, where is Keith?"

"He's out in the living room trying to straighten up some of the mess."

Karen exited the bedroom to join the new man in her life, Keith, and lend a hand in cleaning up.

"Joe," Michelle began to speak, "sweetie, I'm so sorry for yelling at you and especially in front of people. Please forgive me. That was not the way I should have handled the problem."

"Michelle, it's fine. I went behind your back, and after we both agreed not to bring guns in this house, I still went ahead and did so. So, I'm also asking you to forgive me."

"I do, Joe."

"Me too, Michelle." Both smiled and gave one another a kiss. "Now, let's go see what Keith and Karen are doing in our living room.

"Let's," Michelle said, putting her arm in Joe's arm and letting him lead the way.

"Hey, you two!" Joe said.

Keith looked up from picking up some paper that was scattered across the floor. "Oh, look Keith," Karen hollered, "the old couple is back together again!"

"Is everything alright?" Keith asked.

"Of course," Joe said. "Marriage isn't always a bed of roses but strong love with God and your spouse conquers all. Remember what God puts together, no man put asunder. Something like that! You know what I mean right, Michelle?"

187

Michelle smiled at her husband and said, "You got it, baby. Now look at all this mess! Joe, what is missing?" Michelle asked.

"I don't know, honey. It looks like they were looking for something."

"Really Joe," Karen said. "I see you went to cop school!" Joe just looked at Karen and smiled.

"Oh, my goodness, Joe!" Michelle hollered. "Where's my jewelry box?"

"I don't know! Wasn't it in the bedroom?" Joe asked.

"No! I left it in here last week! Karen and I were going through it!"

All four friends quickly started a search for the jewelry box, but nobody could find it anywhere in the living room.

"Joe!" Michelle called to her husband with the sound of sadness in her voice. "Joe, I'm not feeling well. I want to lie down." Joe quickly rushed to his wife's side. Karen and Keith dropped what was in their hands and went over to help Joe walk Michelle back into the bedroom.

"I want you to stay in bed, okay honey! Please Michelle, don't get back up."

"I'll stay with her, Joe." Karen spoke. "You and Keith go and finish cleaning the living room." Karen looked at her friend whom she loved so dearly. Michelle wasn't looking too well. "I'm going to get a cool cloth and put on your forehead, okay sweetie," Karen said to Michelle.

"Okay," Michelle answered.

Now I know she isn't well, Karen thought to herself. *She's letting me take care of her without any complaints.* This really had Karen concerned now. She went into the bathroom, got a cool cloth, and returned, placing it on Michelle's forehead. Michelle had taken her clothes off and was not under her bed covers.

"Karen," she whispered, "would you be so kind as to get me a bottle of water?" Karen left to get the water but stopped first to talk with Joe.

"Joe," she said, "I think Michelle is really sick. She agreed to letting me put a cool cloth on her forehead without a fuss and she now wants a bottle of water, plus she doesn't look well, Joe. I'm really concerned, Joe."

Joe left Karen still talking and walked into the bedroom to check on his wife, Michelle. "Honey," he said as he crawled into the bed next to her, "Michelle! Michelle!" Joe shook his wife.

Michelle hollered, "WHAT JOE?" Michelle yelled back, which was a low yell, "I'm in prayer! What is wrong, Joe?"

"Woman, you just scared the dickens out of me! You didn't answer, and Karen was saying you didn't look so well, which you don't."

"Joe, I'm tired! I haven't had much rest since the surgery. I was supposed to stay home but I went to church. It was meant for me to leave this house because this house was being robbed. Joe, you and Karen have got to stop this. You both are going to drive yourselves loony ad I'm not going there with you and her. See, this is why I don't tell you all too much about my health. You and she get nutty! Now, please Joe, go back and finish what you and Keith were doing and let me get some sleep! Love you Joe, now go and send that nutty friend of mine back in here with my bottle of water so I can tell her a thing or two!" Michelle said with a small laughter.

Joe left to find Karen who was in the living room with Keith crying in his arms. "Are you serious, Karen?" Joe said. "Michelle is fine, and she is calling for you and her bottle of water."

"Karen, look," Keith said, "Michelle is a woman of God. If she says she is fine and just tired, then believe her, baby."

"You're right, Keith!" Karen whispered. "I just love my friend, Keith."

"I know you do, baby," Keith said while holding Karen close to his chest. "Now, go on back to her," he said and gave Karen a kiss on the forehead.

Karen went back into the room to find Michelle sitting up and smiling a small smile. "Girl, if you don't get your butt in here and sit and talk me to sleep, I'm going to get out of bed!"

"Michelle, if you scare me like that one more time, I promise you I'm going to buy a house in another state and live there!"

"Girl, please hand me that bottle of water! Anyway, I won't let you move to another state. If you do, I'm going to follow you, now!" Michelle said, laughing with her friend.

"Here, take your water, Michelle! I'm going to sit here in this recliner and take me a nap while you take one also. We both can use a nap about now, it's been one busy afternoon." Both women closed their eyes and went off into a deep sleep.

"Joe! Tell me about your wife. Is she very ill?" Keith asked.

"No, she's not. At least, I don't think so. To be honest with you, Keith, I don't really know what's going on with Michelle's health. I know she's a breast cancer survivor and from the looks of it, she's a second time survivor. Keith, sometimes my wife can be a mystery to me. I mean it. Like at times, I don't know what she or Karen are up to. Remember in the hospital, when Karen asked me if Michelle ever discussed Little Girl with me? Well not much. What they both don't know is that I have overheard them a few times talking about this girl named, Little Girl. From what I have overheard, both of them seem to be interested in this girl. Michelle seemed eager to tell Karen. Karen seems eager to know more and more about this girl."

"Joe, what about your wife? Is she ill?"

"Man, I just told you! She's a second time cancer survivor. You heard the doctor, she will have to take chemo for a while. I believe she will be just fine. In fact, as she would say, she's blessed!"

"Amen!" Keith responded back. "So, let's finish cleaning this place up and order some food from the restaurant. I'll have someone bring it to us,"

Keith suggested.

~Little Girl and Kim~

Little Girl woke to the cries of baby Kelly. Walking into Kim's bedroom room, she was sound asleep unaware of hearing the baby's cries. "Come here," Little Girl said as she reached into the baby crib and picked up baby Kelly in her arms. "Come on, let's go into the kitchen and see if I can find you a milk bottle already made."

Little Girl found a bottle, heated it up on the stove, then began feeding baby Kelly. After the baby was fed, Little Girl changed her diaper and placed her back into her crib, then walked back into her room and laid in the bed. *I want to go home,* she said to herself. *I want to stay here also.* Little Girl just didn't know what to do with herself. She had no one to help guide her in her life. Instead of trying to fall back to sleep, she went into the kitchen and dialed Charley's phone number.

"Hello!" came Charley's voice on the phone.

"Charley! It's me, Little Girl. Can you come down here with me?"

Charley said, "Yes babe, I'm coming. Give me the address and I will be on the next flight out."

"Charley," Little Girl said, "where are you going to get the money?"

"Baby, I have enough money to come see you and bring you back with me when you are ready to come home."

"Okay, Charley. I will see you tomorrow." Little Girl hung up the phone, returned to her room, and laid there thinking about Charley. She realized she did miss him. She also thought about baby Kelly. *What if I had a baby? Then, I'll have someone to love and really love me back,* she thought to herself. She thought about that for a while then went off to sleep.

When the sun arose the next day, Kim was in the kitchen on the phone as Little Girl walked in.

"Hey Kim!"

Kim turned and said to Little Girl, "You invited Charley, Pam, and Pam's boyfriend, Jason, to my house without asking me?"

"I'm sorry, Little Girl said, "but I just invited Charley. I didn't think you would mind for him to come. I never invited the other two."

"Well, they are all here now. I just got off the phone with Pam. They are taking a taxi from the airport. Little Girl, I don't mind them coming, I just wish you would have said something to me. My house is a mess. I haven't enough food to feed everyone and where is everybody going to sleep?"

Little Girl started feeling bad. "I'm so sorry, Kim, really I am."

Kim and Little Girl ran around the house tidying things up when there came the knock on the door. "I guess that's them," Kim smiled and said. Kim arose and answered the door with a pleasant greeting.

Pam came in rushing Kim with hugs and kisses. "How have you been, girl? It's so good to see you, girl! It's been a long time!" Pam introduced Charley and Jason to Kim and everyone said their hellos. "Where's Little Girl?" Pam asked.

Little Girl had left the room as soon as the doorbell rang and retreated into her room. She wanted to fix herself up for Charley. When she was through, she walked into the living room.

"There's my baby!" Charley said and reached out to give Little Girl a hug. She hugged him back then everyone sat and started talking and laughing.

Charley and Little Girl moved their conversation into the room Little Girl was staying in during her visit. "So, Little Girl, when are you coming back home?"

"I don't know, Charley," she said. "I like it here." Then she proceeded to tell Charley all the things she had done since she was there and the joy it brought to her. She told Charley that, "Kim prays a lot and it just feels nice and quiet here."

"Do you want to move here?" Charley asked Little Girl.

"No Charley," she answered him back. "I did but nah. I think I'm going home with you. I like Kim. She really is a good friend and I think her baby is so beautiful. Come on Charley, let's go back in the room with the rest of them."

"Hey, what have you two been in there doing?" Jason asked.

"Just talking," Charley said.

"Who's hungry?" Pam asked. Everyone said "ME!" Turning to Kim, Pam asked, "Where can we order some pizza?"

"I'll call the pizza place," Kim responded.

Little Girl looked at her friends. They were all talking about school and their future.

"Yeah, Jason is going to help Little Girl get her GED, so she can go on the college and study education," Pam said. Little Girl was feeling that familiar feeling of being a black sheep, different, and dumb. She continued to listen and fake a laugh and smile with them. "Little Girl, come show me where the bathroom is," Pam said to her.

"It's just right down the hall to your left," Little Girl said.

"Come with me, I have something to tell you while Kim is on the phone ordering out pizza." So, both girls walked down the hall and went into the bathroom.

"What is it Pam?" Little Girl asked.

"Oh, it's nothing! I just want you in here with me while a take a line or two."

"A WHAT?" Little Girl said.

"Ssshhh, be quiet!" Pam whispered while pulling out a small white paper with white powder in it.

"Pam, I thought you only swallowed pills."

"I know, but I used to take a little of this once in a while to keep me up in class, now I just crave it more now."

"Here, take a line with me," Pam said to Little Girl. Little Girl didn't want to, but she reminded herself she needed to belong, so she was going to do what she needed to fit in. So, for the first time, Little Girl snorted cocaine. "How do you feel, Little Girl?" Pam asked.

"I feel nothing! What am I supposed to feel?"

"Here then, take another line." Pam made the line a little thicker than the first.

Little Girl snorted that and said, "WOW! That's something. I feel like I'm alive, I guess!"

Pam laughed, "See, it's an upper. Here, wipe your nose and let's get out of here before Jason figures out what I'm doing." The girls went back and sat down. Little Girl smiled at Charley. She started feeling funny in her body.

"Charley, come here in the room with me." So, Charley and she went back into her room. She sat on the bed, then motioned Charley to sit also. Little Girl started talking and talking and talking.

"What's wrong with you?" Charley asked, looking at Little Girl.

"Kiss me, Charley!" she said.

Charley reached over and kissed her. In about another ten minutes, Charley and Little Girl were under the covers. After their moment of being together, Charley said to Little Girl, "What did you take when you and Pam went into the bathroom? I know Pam, she has been doing cocaine a lot lately and Jason is beginning to get pissed off about it. They used to do it every now and then among other things, but Pam has gone overboard with it."

"I just snorted a line, that's all Charley."

"Little Girl, let me tell you something. I don't want my girlfriend doing drugs. So many do on campus and some overdose on that stuff. I want to finish college and get my life together. I'm not throwing my life away on drugs and pills."

Little Girl looked at Charley and thought to herself, *You didn't say no when you just slept with me.* "Okay, Charley. I won't do it again. I promise."

So, they dressed and went back into the living room with the rest of their friends. After everyone ate and talked some more, Kim showed everyone where they would be sleeping that night.

"So, how long are you all staying?" Kim asked. "I would love to show you around."

Pam said, "Kim, I don't know. It depends on Jason.

Jason looked at his girlfriend Pam. He knew what she meant. If she couldn't find any cocaine down here, she was going back soon. Jason was worried about Pam and didn't want to leave her. He also didn't want an addict for a girlfriend, but he did love her a lot.

"Kim, can I speak with you in private?" Jason said.

"Sure," Kim answered back.

Everyone else looked puzzled. "What did Jason have to talk to Kim about? He just met her."

Kim and Jason walked outside to the apartment parking lot. "Kim, is there a place here I can get Pam into for doing too much cocaine? I love her so much, but she is now abusing the drug. I think she has become addicted to it."

"I don't know, Jason," Kim said, "but I will look into it today. I'll make a few phone calls but I will leave the house so she doesn't hear or know what I am doing."

"That's great," Jason said.

"Look Jason, I have my keys with me. You go back in and just tell them

I'm going to buy a cake to celebrate us girls being back together."

"Okay, Kim. See you when you get back." Jason went back in.

"Where's Kim?" Pam asked.

"She went to go buy a cake to celebrate you three girls being back together," Jason answered her, feeling bad he had to lie to Pam.

"So, what did you want to talk to her about, Jason?" Pam asked with an attitude.

"I wanted to talk to her about a celebration for you three girls. What's with the attitude towards me, Pam?"

"I'm sorry, Jason. Just forget it, okay?"

"Okay," Jason said to her.

Little Girl sat listening to it all. She knew from past experience how drugs made someone feel paranoid. That's how Steve, her only true friend that died from drugs, used to act, and even Shirley from the shelter would act like that also. She, too, died. Little Girl began wondering about Pam, *I hope Pam stops.* She did not want to lose another person she knew from drugs. Little Girl wasn't feeling well. She started feeling strange inside. *What's wrong with me?* she thought to herself, so she grabbed Pam by the arm and almost dragged her into the bathroom. "What is that stuff you gave me, Pam? I feel like throwing up."

"Don't worry, Little Girl. You are not addicted to it. It does that with some people the first time they snort."

"Pam, what was that you gave me?" Little Girl asked again, this time with anger in her voice.

"Dag, Little Girl! It was cocaine with a little heroin mixed in it."

"WHAT THE HELL? Are you stupid, Pam? That's what killed our friends, Steve and Shirley. Don't give me anymore and you need to stop yourself."

"I am as soon as I finish this last bit. I'm going to stop for a while," Pam said.

"You hid that from me! I'm thinking I'm just snorting cocaine and you knew it had heroin in it. What other hidden secrets are you hiding, Pam?" Little Girl was furious with Pam. "Are you sleeping with more than one person, you and Jason, for money? You sell pills for money, Pam? What other hidden secrets do you have?" Little Girl was now yelling at Pam.

"Let me tell you something, Little Girl! If it weren't for me you would still be homeless, living in the streets, or at some nasty shelter. So, don't go to yelling at me for what I do. At least I have a roof over my head and I'm in college studying to be someone. You are just a drifter, Little Girl. You don't have a soul who cares one thing about you!"

When Pam had finished saying what she said, she realized what she said and began to feel bad, but it was too late. Charley and Jason were already at the bathroom door, had opened it, and saw the whole argument. Little Girl turned, looked at everyone, stormed into her room, and locked the door.

Charley knocked on the door, "Little Girl, let me in, baby! That wasn't Pam talking. That was the drugs." Little Girl couldn't care less what it was. What Pam said had truth to it. Little Girl didn't have anyone who really cared or loved her, everyone lies to her. She didn't have a place she could really call home; that was her home.

Little Girl changed her clothes while she was in her room, picked up her pocketbook with enough money to get her to where ever she needed to go, opened the room door, looked at Charley, Jason, and Pam who was crying uncontrollably, and walked out the front door.

Hidden Secrets

Are hidden

Or are they?

There are no secrets,

For He sees and knows all.

God.

Secrets: To keep from the knowledge of others.

What does Jesus say about hidden secrets?

Psalms 44:21, "Shall not god search this out? for he knoweth the secrets of the heart."

Luke 12:2, "Nothing is covered up that will not be revealed or hidden that will not be known."

Ecclesiastes 12:23, "For God will bring every deed into judgment, with every secret thing, whether good or evil."

Author's Own Thoughts:

Secrets are not good.

7

IF I HAD ONE WISH

~LITTLE GIRL~

Little Girl sat on the bus gazing out the window. It was just three hours ago that she was with her friends or were they her friends? She didn't really know. Pam was a liar, Charley didn't mind sleeping with her even though he knew she had snorted cocaine but decided to only say something about it after he got her body. Jason, she didn't know or trust that well and Kim she liked yet just didn't understand. The only one she really fell for was baby Kelly. She was going to miss her.

Little Girl almost felt good about leaving. She kind of wished she had said goodbye to Kim. She also wondered what Kim had to say when she returned with the cake for a celebration that was not going to take place. *I wish I had that book, the Bible with me so I could read a few more pages in the front. I want to finish one of those books that Bible had in it. There are so many books in one book,* Little Girl thought to herself, so she sat looking out the window of the bus, looking at the everything the bus passed. Finally, she dozed off to sleep.

When Little Girl awakened, she was at her destination back home in New York. As she got up and walked off the bus with just her pocketbook and a few more dollars she had left, she looked around. It looked so different from where she just came from. The crowds of people were rushing here and there. There was hardly any grass, just concrete streets and sidewalks. There were lights everywhere and noisy car horns. "Yuck!" She said out loud.

Little Girl knew she had to find a shelter that would take her, so she went into a phone booth and began scanning through its pages. *There's one*, she said to herself. She went down into the train station, paid for her token, and hopped on the train to find the shelter. As she sat there, her mind raced back to her long-ago friend, Steve. This was how they met. Now he's dead; she quickly put her mind on something else, wondering what this shelter would be like. It's been a long time since she's been in one.

Little Girl finally reached her stop and began to walk a few blocks. The sun had begun to go down. *This must be it*, as she walked up to one of the ugliest buildings she ever laid her eyes on. She walked into the front door and up to a window. The place reeked of stench. "How can I help you, miss?" the lady said behind the desk.

"I need a place to stay," Little Girl responded.

"Okay, follow me," the lady said.

Little Girl followed the lady up a flight of stairs and down a long hallway. There were rooms on both sides of the hallway. The smell was sickening. *Do these women wash*, Little Girl thought to herself.

"This will be your room," the lady said, "and if you have anything personal, I would advise you to sleep with it. Here are two sheets, a blanket, and a few toiletries. Breakfast is at 7:00 am, lunch at 12:00 pm, and dinner at 6:00 pm. Do you have any questions?" asked the lady.

"Yes," said Little Girl, "do I need to sign any papers?"

"Someone will come to you in the morning around 5:00 am to talk with you and find out your situation to see if you qualify for any assistance. Doors lock at 12:00 am, so if you aren't in, you will be locked out until the next day. We allow that three times, then you will be kicked out and your space will be given to some else. Your belongings will be put in a plastic bag and tagged. You will then have one week to retrieve them.

"Well, I have some paper work to finish. My name is Ms. Daisy and you are?"

"My name is Little Girl."

"Very well, Little Girl. I will leave you to look around. Oh, the bathroom and showers are down the hall. Some rooms have their own bathroom. Yours doesn't. Sometimes the women will change rooms with one another. Well, see you later Little Girl."

Little Girl looked around the room. There were five other beds in the room. One had someone asleep in it. She walked over to her bed which was against the wall with no window. Little Girl made her bed and sat on it holding her bag of toiletries in her hand. *What am I going to do now?* she thought to herself. She reached in her pocket and pulled out a sleeping pill, placed it in her mouth, and swallowed it.

After about thirty minutes, her eyes closed, only to be awoken with a push and a voice yelling, "This is my bed, BUM!"

Little Girl was groggy from the sleeping pill but managed to open her eyes. There stood next to her bed was a rough looking girl with a torn shirt and a scar that ran across the top of her eye. "This is my bed, BUM!" she said again.

Little Girl got up without a saying word, gathered her sheets, and moved to another vacant bed. This one was next to a wall with a large crack running up the wall. Little Girl was too tired to make this bed, so she threw the sheets on the bed and crawled onto it, covering herself with her blanket. When Little Girl awoke, it was 12:00 pm, the next afternoon. The five beds that were in the room, all five had women either sitting on laying across it.

"Hey, so you're awake," came a voice from across the large room. Little Girl scanned the room to see who the voice belonged to. Sitting right across on the opposite side of the room was a young woman looking straight at Little Girl.

"Yeah," Little Girl answered back.

"Come over here," said the young girl. Little Girl approached the young woman and without being invited to, she sat her on her bed. "I'm Pat, but everyone calls me, Bucky."

"I'm Little Girl, and everyone calls me Little Girl."

"So, what brings you to this nasty place, Little Girl," Bucky asked. "Are you running from the police? Did you have a fight with your boyfriend? Did you get kicked out your apartment?"

Little Girl looked at Bucky and thought to herself, *This girl is nosey.* "No, to all your questions," Little Girl said.

"What time is it?" Bucky asked, looking at the other woman in the bed right next to her.

"It's about 1:30 pm. Why?" said the woman.

"Well, gotta go," Bucky said to Little Girl. "See you later tonight if I come in."

Little Girl said, "Bye," and then returned to her own bed.

~Michelle and Karen~

Karen woke from her short nap to find Michelle looking through some papers she had scattered across her bed. "What are you looking at Michelle?" Karen asked.

"Oh, I'm just reading some old poetry I wrote through the years."

"Michelle?" Karen wanted to know more about Little Girl. "Girl, I wish you would finish telling me about this Little Girl. You can't just start telling a story and then decide not to finish."

"Karen, okay, since the men are in the other room cleaning up, I'll tell you some more. Now, where did I leave off on the story?" Michelle responded back.

"Karen," eager to hear more, quickly remembering said, "You left off where Little Girl went back home, started staying at a shelter again, and met some girl name, Bucky."

"Dag, Karen!" Michelle said laughing. "You are eager to hear some more. Well......"

~Little Girl~

Little Girl walked down the flight of stairs of the shelter. As she walked on to the first floor, *Wow*, she said to herself. There were a lot of women. Looking around, she saw some women leaning on the wall talking to themselves. Some were in a small group laughing. As she continued to walk further down looking for an office where maybe she could talk with someone since no one has come looking for her, there was a small room with chairs and a television with more women watching. Some were nodding, and some were just gazing into the whatever was playing on the television. She walked up to a door that had *Counselor's Office* on the door, knocked, and waited for someone on the other side of the door to answer.

"Come in," said the voice. Little Girl entered into the office. There was a beautiful woman sitting behind one of four desks. "Hello," she said. "How can I help you?"

Little Girl explained to the beautiful woman that the lady last night said someone would speak to her about qualifying for someone assistance. "Okay," said the beautiful woman. "Let me introduce myself. I'm Mrs. Carrington, and if you will give me a minute, I will see who your counselor is.

"Well, look here," Mrs. Carrington smiled, "looks like it's me! I'll be your counselor during your stay. Grab one of those chairs and pull it up to my desk," she said pointing. Little Girl smiled and did as the woman said for, *the woman had a nice personality*, Little Girl thought to herself. Mrs.

Carrington began asking some questions to Little Girl which were all answered with a *no*. Then, she said, "Little Girl, have you ever seen a therapist? I have to ask all these questions. You don't have to tell me why, just let me know, okay."

Little Girl answered, "Yes."

"When was the last time you seen your therapist?"

"About a year ago," answered Little Girl.

"Okay, just one more question then we are finished with this part. Do you have anyone I could write down in case something may happen?" Little Girl looked at Mrs. Carrington and without any warning, started crying. Little Girl cried so hard. "It's alright," Mrs. Carrington said as she walked from behind her desk to give Little Girl a small hug. "If there is no one, its fine. Listen to me Little Girl, you will be fine. You're almost twenty years old. Whatever has happened to you in your life, God was there and has seen you through it. I'm going to see about getting you on welfare and then you may be able to find yourself either a room or a small apartment, depending on the amount of the check. You also will be eligible for food stamps," Mrs. Carrington said to Little Girl.

"So, that will be it for now, Little Girl. I am going to set up an appointment with the clinic right down the block so you can start seeing a therapist again."

Little Girl listened to Mrs. Carrington and just spoke in a soft voice with a, "Yes." She left the office and walked outside the building feeling very alone. She just stood on the walkway of the building looking around at her surroundings. Across the street was a fruit stand, a little further down the block she noticed people going in and out of what looked like a pool hall and next door to that was a Chinese Restaurant. She started to walk down the sidewalk to a little store she noticed on the corner. Once inside the store, she saw some of the women from the shelter playing a pinball machine and some others standing around talking with the man behind the counter. Little Girl walked over to a cooler, grabbed a cream soda, and a bag of onion and garlic potato chips.

At the counter, the man said, "Seventy-five cents," to her. She handed him the money and left the store. Her curiosity about the pool hall got the better of her so she entered there, standing inside. She noticed more of the shelter women playing pool and drinking beer. In the rear of the building was a very dark skin man with curly hair looking at her.

"Hey, Barbara! Who's this new one in here?" Little Girl heard him say to the woman standing at one of the pool tables.

"She's from the shelter. I saw her come in last night. I haven't met her though," Barbara answered.

Little Girl turned to walk out when someone asked if she wanted to shoot a game of pool. Not wanting show how nervous she was, Little Girl answered, "Sure, but I have to tell you, I have never played before."

"Aww, that's okay," the woman who asked her said. "It's just for fun. We won't play for money. What's your name?"

"Little Girl! What's yours?" Little Girl asked her back.

"I'm Geraldine, but people around here gave me the name, Shark."

"Shark?" Little Girl said with a question.

"I know it's strange, but I'm very good at shooting pool and playing poker," Shark answered. Shark showed Little Girl how to shoot pool.

Little Girl had grown into a young woman who was tall and model-like. Her hair was now down on her shoulders. She was model-like, yet tomboyish at the same time. While Shark and she played pool, the man in the rear kept looking over at her every time he got the chance. Little Girl did not let on that she knew he was looking at her.

"Shark," she asked, "who is that man in the back?"

"Oh, that's James. He owns the place. He's the numbers man. Everyone around here who plays the numbers either bring their numbers here or take them to King Pen who owns the fruit stand down the block. Both are nice men. They kind of look out for the women in the shelter if any of the neighborhood boys try to rob us."

"You're in the shelter?" Little Girl asked.

"Yeah! Every woman you see in here lives there. The men just come in here either to gamble or look at us women and to see who the new ones are. It's almost time for dinner at the shelter," Shark said. "Come on before the line is too long."

As Little Girl stood in line with Shark, she saw a young white girl pulling her hair out of her head. "SHARK? Look at the girl over there! She's pulling her hair out!"

"That's Sarah," Shark said back. "She's lost her mind from a bad trip on acid, LSD." Just as Little Girl was about to say something else, a counselor went up to Sarah and gently took her hand and led her out of the dining area.

"What's going to happen to her?" Little Girl whispered.

"They will take her back to the mental hospital. I think this time they won't let her out."

Little Girl received her tray and sat at a table with Shark and about ten other women. The table benches held five women on each side.

"So Little Girl, what's your story? Everyone has a story."

"It's too long to tell," Little Girl answered.

"Yeah, I hear ya," Shark responded. "Mine is too. Do you ever wish you didn't have a story? I mean, not the ones we have now?" Shark asked.

"I sure do wish," Little Girl said.

"Hello Little Girl," Bucky said as she approached the table. "How are you doing? Hey Shark, how's it going?"

"Great Bucky!" Shark answered. "You met Little Girl?"

"Yeah, she stays in my room. What are you doing back so early?"

Shark looked at Little Girl and said, "Bucky leaves every day to visit with her two kids."

Little Girl looked towards Bucky's way and asked, "Where are your kids?"

"My kids are staying with my oldest sister until I can find a place. I got evicted."

"Why didn't you just live with your sister?" Little Girl asked.

"She only has a one bedroom and my kids sleep in the living room. Plus, I don't like her husband. He's a real snob, you know what I mean?" Bucky had now squeezed in between Shark and Little Girl at the table.

"I'm finished eating. Come on let's go to Mr. Foly's," Shark said.

"Who's that?" Little Girl asked.

"He owns the store at the corner."

Little Girl walked with Bucky and Shark to Mr. Foly's. She started thinking while walking about Charley, Kim, Pam, and Jason. She still had Kim's phone number in her pocket. *I wonder if I should call her to let her know I'm alright.* She quickly filed that thought to the back of her mind.

"Hey Mr. Foly!" Shark said, greeting the old man who owned the store.

"Hello Shark! What's shaking?"

"Nothing, Mr. Foly," Shark answered back. "I want you to meet the new girl at the shelter. This is Little Girl."

"Glad to meet you, Little Girl," Foly said while shaking Little Girl's hand. "Since you are the new one, I do this for all the new ladies that arrive at the shelter. You go and pick five items in the store. Don't worry about paying; it's all on the house."

Little Girl felt funny going to pick out something free. *Nobody ever gives anything free without wanting something back,* but she still picked out some snacks she, Shark, and Bucky could eat on, then slyly handed Mr. Foly two dollars without Shark and Bucky seeing. "I pay for what I want," she whispered.

"Let's play pinball," Bucky told Shark.

"Okay, but this time, don't tilt the machine, Bucky."

Little Girl sat in a chair next to the pinball machine and watched the two young women play and laugh.

"Little Girl, how old are you?" Shark asked.

"I'll be twenty this coming summer."

"Wow, you're a young one!"

"You wish you were that age again!" laughed Bucky to Shark. "Shark is twenty-five!" Bucky blurted out. Little Girl could not believe that the woman she played pool with was that much older than her. She looked the same age. "Beat ya!" yelled Bucky to Shark. "You wanna play, Little Girl?"

"No, thank you. I would like Shark to finish teaching me how to shoot pool though."

"Come on, then."

The young women crossed the street and walked into the pool hall. This day, the pool was packed with men and women drinking beer and just hanging around.

"Here Little Girl, take this dollar up to James. Tell him we are going to play for about an hour."

Little Girl hesitantly walked to the back of the place and straight up to the man named James. "Here's a dollar. Shark said to give it to you. She said we will be playing for an hour."

James reached and took the dollar and smiled at Little Girl. "Thanks baby," he said in return. "Tell Shark she better save a game for me. I want to win my ten dollars back," James said.

The three young women shot a few games of pool then watched Shark beat a few people out their money on the pool table.

"Here, Little Girl! I got us all a beer," Bucky said, handing out the beer she purchased. Little Girl did not want to drink, but she wanted to belong and fit in with these new people in her life, so she took the beer and drank it.

After finishing the can, Little Girl asked for another. "I'll pay for it," she said.

"Are you sure?" Bucky asked? You know we can't get back in the shelter if we are drunk."

"Don't worry," Little Girl answered back. "I won't get drunk. I'm just thirsty," but the real truth was Little Girl didn't want people to think she didn't care for drinking. So, Bucky went to the back to purchase another beer for Little Girl.

"Let me have another beer, James," Bucky asked.

"Whose drinking all the beer?" James asked Bucky.

"Little Girl is. This is just her second; don't worry James. I won't let her get drunk. I see you staring at her a lot."

"Go on, girl," James said. "I look at everyone in my place. Here, take this beer and give her money back. Tell her it's on the house."

"If you say so!" Bucky laughed taking the beer and headed back to Little Girl. "Here," she handed Little Girl the beer and the money. "James said it's on the house," Bucky said.

"Oh, no! I pay for whatever I want," Little Girl responded. She remembered THE MAN and what she and Steve went through owing money. So, she walked to the back of the pool hall and handed James the money with the words, "I pay for what I want," and walked away back to where Shark and Bucky were. James looked at Little Girl and smiled.

"Hey, Shark! Are you finished playing yet? I'm bored watching you," Bucky yelled across the hall.

"I'm almost done, Buck!" Shark yelled back. "Just let me win this last ten dollars." In ten minutes, Shark was standing with Bucky and Little Girl.

"Come, let's go to the Chinese Restaurant and get some chicken and bread. I have enough for all three of us," Sharky said.

After the girls ate their food, they headed back to the shelter.

"I didn't realize it was so late," Little Girl said, trying to hide the buzz she got from the two beers she drank at the hall.

~Michelle and Karen~

Michelle continued to talk about Little Girl when Joe and Keith walked into the room.

"Hello ladies," Joe said while walking over to his wife, Michelle, and grabbing a hold of her hand. "Keith ordered some food from the restaurant to be sent over. Plus, Keith and I are almost finish cleaning the living room and the rest of the house. So, what have you two been talking about in here?"

Karen looked at Michelle with a, *Is it okay if I tell what you have been talking about*, kind of look. Michelle read Karen's expression and simply said to her husband, "I've been telling the story of Little Girl."

"Who is this Little Girl and what is so important about her if you all don't mind me asking, that you all keep talking and wondering about her?" Keith asked looking at Karen, the woman he has now fallen in love with.

Replying to his question, Michelle said, "Little Girl is a girl I knew and know very well."

"Well, I wish one day to meet this person you talk about so much and seem to have such a connection with," Joe said.

Michelle looked into her husband's eyes and with a calm voice said, "Have faith and hope and if it is in our Lord's will, then it will be done."

"So, will we get to meet Little Girl?" Keith asked. Karen shoved Keith slightly as to say, *Leave it alone*. Getting the hint, Keith said no more about asking to meet Little Girl and left that to Joe and Michelle.

"I hear someone knocking," Karen spoke out, interrupting the conversation.

"That must be the food Keith ordered. I'll get it," Joe spoke.

"I'll come with you," Keith said also and following Joe to the door.

"Guess we have two nosey men on our hands!" laughed Michelle as she stretched across her bed.

"Yeah, we do!" Karen laughed back. "So, are we going to finish talking about Little Girl or do you want to rest some?" Karen said as she reached over to drink a glass of water she had sitting on Michelle's nightstand.

"You know what I want to do right now, Karen? I want to read some of the Bibl. I think I'll read a little of Philippians."

Michelle reached for her Bible and turned to the book of Philippians 4:6,7, "Do not be anxious about anything, but in everything by prayer and supplication with thanksgiving let your requests be made known to God. And the peace of God, which surpasses all understanding, will guard your hearts and your minds in Christ Jesus."

"I like that verse," Karen said to her friend. "I love that when it reads, *Do not be anxious about anything, but in everything by prayer.* Do not be anxious," Karen repeated herself.

"Yes, Karen," Michelle said. "Don't be anxious. You see, Karen, I can feel you are so anxious to meet and know if Little Girl is me. Let me tell you something," just as Michelle was talking, Joe and Keith returned with the food.

Karen threw her arms up in the air and screamed playfully, "WHAT NOW?"

Joe hesitated for a moment then said, "I was just going to say, *Here you go ladies, some food to fill our bellies up with.*"

"Joe, is that all you and Keith think about is food?" Karen said.

"Yeah!" Michelle agreed. "Put our food in the kitchen and Karen and I will eat later."

"Very well," Joe said as he shrugged shoulders and walked out the bedroom with Keith at his heels like two little boys who had just been scolded by their parents.

"What's wrong with those two?" Keith asked.

"I don't know! Just being women, I guess," Joe responded.

"Now, what were you saying? You know I that am anxious to find out if Little Girl is really you!" Karen said.

"Karen, let me explain something to you." Michelle began to finish what she had begun to say. "I want you to be patient with me about Little Girl. The reason I read those two scriptures to you is for you. You see, God wants us to be patient and to wait on Him and in His time. Through prayer, He will reveal to us what He wants us to know at the right time. Study those two scriptures when you go home. Meditate on them. Plant them in your heart."

Karen then asked Michelle, "Why are you telling me this story about this girl?"

"By the time I finish telling you Karen, you will have the answer to that question. You will see why I have told you this story and the true glory of God and His works."

If I had one wish Jesus, I wish

For You to reach down and tear off a piece

Of Your heart and I would place it in my right shirt pocket.

If I had a second wish,

I would take the contents of my pocket

And place it under my pillow

For I would allow no harm to come to it.

If I had a third wish,

I would buy a canvas and take all the bright and

Soft colors of the rainbow and

Paint your eyes and smile.

If I had a fourth wish,

I would record your voice

So You could speak to me each night the stars

Appeared in the heavens.

If I'm allowed one last wish,

It would be to let You know

That Your love

Is like the world of all worlds

That never ends.

I love You, Jesus....

Thank You for loving me before I knew me....

And still loving me....

What does Jesus say about wishing?

John 15:7 (BSB), "If you abide in me, and my words abide in you, ask whatever you wish, and it will be done for you."

Mark 11:24 (NLT), "Therefore I tell you, whatever you ask in prayer, believe that you have received it, and it will be yours."

James 1:6 (BSB), "But let him ask in faith, with no doubting, for the one who doubts is like a wave of the sea that is driven and tossed by the wind."

Author's Own Thoughts:

Our Lord in heaven stands on His word. I so longed and wished to write this book with my faith in our Lord Jesus and believing in my heart, where He lives, and through prayer and standing from that His word is the truth and the only way to life. You are now reading the answer to my prayer. Thank You, my Father in heaven for You truly are an awesome God.

Please, just let Him have His way in you... for God loves you so....

8

RAPE/ADDICTION

~Little Girl~

The wind blew hard. The snow on the ground was ankle deep. It was now two years since Little Girl entered the women's shelter. Little Girl had left and came back five times. She began seeing a therapist and also was approved for welfare with food stamps. She was now well known in the neighborhood of the women's shelter. James, the owner of the pool hall, had become a good friend to her. Bucky and Shark had moved on with their own lives elsewhere. Mr. Foly would let Little Girl work once in a while at the corner store, so she could earn extra money for her pockets. Little Girl was turning twenty with no foundation in life. She was just coming and going wherever she felt.

As Little Girl stepped on the front steps of the shelter, which she considered her real home, it could be she was now familiar with the rundown neighborhood and its people. Even the young gangster boys would look out for her. Little Girl checked her pockets, it was there so she stepped down and started to walk towards the train station.

"Excuse me, lady!" yelled a man's voice from inside a black old used Cadillac. "You wouldn't happen to have a match."

Little Girl had taken up smoking cigarettes. "Sure, I do," she answered back and walked up to the car. Without even a blink of an eye, in front of her was a gun being pointed to her head. "Get the *F*... in the car, you *B*..."

Little Girl stood frozen and unable to move, but the click of the gun woke her. She stepped into the car which had two other men in it. "Hey man, we got us a pretty one this time." The man with the gun reached and grabbed Little Girl's hair and bit her on the face, drawing blood. "Hey man, don't hurt her too much! I have to have my turn."

"Me too!" said the other man.

Little Girl fought unsuccessfully with all her might trying to stop the man in the back seat from ripping off her clothes. As her naked body was now exposed, he proceeded to bite on her and punch at her breast.

"Now, that's what I'm talking about," when he was through with her.

"Hey Kevin, switch back here with me!" he said to the driver. "I'll drive a little."

The second man took Little Girl, turned her over, and proceeded to find any hole that was available. The pain was so unbearable Little Girl could no longer whimper or cry. Her skinny body just laid across the back seat of the car, bloody and scarred.

"Come on now! You said I could do that first!" the third man yelled back. "Man look at her. Is she still alive?"

"Aww man, she's alive," spoke the driver. "Jump back here and even if she's not, who gives a F...? She's just some dumb shelter woman. Ain't nobody gonna miss her. Here take her for a while. I'm getting too much blood on me."

Little Girl listened to every word that was being spoken. All she wanted was to end all the pain. If they killed her, she would not care as long as the pain vanished.

The third man moved to the back of the car and grabbed Little Girl as if she was a ragdoll. He looked into her eyes and for a second, he thought he was looking into a little girl's face. "Man, how old is she? She looks like a little girl. I don't do little girls, man."

The driver turned around and said, "Man, she lives at the shelter. I told you."

He slapped her hard across the face to see if he could change her look. Then again. This time, he punched her in her eye then started in on her with his heavy body against her weightless body. "Open your mouth, B…". After he finished, he yelled to the front of the car. "Where are we dropping this one off at?"

"Man, right down in the alley from the shelter."

Little Girl felt a thump. It was her half naked, bloody, and scarred body being thrown onto the snowy ground. She laid there alone, blood oozing from her scars. She had no thoughts. Her pain seemed to numb itself. Little Girl felt nothing now. Even her cries no longer existed. As the snow seemed to fall slightly from the sky, a woman who lived also on the streets, came stumbling into the alley holding a bottle in a brown paper bag. "Hey, miss! Hey lady, are you all right?" Little Girl heard not a sound.

~Michelle and Karen~

Karen stood up from the chair in which she was sitting and walked over to Michelle. She sat next to her, handing her a tissue for Michelle's tears were falling so hard into her lap.

"Michelle, you don't have to tell anymore of the story if you feel it's too tragic," Karen said to her friend.

"Karen, I'm okay. I don't mind telling the story, but I have to admit, some parts are painful."

Karen picked up a tissue for herself. She, too, had been crying. She then squeezed her friend's hand and asked, "Did Little Girl die?" Karen did not think Little Girl was Michelle at that time.

~Little Girl~

There were IV's running in both arms of Little Girl. There was also an oxygen tube was on her face. She had bandages covering parts of her body. Little Girl's eyes and lips were puffy and swollen half shut from the slaps and punches to her face. A small moan escaped her body.

"You're waking up," said a small gentle voice coming from a chair that was sitting in the corner of the hospital room. The voice was coming closer. There stood over Little Girl's bed a nurse dressed in white. "I know you must be in a lot of pain. We have given you some pain medication through your IV." Little Girl looked at the nurse through the little space from her eyes.

"The doctor is out there talking with the police right now. He doesn't want them in here bothering you. So, you just rest sweetie, and if you need me, I'll be right over there in that corner," the nurse said, giving Little Girl a gentle squeeze of her hand. Little Girl dozed back off.

Three days passed when she finally opened her eyes enough to focus on her surroundings. She moved her legs and pain shot up her body. "OUCH!" she whimpered.

"Take it slow," the nurse said.

The nurse sat there every day when she came into work at the hospital. She would not leave the room. Her heart was so full for Little Girl and the damage that was done. She stood over the bed and checked on Little Girl's IV and the bandages.

"Sweetie, you will heal, but it's going to take some time. You had to receive some stitches down there and on your bottom area. You're young, so the scars on your face will heal quickly."

Little Girl parted her lips and began to speak very softly. "Why? What did I ever do to people to always be hurt?"

"Sweetie, there are a lot of nasty monsters out there. It's not your fault. I don't want you to think this is your fault."

"Can I have a mirror?" Little Girl asked the nurse.

"Why not wait a few more days on the mirror," said the nurse. "I haven't introduced myself," the nurse said, trying to change the subject. Little Girl knew that.

"How's my patient doing?" The doctor said as he walked into the room. "Well, young lady, I see you are waking up and alert a little. How's she doing Nurse Patty?"

"I was just introducing myself when you walked in, doctor."

"Young lady, can you tell me your name and who we can contact for you?"

"My name is Little Girl and I have no one. It's just me. Nobody cares about me or likes me."

"I see," said the doctor. "Well Little Girl, we are going to keep you here for a while then we want you to visit the ninth floor. We have some very nice doctors up there that will help you through all of this. Meanwhile, the police are going to ask you some questions. I don't want you getting upset. If it becomes too much for you, then you stop talking, okay?"

"Yes," Little Girl responded back.

~Michelle and Karen~

Michelle stopped talking. Karen said, "I think we need to eat something. Let's go get the food Keith had delivered. You stay in bed," Karen said. "I want you to rest. We talked about Little Girl enough for today. Plus, you have chemo to take tomorrow, so you need to be well rested. I'll go get the food."

Michelle felt exhausted. She was tired and had become sleepy, so she pulled the covers up on her, fixed her pillow under her head and closed her eyes. Michelle started to talk to God. She knew that only her Lord was her refugee and peace. Before she knew it, Michelle was sound asleep in a very calm and peaceful sleep.

Karen returned with the food and saw Michelle sleeping. *She looks peaceful and calm*, Karen said to herself. Karen left the bedroom and went to join Joe and Keith who now were watching television in the living room.

"How's she doing?" Joe asked as Karen sat next to Keith on the couch.

"She's asleep," Karen said. "Joe?" Karen started to ask a question but changed her mind.

"What Karen?" Joe said.

"I was just thinking, when you look at Michelle, I mean really look into her eyes, it's like you can see a story there. I know that doesn't make any sense. I just can't explain it, Joe."

"Karen, I know what you are saying. Look Keith, do me a favor and take your woman home. I think she needs some rest also."

"I believe so," Keith answered. "Come on sweetness," Keith said taking Karen's hand in his. "Joe, you call us if you need anything, man. I'm going to sleep over at Karen's house," Keith said. "And yes, I will be sleeping in your guest room."

"Goodnight Keith. Thanks for helping out. I'll tell Michelle you two said goodnight," Joe said as he walked the two to the door and closed it behind them.

Joe stood at the door for a moment. He thought of his wife. For some reason, he felt a sense that his wife was here physically, but another part of her seemed to drift away. Once again, he stood at the door, and this time Keith with him, listening to the story of Little Girl. It hurt his and Keith's heart so bad at what those men did to Little Girl that he and Keith had to go into the living room and sit silently, letting the TV watch them. Joe also could not shake the thought of Karen thinking that Little Girl might be Michelle.

Joe had come along way with Michelle and their children. *Maybe*, he thought, *if I work less and start spending more time with her. She likes to laugh.* Joe found himself talking to God. "God, I don't know You like my wife, Michelle, but I know You are real. I've seen the things You have done for her. God, please help me help my wife. I don't know what is going on, but I feel something inside of me that I can't really explain what it is. It's like she's here, yet she's not. What's happening to her? I love her God, in Jesus name, amen."

Joe cut the lights off in the rest of the house and went into the bedroom where his wife was sleeping. He went to bed with his clothes still on, climbed into the bed, and just held his wife in his arms. He felt a closeness for her that he had never felt before. It was like all he wanted to do was protect her as if she was a little girl who fell and hurt her knee. Joe felt tears slowly rolling down his face. He whispered to his wife, Michelle, "Nothing will ever hurt you again." He didn't know why he said that; he just felt that. Joe fell asleep holding his wife.

Michelle felt her husband and heard his words. She kept her eyes closed and felt her husband's love for her holding her. Michelle laid in his arms thinking about him, Karen, and Keith. "Don't they know, Lord, that I don't feel sad about anything? Sometimes, I have to empty my pitcher. I think they want to protect me so much." Michelle smiled to herself. "They can be so silly at times, Lord, and I love them." Michelle then turned her thoughts back on Little Girl. *People don't know your strength, Little Girl.*

~Little Girl~

After spending two weeks in the hospital, Little Girl was transported to the ninth floor on the West Wing. That was where rape victims were treated through therapy and counseling. She had been on the West Wing now for two weeks. The counselors had a very difficult time trying to get her to open up about the attack or about anything that might be bothering her.

"Little Girl, this is your last day here. Is there anything you might want to say?" her therapist asked, sitting behind a huge desk.

"Nope," Little Girl responded. "I just feel like it's time for me to leave. There is nothing you or anyone can do about anything that happens to me."

"Well then Little Girl, I've set you up an appointment with a therapist near the shelter you say you live. I want you to continue on the meds I've prescribed for you. Also, don't overdo the pain medication. Now, the floor aid will take you down to a car that will drive you back to the shelter. Do you still have the detective's phone number?"

"Yes, I do," answered Little Girl.

Little Girl said bye and left the building with the aid who helped her into a car which drove off on its way back to the woman's shelter. Little Girl reached into her pocket and pulled out a pain pill. She swallowed the pill without any water. She then opened the bag the hospital gave her. The bag had a set of new clothes, sneakers, and toiletries including a mirror. She pulled out the small mirror and gazing into it, she saw the scars. The more she looked at herself, all she saw was the word, *Why? Who are you? What is your real name? Why don't you use your real name? Where do you belong? Does anyone really care about another human being? Why do people hurt each other?*

"Okay miss," said the driver. "We are here, the shelter."

"Thanks," said Little Girl. She got out the car and headed up the stairs to the shelter doors.

"Little Girl come here!" It was James across the street yelling from the poolhall.

Dag that man has a big mouth, Little Girl said to herself. She turned and walked across the street to where James was standing.

"Woman, who the hell did this to you? You do know it's out in the streets. Some of the gangster boys are looking for whoever did this. We just want you to tell us what he looks like."

"James, it was three men, not one," Little Girl answered and not wanting to talk about it. Little Girl filed the details in her private file cabinet in her brain with all the rest for she knew people didn't really care about what happens to her. They just want something to talk about.

James was so mad he had not realized that he had torn up some of the numbers people had turned in.

"I don't want to talk about it, James."

"Look Little Girl, you are coming and staying at my place. I have a three-bedroom house. You take one of the bedrooms. It's not in this neighborhood. Don't bother going into the shelter. Come on in the hall while I get someone to watch over it until I get back"

They both walked into the poolhall. The people looked over at Little Girl, some waved. One came over and handed her a beer and said, "Don't worry, Girl. We will find them."

Little Girl reached into her pocket while listening to some of the people who had now picked up enough nerve to come over to her and took two more of her pain pills. This time she swallowed them down with some beer. Little Girl listened to the people talk about what they heard. It all seemed like a fog to her. Their voices seemed far away.

"You ready Little Girl?" James said as he approached her.

"Yeah, I guess so. Come on James, let's get the hell out of here." James took a double look at Little Girl. He never heard her talk like that. "Are you coming James or what? Come on then," Little Girl said again, this time with more force in her voice

James and Little Girl got into his car and drove away to their destination. After thirty minutes, James pulled up into a driveway where a two-story brick house stood with painted windows in front, a large front door with a car garage, and a fence surrounding the entire house. James opened the car door for Little Girl and led her up the pathway the house. He then guided her into the large foyer and then into the living rooming. In the living room, there was a large floor model television with an oversized remote sitting on the coffee table which was glass. Little Girl sat on one of the two couches and felt like just falling asleep; it was so soft.

"Follow me into the kitchen," James said to her. Into the kitchen they both went. A large round glass table was in the middle of the floor with six chairs going around it. "Here sit," James said. Little Girl sat in one of the chairs. "I'm going to fix us both some dinner. How about a couple of T-bone steaks and a baked potato with a salad?"

"Sounds good," Little Girl said back.

"Very well. You go into the bathroom down the hall on your left and wash your hands."

After washing her hands, Little Girl sat back down in the chair. "Oh no," James said with a smile. "You are going to learn how to cook."

"I know how to cook," Little Girl answered back. "The Man taught me when he wouldn't let me and my friend, Steve, leave."

James looked at her and simply said, "That's for another time. Right now, I want you to eat, take a bath, and go to bed. Don't worry, you will never see me come in your room, even if you were to invite me. While you sleep, I have to run back to the poolhall and check on everything. I don't want anyone knowing where you are so don't make any phone calls."

Little Girl looked at James and said, "Who would I call James? And may I please have a beer?"

"Sure," he said. "Just open the refrigerator and help yourself. This is going to be your home until you find out what exactly you want to do with yourself. Do you understand, Little Girl?"

"Yeah, I do James, but why are you doing this? I don't have money to pay you or will I have to do something to stay here? All you men don't do anything for free. You all expect a woman to do something for her keep."

"Look Little Girl, I don't know what your past is like, but you will turn twenty soon. It's time you start thinking about what you want out of life. And as for wanting anything out of you, yeah, I do. I want you to be happy and grownup, and please one day, start using your real name.

"Now, you come over here and start cutting up this stuff for the salad while I get the steaks done."

"James, can I ask you a question?"

"Sure, Little Girl."

"How can you afford this big house and all this stuff? Do you sell drugs, too?"

"No, I don't, Little Girl. If you notice, I'm at the poolhall in the evening during dinnertime. I work during the day and I work hard for what I have. I'm not a lazy man. I'm divorced from a woman whom I was married to for five years. I haven't any children. Most women throw themselves at me, but I am not interested in those money grabbing women nor am I interested in you as a woman for me. I plan on closing down the poolhall next year. I will have enough money then to relocate to another state and set myself up with my own investment firm or even rehabilitation center to help some of these addicts off the streets.

"Now the steaks are done, so look into the drawer and get some silverware and plates and let's eat."

While they ate, Little Girl drank her beer and slipped a few pain pills in her mouth.

"James, how can I get a real job?"

"You can't right now, Little Girl. We are going to work on finding out if you have any blood relatives somewhere out there. We are going to get your social security card and birth certificate."

After dinner, James showed her to her room then said he would be back later.

Little Girl took her shower and laid in the king-sized bed, a size she had never slept in. When she felt he was gone and wasn't turning around to come back, she got up and began walking around the house, looking into every room. *These rooms are huge*, she said to herself. As she came to the room at the end of the hallway, looking in, she could tell it was James' room. It contained a large bed, a bathroom, a tall dresser, and a floor model television. *Wow*, she said to herself. *I wonder what he does.* So, she went into his room and started snooping. She walked into his walk-in closet and went through a shoebox that held some papers in it. As she began reading some of his papers, she noticed a safe on the floor in the closet. It was locked. *Where is James getting his money from?* She did not find anything in his closet and she was getting sleepy from the pain pills and beer she drank so she went back into her room and fell asleep.

James returned home around 2:00 a.m. He looked in on Little Girl who was fast asleep, went into his room and turned on the TV, then reached on his nightstand and picked up his book he had started reading a few weeks ago. He turned to the book of Psalm.

~Karen and Keith~

Karen and Keith sat across from one another in Karen's dining area talking while sipping on tea.

"So, what do you think about us?" Keith asked.

"What do you mean?" Karen answered back.

"Do you think this relationship is promising? I mean do we have a future together, is what I am talking about?" Keith said.

"Yes, I do, Keith," responded Karen.

"Well, I don't want to rush anything, but I will say this Karen. I am falling in love with you and want to wait till next year when I will ask you to be my wife. I'm not going to tell you what month, time, or date, but I want you in my life. I want us to build a life together. I see you're a beautiful woman Karen, inside and out. You have a lot of love to give to other people. I can see how much you love your friend, Michelle. Very rarely these days does someone see true friendship from the heart that two friends have for one another."

Karen sat listening to Keith, smiling from ear to ear. She was smiling so hard one could see the cavities in her teeth.

"Keith, I, too, am falling in love with you. It's like you were sent from God and at the right time in my life. Also, you are a man of God. Trust and believe, I will be marking on my calendar as each day passes until next year.

"Let's go into the living room and watch a movie," Karen suggested.

So, the two got comfortable on the couch with Keith's arm wrapped around Karen and Karen laying her head against him. The two escaped from the world and went into their own world watching movies.

"Karen, let me ask you something," Keith said as he removed his arm from around her and took her hand in his. "What is this addiction you have with this story Michelle has been telling you? When I watch you or hear you talk about it, you seem to get anxious, almost like an addict waiting for its fix. You really seem like you are addicted to this story," Keith said again, this time smiling to let Karen know it's okay.

"I know Keith, and then I don't know. There's something important in that story. It's a true story about this girl whom Michelle knew or knows. The girl seems to have been very close to Michelle or is still close to her. I don't know. Sometimes, when Michelle's telling me the story, I wonder if she's talking about herself. Then she will say something in the story and I would be like, no she's not talking about herself, but for some reason, Michelle wants to tell it and I am, like you said, anxious to hear and can't wait sometimes for her to start telling the rest of the story. Keith, I just don't know what the connection is," Karen finished saying.

"Well, we will leave it alone for now. Let's call it a night. I'm tired and I know you are exhausted. Let's pray first before going to bed."

They both held hands while Karen began to pray. "Father, we want to give thanks for another day. We want to glorify Your name. We ask Lord for a special healing for our dear friend and your daughter, Michelle. Please send down Your healing angel Raphael for her. Lord, we know we are not worthy, but You love and have mercy on us anyway. You are a loving God. Clothe us in the blood of Jesus, amen."

Karen and Keith kissed goodnight and went into their separate bedrooms.

~Little Girl~

The sun rays shined through the window in the room Little Girl was sleeping. Little Girl opened her eyes and gave her body a little stretch then planted her feet on the soft carpet covering the entire room floor. She rose from the bed and went into the bathroom in her room. There, on the counter, was a note with female toiletries and a brand-new outfit: pants, underwear, shirt and sneakers. *How did he know my size?* she thought to herself. She cleaned herself up, got dressed, and read the note. The note read:

Little Girl, I've gone to meet a friend of mine who maybe can help you get your birth certificate. I also need to stop and check in on the pool hall. This is your home now so feel free to help yourself to whatever. There's a pool table in the basement; you are welcome to play on it. See you as soon as possible.

P.S. Please make sure you eat.

Little Girl said out loud to herself, *Why is James being so nice to me?* She walked back into her bedroom and poured a few pain pills out of the bottle into her hands then swallowed them. *I wonder if James has anymore beer.* So, she headed for the kitchen when something caught the corner of her eye. There, in the dining room was a liquor cabinet. *Hey, maybe I'll try a drink; it's been awhile. The last time I drank was with Pam.*

Little Girl grabbed a bottle; she didn't care which one and proceeded into the kitchen for a glass and some ice. She poured herself a hefty drink. Taking a sip, *Wow, this stuff burns*, but she continued to drink until the glass stood empty. Little Girl was now tipsy, but she realized, *Hey, I don't feel any pain.* So, she poured another glass and drank that. Feeling past tipsy now, Little Girl said out loud, *I better eat something.* So, she searched through the refrigerator and found some left over fried chicken. She put that between some bread, stumbled into the living room, and turned on the television set.

"Little Girl! Little Girl!" James had returned home to find Little Girl in a drunk sleep. She reeked of liquor. "Little Girl!" James shook her gently, but Little Girl was out from the drinks she drank. James reached on the top of the couch and covered her up. He took the plate of the half eatened chicken and the half of glass of liquor and headed into the kitchen.

James wasn't worried about Little Girl for he knew she was the victim of a serious crime and was lucky to be alive. *She is hurting, so I'll let this ride this time*, he said to himself. James then started to prepare a lunch for himself and Little Girl.

"Whatcha making?" came Little Girl's voice. She was standing in the doorway of the kitchen. "When did you get home? I didn't hear you come in."

James looked at her with a reply of, "Because you were passed out drunk on the couch!"

"I wasn't drunk," Little Girl snapped back.

"Very well, if you say so," James said. "I'm fixing lunch now for you and me. You need to eat something. Did you read the note I left in your bathroom?"

"Yes, I did," Little Girl answered back. "What happened?" James stopped what he was doing and sat at the table and motioned Little Girl to do the same.

"My friend needs some information. Anything you can tell me that might help."

Little Girl was not in the mood to think. Her head felt like someone was banging a hammer on it. "All I can remember is I was in one foster home and…"

James cut her off, "Your foster parents should have a copy of your birth certificate and other things. Why don't we try to contact them?"

"NO!" Little Girl yelled out. "I will not contact those people, but I do remember the name of the orphanage I belonged to."

"That's a start," James said back. He rose and retrieved a pen and paper out of one of the kitchen drawers. "There," he placed it in front of Little Girl. "You write down anything and everything you can remember. I will see what can be done."

Little Girl began to write down some names and addresses according to what she remembered then handed the paper to James. "I'm going to the restroom," she said. As she went into her room, she reached for her pill bottle and took two more pills out. *Dag, I have only three left*, she moaned to herself. She then went back into the kitchen after swallowing her pills.

"James, I have a doctor's appointment tomorrow. I forgot to tell you. It's at 8:00 a.m. Will you take me?"

"Of course, I will," James said. "Now eat your food I've fixed."

The two sat eating their lunch.

After eating, James said to Little Girl, "I want to know your story. I want to know how your life has got to be where you are now."

"You're kidding me, right James?" Little Girl said with a smirk. "I'm not about to sit here and talk about everything that has happened to me. I will tell you I like strawberry milkshakes, and would you please bring one back?"

"That's fine, Little Girl. I have to leave and go check on the pool hall. I was supposed to do that while I was out, but I decided to come home first and check in and see if you were doing alright."

"Okay James, I'll be fine here until you get back."

So, James left the house and Little Girl was alone, just her and her thoughts.

~Michelle and Karen~

Karen got out of her car and went into the doctor's office where Michelle was taking her chemo.

"Hello beautiful," Karen said as she walked up to Michelle, giving her a kiss on the forehead. "How are you feeling?" she asked Michelle while pulling up a chair to sit next to her.

"I'm blessed; won't complain," Michelle added back. "My children are on their way here any minute now."

Michelle's children, just as she was talking to Karen, walked into the room.

"Hey mother!"

"Hello mom!"

"Hi Nana!"

"What's up mama?"

"Well, what brings you all here today?" Michelle said, laughing and joking with her children.

"Daddy called us and said we should not be too busy to come and check on our mother."

"Yeah!" Thomas said. "Daddy made us feel kind of bad that we haven't been coming home more to visit."

"Nana," Angel said, "are you going to be okay? I want to come and stay with you for a while. Can I please Nana?"

"Sweetie, you come as soon as your mama says yes." Michelle gave Suzy a, *You let that granddaughter come,* kind of look.

Suzy said to her mother, "Mama, as soon as you are a well enough, Angel can stay a week with you."

"Why do I have to wait mama?" Angel argued back to her mother.

"Yeah, why?" Alice said. "I think we all should come and stay with mama and go to work from there." Thomas gave Alice a look that meant, *Girl be quiet.*

Karen opened her mouth and said to everyone. "Look, you all can stay at my place and I'll stay with your mother. You all know my house is huge. There's enough space for all of you. This way, you will be closer to your mother. How does that sound to everyone?"

"That's fine with me," Suzy said.

"Won't argue with that one," Thomas said.

Michelle motioned to all her children to come and give her a kiss. Then, "Go make arrangements to move into Karen's house for a while."

She turned to Alice and asked her youngest daughter, "Sweetie, how are you going to get back and forth to school?"

"Mom, I have to talk to you about that, but I'll wait, okay?" Alice responded back.

"Alright then, all of you go and take care of your business," Michelle said again.

When all had left the room, Michelle looked at Karen. "Are you crazy? Did you just meet my children? Those are my children that you are leaving in your home!"

Karen laughed, "Girl, remember I am selling my house. Plus, why not? I think it's a good way to bring everyone together at one time. You all are a family. And aren't I a part of this family? Everybody is always too busy doing something or going somewhere to stop and say, *Hi mom. How are you doing today? Just called you, mom, just to say hi. I don't need anything just wanted to say, I love you, mom.* Those children don't know how blessed they are that they have a mother and a father. Michelle, children now a days don't take the time to stop and smell the, what's it called?" Karen laughed about forgetting the rest of the saying.

"It's roses!" Michelle laughed finishing the sentence for Karen.

"Michelle, you are through now, ma'am," the nurse said while taking the IV out of Michelle's arm. "Now remember, the doctor said you will be sick for a while so go home and please eat something."

"She will," Karen said to the nurse.

"Come on Karen, let's get out of here. Where did you park?"

Both women walked to the car and drove back to Michelle's house. During the ride, Michelle had thrown up all in Karen's car and on herself. Once pulling into the driveway and then entering the house, Karen asked Michelle, "Do you want me to call Joe?"

Michelle said, "No. He's working and what can he do here? I'm good, Karen. People get sick from chemo. It's no big deal, alright. Now, let's go into my room so I can clean myself up from all the throwing up on me."

"Then, can you finish telling me the story?"

Michelle stopped in her tracks, turned, and said to her friend, "Are you addicted this story?"

"Hey, that's the same thing Keith said to me the other night!" Both women laughed.

Sighing, Michelle just simply said, "Yes, Karen, I will tell you some more of the story. Now let me go clean up while you run out for some shakes."

"Michelle, really? Girl, I do not feel like going anywhere now that we are home."

"Please!" Michelle asked with a little girl's voice and poking out her lip. "Please, pretty please!"

"Fine! Go clean up and I will be right back."

"Thanks girl! Love you too!" Michelle said with a big smile.

After cleaning herself up, Karen had returned with the shakes. She handed Michelle her strawberry milkshake and both women went into Michelle's kitchen, sat at the table, and Michelle began to tell the story of Little Girl.

~Little Girl~

Little Girl and James returned from the doctor's office with her prescription of pain pills filled. James noticed the joy in Little Girl as she held onto the bottle.

"When do you go back to the police station and talk to the detectives?" he asked her.

"They said they will come to where I am. I just need to call them and tell them where I live now. I also need to go down to social services or to the shelter and pick up my check and food stamps," she answered back.

"We can do that tomorrow when I meet up with my friend who can help us out with finding some more information on you. In fact, he is supposed to call me tonight and let me know something," James said to Little Girl.

Little Girl, while listening to James, opened her pill bottle and swallowed two pills.

"Little Girl, how many of those are you supposed to take at a time?"

"James, I am in a lot of pain right now, everywhere in my body, so, I took two. Why?"

"You know you can become dependent on those pills. You're addicted to them," James said to her as he pulled up into his driveway.

"I doubt if I become addicted to these pills or anything else, James," Little Girl snapped back. "In fact, I don't want to talk about it, if you don't mind."

James was beginning to notice the change in Little Girl since the incident that happened to her. She has become snappy in her attitude, defensive in most things that are said to her.

"Hey Little Girl, when is your next appointment with your therapist?" James asked.

"I don't need any stupid therapist that wants to pry into what's going on with me. All they do is sit and write on a notepad and shake their heads. They don't really care about people," Little Girl said in an angry voice.

James and Little Girl were now in the house, still talking about her seeing a therapist. Feeling he was losing the battle, James said no more and went into his bedroom, leaving Little Girl sitting alone in the living room. Used to being left alone, Little Girl opened her pill bottle and took one more pill then walked in the kitchen to find a beer to wash it down with. After what seemed about an hour and watching TV, she became sleepy and dozed off. She awoke to hearing James on the phone.

"I see," she heard him say. "What is the name of her sister and brother? Okay, I got that. Now where is her biological mother? You're still working on that? Okay. Oh, she has family in *where*? Okay, I got that too. Were you able to get any phone numbers? Great! Thanks. It's a start; let me know when you find anything else."

James hung the phone up and went into the living room where Little Girl was now sitting up sipping on a soda.

"Got good news, Little Girl! You have brothers and sisters, but only one brother and sister live in this state. Your sister right now is in college and your brother, well he can't be found at this time. You also have an aunt in the state of Virginia where your other brother and sister live. Your biological mother cannot be found also right now. My friend was able to get a phone number of your aunt in Virginia so when you are ready, we can give her a call."

Little Girl sat straight up with a glow on her face for she has family, a real family that is her own. So many questions started to arise in her.

"James, I think I'm going to be sick," and she ran off to throw up in the bathroom. After her incident in the bathroom, she returned to the room with James.

"I'm not ready to call anyone yet," she said while rubbing her stomach.

"That's understandable," James responded back. "Whenever you are ready to make the call, just let me know."

Little Girl also wondered to herself, *Who did James know that was able to find these people?* And what if James lied about not wanting anything from her for helping her? *Maybe I should leave,* she thought to herself. *I'll wait,* she thought again to herself not sure what to do at that time. She filed her thoughts in the back of her mind to figure out in the future.

"Are you alright, Little Girl? You don't look so well."

"I'm fine, James," she answered. "I'm just sleepy. You don't mind if I go and lay back down on the sofa?"

~Michelle and Karen~

Michelle stopped talking and just started laughing.

"What's so funny?" Karen asked with a puzzled look on her face.

"It's just that if you could see your face," Michelle said in the middle of herself laughing. "You look so, I don't know, just funny, I guess."

"Ha! Ha!" Karen said cranky like. "So, you stopped talking just to tell me I look funny? Really Michelle?"

"Oh, come on Karen. Don't feel like that. You know I don't mean any harm. Come on, let's go sit on the front porch for a while and I will tell you some more about Little Girl. First, let's grab something to snack on."

"I don't want anything to snack on. I will grab a bottle of water," Karen said.

The two women took what they wanted from the kitchen and went and sat in one of their favorite spots, the front porch of Michelle's house. After getting comfortable in their favorite chairs (Michelle on the long stretched out chair and Karen on the swing), Karen gave Michelle an, *okay, can you finish telling the story*, kind of look.

Michelle, looking up at the sky smiled and said, "Thank You, Lord for my friend, Karen," then turned to Karen. "Girl, I think you need to find a program for your addiction to this story!" she said joking.

Ignoring Michelle's comment, "What is wrong with Little Girl? Why doesn't she want to call her aunt? Doesn't she want to see her own family? I mean, if it were me, I wouldn't wait another minute to call."

"You're not Little Girl, Karen, and you really couldn't say what you would have done in a situation like hers."

"Okay, maybe you're right, Michelle, but I would like to think that's what I would do! Anyway, she doesn't know yet that James reads the Bible? And.."

"Karen!" Michelle cut her friend off before she could say anything else. "Let me finish telling you some more about Little Girl before you start with all the questions and answers."

~Little Girl~

Little Girl picked up the phone to call the number James had given her. As she began to dial, her nerves were like butterflies fluttering all through her stomach. She heard the phone ring on the other end and someone picked up.

"Hello!" she heard the woman's voice. "Hello!" the woman said again.

"Hello," Little Girl found herself saying back.

"Hello again," said the woman. "Who would you like to speak with?"

Little Girl hesitated for a moment, then began to speak. "I'm looking for my aunt. Someone gave me this number. My name is Little Girl."

~Michelle and Karen~

"Wait a minute!" Karen interrupted. "You mean to tell me Little Girl did not tell her Aunt her real name? Why?"

"Karen, would you please be quiet so I can tell you what happened!" Michelle snapped back.

~Little Girl~

Little Girl's voice cracked as she began to tell the woman on the other end of the phone who she was.

"I was told this is my aunt's phone number. I was in foster care when I was young and never met my real family and I am looking for them."

"Who did you say you were?" said the woman.

"Everyone calls me Little Girl, but my real name is…." Little Girl gave the woman her real name.

Seven

~Karen and Michelle~

"No, you did not just do that to me, Michelle!" Karen screamed. "You know you are wrong! You are just wrong! What is Little Girl's real name?"

Michelle once again ignored Karen and continued with the story.

~Little Girl~

"Oh, dear Lord!" shouted the woman. The woman repeated herself at least three more times. "Baby, I am your Aunt Sue! Baby, where are you?"

Little Girl bursted out in tears. She felt something she had never in her life ever felt. It was a feeling of belonging to someone who was real, a real person whom she felt was hers.

"Baby, are you alright?" Little Girl's Aunt Sue said.

"I don't know," Little Girl answered back.

"Give me your phone number," her Aunt Sue said. So Little Girl gave her the phone number.

They talked for about two hours. Aunt Sue was telling Little Girl about her younger brother and sister and her older brother.

"I really have an older brother?"

"Yes dear, you have an older brother and a lot of cousins and a grandmother with aunts and uncles."

Little Girl started crying even harder now.

"Listen," Aunt Sue said to her, "I want us to hang up now and I want you to rest. This is a lot to take in at one time. Is there anyone with you, Little Girl, or would you like me to call you what your mother, my sister, named you?"

"I'm used to Little Girl. And no, no one is here right now. It's just me."

"Then you go get you a glass of water and rest some. I will call you back

239

later this evening. There is so much to talk about and I also want you to talk with your younger brother and sister."

Little Girl, even though she was going on twenty, felt like a child all over again.

"Yes, okay," she answered her Aunt Sue back with tears so big falling from her face. She then hung up the phone.

Little Girl walked over to the sofa, sat down, and let the tears from years of wanting to know who her family was flow and flow and continue to flow. She wound up crying herself to sleep only to wake up to find herself running to the bathroom and throwing up again. Little Girl, for some reason, began to think about the three men that took her body and did what they wanted with it and some of the things that she had filed in storage in the back of her mind. She took out her pill bottle, popped another pain pill, went into her bedroom, and crawled under the covers with her clothes still on. She went back to sleep.

The metal was cold,

All three were bold.

Took something can never get it back.

Never asked, just demanded.

Can still hear the cry on sleepless nights.

The metal was cold,

All three were bold.

Laughter to the ears,

a pain of despair.

On the way down, count

the stars.

The metal was cold,

All three were bold.

Slap across the face,

taste of blood,

don't want to die.

The metal was cold,

All three were bold.

Took something can never get it back.

They never asked, just demanded.

Can still hear the cry on sleepless nights.

This is my body,

not yours.

Rape... To take sexually another person's body without consent.

Addiction... A habit forming that is physical or psychological.

What does Jesus say about addiction?

John 8:36, "If the son therefore shall make you free, ye shall be free indeed."

2 Corinthians 5:7, "Therefore if any man be in Christ, he is a new creature: old things are passed away; behold all things are become new."

James 1:12-15, "Blessed is the man that endureth temptation: for when he is tired, he shall receive the crown of life, which the lord hath promised to them that love him. Let no man say when he is tempted, i am tempted of god: for god cannot be tempted with evil, neither tempteth he any man: but every man is tempted, when he is drawn away of his own lust, and enticed. Then when lust hath conceived, it bringeth forth sin, when it is finished bringeth forth death."

Author's Own Thoughts:

Let go and give it all to God.

9

FAMILY

~Little Girl~

Little Girl opened her eyes to James telling her there was a phone call for her. "It's some lady saying she's your Aunt Sue. Little Girl, did you call your Aunt?"

"Yes, James, I called and we had a long talk."

Little Girl ran to the phone and answered, "Hello!"

"Hi Little Girl, it's your Aunt Sue. How are you doing, baby? Did you get you a little rest?"

"Yes, I did."

"That's good to hear," Aunt Sue responded back. "I have a surprise for you. I have your younger sister here with me. I'm going to hand to hand the phone over to her."

Little Girl felt butterflies in her belly. Next, she heard one of the sweetest voices. "Hi, my name is Donna. I'm sixteen years old. When are you coming to Virginia to meet me and your youngest brother, Kenneth? He's the youngest out of all six of us. It's three boys and three girls. You're the eldest sister. We have a brother who is older than all of us. He's just a year older than you."

Little Girl sat listening to all her sister Donna was saying. She was too excited to say anything and just wanted to listen about all the real blood related family she has.

"Are you going to say anything?" her sister Donna asked.

"I guess. I just wanted to hear all I could hear about my family whom I have never met. I have a question for you, Donna? Where's our mother?"

"She's here or there. Right now, she's living with some man who she married a year ago in Mexico. She's fine."

"Does she miss us, Donna? Does she ask about me or where I am?"

"Sometimes, Little Girl, when she comes to visit grandma."

"I want to see my mother, Donna!"

"Well, I want to see my two big sisters!" Donna responded back.

Little Girl started feeling sick again. "I'll call you back. I'm feeling a little sick on the stomach." Little Girl hung the phone up and made a bee line straight towards the bathroom and threw up into the toilet. *What is wrong with me?* she said. She looked at herself in the mirror. She noticed how her face seemed to become a little puffy.

"Little Girl, are you alright?" James said standing in her bedroom. "I saw you hang up and run to the bathroom. Did you throw up again? Come with me," James said. "Put your shoes on, clean yourself up a little, and come on. I want to take you someplace and while I drive, you can tell me about your family."

Little Girl proceeded to get ready and then she and James got into his car. Where she was headed, she had no idea. She was starting to trust James just a little.

"So, how's the family?" James asked.

"Oh James, they sound really nice and want to meet me. I have a lot of cousins and uncles, aunts, and even a grandmother, James. My mother had six children: three boys and three girls."

"I know, Little Girl. I found out from my friend. I just wanted your family to tell you all about themselves."

"Oh James, I am so happy and so scared at the same time. What if they meet me and don't love me, James?"

James pulled the car over to the curb, took Little Girl's hand, parted his lips, and spoke the words, "Jesus loves you. Nobody loves you like Jesus." Then James started the car back up and continued to drive. Little Girl sat back in her seat and thought about the words James said. *Nobody loves you like Jesus*. Then she filed that in her storage in her mind.

"Here we are, Little Girl," as they pulled up to a doctor's building. Little Girl looked around the parking lot and at the tall building while getting out of the car. "Come on," James said to her as she said nothing and just followed him straight into the building and onto the elevator.

Still not saying a word, Little Girl followed him on the fourth floor when the elevator doors opened, then into two doors and up to a desk with a lady nurse sitting behind.

"Hello James," she said. Little Girl thought to herself, *He knows a lot of people.*

"Hi Connie! Is Victor in?" James asked the lady.

"He sure is. Just have a seat and I'll call him for you."

James and Little Girl sat in the waiting room. In a few minutes, a tall white man came walking out and shook James hand.

"How have you been, James? We haven't seen you in church in a few weeks. Is everything alright?"

"I'm great, Victor," James answered back. "I'm here for a very dear friend of mine, this young lady. I would like you to give her a pregnancy test and some blood work on what she's been consuming in her body."

Little Girl looked at James with her mouth wide open and said, "PREGANCY, are you serious James?"

"Come, you two," Dr. Victor said. So, they all went into an examination room where a nurse took Little Girl's vital signs, some blood work, and asked her to pee in a cup.

Little Girl did not know what to think as she sat next to James in the room. "James," she asked, "What makes you think I am pregnant?"

"You have all the symptoms, Little Girl."

"So, what's all the blood taken for?" she asked, crossing her legs and uncrossing them.

"That's to see the levels of pain pills you have been consuming in your body."

As James and Little Girl continued their conversation, Dr. Victor returned with the results from the tests.

"This is what we found, Little Girl. Your pregnancy test is positive, and you also have a V.D., Gonorrhea. I am going to give you two shots on both sides of your butt cheeks that will clear that up. Now, who is the father, James?"

"James," Little Girl yelled, "it has to be one of those men. James, am I going to die?"

"No, Little Girl! Hasn't anyone told you about this stuff?"

"No James! No one has."

"I don't want to keep this baby, James, I don't want it."

"Victor, what do you suggest?" James asked his friend doctor.

"It's not for me to say," the doctor answered back. "It's her decision to make."

"I don't want it," Little Girl yelled again. "I don't want a baby from whichever of the three men that raped me."

"Come in tomorrow and I will clear some of my appointments. We will get rid of it for you. Now, let me give you your shots."

James left the room and heard Little Girl scream from the shots. After everything was over, Little Girl came out into the waiting area where James was sitting. She looked angry and yet sad.

"It's going to be alright," James said to her. "The shots he gave you will clear everything up and tomorrow, you will have the abortion."

Seven

~Michelle and Karen~

Karen was no longer sitting in the swing on the porch. She moved next to Michelle on the long chair. She could see something in her Michelle's face that made her want to comfort her friend if she needed it.

"Michelle, why when you tell some parts of this story, you look so far away? Are you tired? Do you want to go inside and rest some?"

"I'm good, Karen," Michelle answered her friend with a small crack in her voice. The truth was, Michelle's heart was aching for the child that was aborted from Little Girl.

"What time is it, Karen?"

"I guess about six. Why?"

"I feel like taking a walk."

"Well Michelle, if you feel like walking girl, let's go."

The two women walked off the porch and started a walk that Karen would never forget.

"Where are we walking to?" Karen asked.

"Nowhere in particular. I just want to walk and see our Lord's creation, plus get some exercise in. You know, get the blood flowing girl!" Michelle said with a small grin.

"Karen, what's going on with you and Keith?"

"Oh, my goodness girl, I forgot to tell you. The night Keith stayed at my house, and yes, he slept in my guest room, anyway, he wants to ask me to be his wife next year. He said he's not going to tell me the time, date, or when he's going to ask. He said he loves me and truly believes that I am a good woman and have a good spirit. Michelle, I can't believe I forgot to tell you that.

"Michelle, I am in love with Keith. He sees me, and I mean really sees me. I'm not talking about the physical, but me, the me God created, the

247

good me. It's like I don't care if he owns a restaurant or has any money. It's like he was sent from God just for me. I know it probably sounds silly to you."

"Karen, it doesn't sound silly at all. Just knowing you are truly happy, that makes me happy. We have to celebrate."

"What are we going to celebrate, Michelle? He hasn't popped the question yet."

"Doesn't matter, Karen. I know and believe in my spirit that this is going to happen. So, what is it you would like to do this weekend?"

"Michelle, I don't want to celebrate until I have a ring on this finger."

"Very well! You just let me know when you want to celebrate. Now we could celebrate you being in true love!" Michelle said with a laugh.

"Girl, please!" Karen said laughing back.

Neither woman saw the young man approaching them.

"Excuse me, miss," the young man said, "would you happen to have a few dollars so I can catch the bus?"

"Sure," Michelle answered back and then went digging into her purse. Just as she was getting ready to hand him the two dollars and twenty cents, she saw a light coming from out of the distance. Karen, looking at Michelle's face turned to see what Michelle was looking at. Karen could not make out what exactly she was looking at. It was a light. A light that shined not like the sun. The light could not be described except it was bright and clear. It was almost like it spoke but didn't. Michelle, remembering the boy who had just asked her for money, turned back to the boy, handed him the money, and slightly touched his hand. She suddenly felt a sense of peace run through her.

"Thank you, ma'am," he said, looking into Michelle's eyes. He said in a soft tone, "There is no more pain. Peace, be still," and walked away.

Quickly, both women turned back to see the light, but there was no light.

"Wow!" Karen said. "Okay, I know I'm not crazy. Did you see that? I know you saw that."

Michelle heard her friend but was instead focused on the words the boy spoke to her. It's as if he knew the inner pain Michelle had been hiding from everyone she knew.

"Yeah, Karen," Michelle said. "I'm right with you, girl. I saw the light and when the boy left, so did the light. You know what, Karen? I think that was an angel."

"Come on, Michelle! Really?"

"Karen, did you notice all these people out here? Did you see anyone else looking in that direction?"

"No. I didn't. I believe that was for us only."

"Girl, you're right! I sure didn't see anyone else looking."

"Wow!" Karen answered back. "It was a light I never saw before. Do you know people would say we were crazy if we told someone?"

"Karen, everything isn't for everyone to know. When our God, our Lord, wants us to reveal to others what He has shown us, He will let us know."

"Michelle, I will never ever forget this. I mean never. And what did that boy mean when he said to you, *there will be no more pain; peace be still?*" Karen asked.

"I'm going to pray about that," said Michelle. "Do you want to keep walking or head back to the house?" whispered Michelle.

"Girl, let's walk. After this, I just need and want to walk. In fact, Michelle, I don't feel like even talking. Let's just walk."

As the women walked, Karen thought about the light she witnessed and what it was all about. Michelle's thoughts were on the message from the young boy.

Karen broke the silence. "I change my mind! I do want to talk! I think I am ready for a family, Michelle!"

"Really, Karen? Are you talking children, Karen?"

"Yeah, I am, Michelle! I want a husband and I'll settle for one if it's in God's plan for me."

"Okay, what if Keith wants more than one child?"

"Like I said, Michelle, whatever God's plan is for me, then it will be. Keith will be good with that."

"Come on let's head home. I'm tired and hungry. What do you have in the refrigerator for me to eat, Michelle?"

"Don't know! I think there are some leftovers from the food Keith bought."

"Nah, I want something fresh. Hey, I know!"

"Before you even part your lips, Karen, I'm not going to any fast food place and order a hamburger!"

"Dag, Michelle!" Karen said with a laugh. "Well, let's get a sub!" Michelle looked and nodded in agreement.

The two friends talked as they walked back to Michelle's house. They arrived to find Joe and Keith sitting on the front porch laughing and drinking soda.

"Well Keith," Joe said out loud, "look what the wind blew in! I thought you were supposed to be resting young lady?" Joe said to his wife, Michelle. "Our children are in the house. I think they are waiting for you two to get the key to Karen's house."

The two women walked up on the porch. Both went over to their man and gave them a kiss and then proceeded into the house.

"Hey Karen! Where's the key to your house?" Alice yelled out.

"Wait a minute! Don't you see your mother standing here?" Karen snapped back.

"It's okay, Karen," Michelle said. "I'm used to it. They don't mean any harm. I think they are anxious to get to your house and swim in that large pool you have."

"I'm not," Suzy said. "To be truthful, I'd rather stay here with you, mom."

"Awww, sweetie! I'm fine. You go with your brother and make sure he doesn't drown!" Michelle said with a giggle.

"Nana, can I stay here with you and Karen and Papa?"

"Next weekend, okay?" Michelle said to her granddaughter. "Where's Thomas anyway?" Michelle said looking around to see if she could spot him somewhere.

"He's in the bathroom taking a shower and changing," Alice spoke.

"Mom, I'm hungry!" Suzy moaned.

"Me too!" said Alice and Angel at the same time.

"Look, I have plenty of food in my house. Here's the keys. Go and tear it up if you all want," Karen said smiling at Michelle's grown children.

"Thanks Aunt Karen!" they answered back while Suzy reached for the keys. They had gotten used to calling Michelle's best friend, Aunt. They all loved her as if she was blood related.

As they were leaving, they gave their mother a hug and kiss and yelled for Thomas who came running into the living room where they all stood.

"Hey mom! Love you," he said and gave her a hug and kiss also.

Michelle stood and watched her children exit the house and drive away. She smiled and thought to herself, *That's my family whom I love unconditionally.*

~Little Girl~

Little Girl laid in her bed staring into space. Her procedure (abortion) ten hours ago left her in pain. Little Girl hadn't any more pain pills and the doctor refused to fill her prescription again. She laid there allowing herself to reach into her storage in her mind and pull out some of her past events. She had come so far and through so much. *Why am I still alive?* she asked herself. *For what purpose could I be to anyone?* So, after going over some of her events of the past, she stored them back into her storage space in her mind and heart. *Maybe I should call my Aunt Sue,* she thought to herself. And with that thought, she got up and went into the kitchen to use the phone.

She listened to the ringing on the other end of the phone and wondered if her aunt would pick up. She suddenly heard her aunt's voice.

"Hello!" her aunt said.

"Aunt Sue, this is Little Girl. I just wanted to call you and hear your voice."

"Hi baby!" Aunt Sue answered back. "Is everything alright?"

"Yes!" Little Girl said, lying to her Aunt. "Can I come tomorrow and meet you and the rest of my family? I want to get away from here for a while."

"Oh, my goodness! Of course, you can. Are you coming by bus or flying?"

"I'm going to come by bus," answered Little Girl.

"Well young lady, you just call me back with the time your bus arrives, and I will be there at the bus terminal to pick you up. I'll have your younger sister and brother with me, okay," Aunt Sue said.

Little Girl hung the phone up and went straight into James' room to tell him she was leaving tomorrow to meet her real family. After talking over the arrangements with James. He went into his closet, pulled a suitcase, and a small carrying bag.

"You can use this to pack," he said to her. "And Little Girl, I want to let you know that you always have a place here to come back to. Also, I want you to do something, not for me, but for yourself. I want you to read the Bible. I read the Bible every night and I also pray. I believe God has plans for you."

Little Girl looked at James with a shock on her face. "You read the Bible? Why? I knew this girl who lives in North Carolina who reads and prays a lot," Little Girl said while looking straight into James' eyes. Little Girl never noticed his eyes. His eyes were like a comfort in them. "Okay, James," she answered back. "Now I have to go and pack. Are you going to call the bus terminal?" Little Girl said while starting to feel anxious. "What am I going to say to these people when I get there? How am I supposed to act? James, I'm getting nervous already and haven't left yet."

James reached out his hand and took Little Girl's hand into his. "Listen, you just be yourself. You are a special person with a lot of love to give others. I know what I am talking about," James said to her. "Now, close your eyes; I'm going to pray."

After James prayed, Little Girl asked James. "Can I ask you something, James? Why do you run a pool hall and run numbers?"

"Little Girl, I prayed to God to deliver me from all my sins. You don't know this but when I leave here and tell you I'm going to the pool hall, I've been going there to get things in order to close down the place. I've bought a little store not far from here that I plan on opening up sometime next year. I will be selling candy, a few groceries, and other little items people will need."

"That's wonderful, James," Little Girl said with a smile. "Maybe I'll come back and help you run it if that's okay with you."

James laughed and just simply said, "It would be a pleasure to have you help me," he answered. James kept his smile while looking into Little Girl's eyes. For the first time, he noticed she had the eyes of a little girl. Somewhere in that grown up body, there was still a little girl hidden. James' heart felt a compassion for her.

"Okay," Little Girl spoke, "now I have to go and pack while you make the phone call for my ticket to Virginia."

~Michelle and Karen~

Joe and Keith walked into the house once the children drove off.

"So, what are you two ladies up to?" asked Keith.

"Well, Michelle and I are headed to the sub store to buy something to eat."

"Hey, you don't want anything from the restaurant?" Keith asked.

"Nah, honey," Karen responded.

"We are going to the sub store. Would you two like us to bring you a sub back?"

"Nope!" Joe said. "We will finish what's in the refrigerator."

"Very well," answered Karen, "see you two in a little while."

"Come on, Michelle," Karen said, "let's take my car."

The two women headed out the driveway when Karen boldly came out and asked Michelle, "The story about Little Girl, is that you? Are you talking about yourself and if so, why now? Why have you decided to talk about her after all these years of knowing you?"

Michelle smiled at her friend and responded with, "Karen you are too nosey but since you keep on insisting on wanting to know, I will tell you this much. I know Little Girl."

Karen's face turned red with anger. "I KNOW YOU KNOW HER!" Karen yelled.

Michelle calmly looked at her friend, "Karen, there is no need for you to raise your voice at me. I have my reasons, so please respect them and just listen when I tell you about Little Girl.

"Anyway, there is something I wanted to ask you. I want to go back to work, Karen."

"You what?" Karen asked.

"Yes, I want to go back to work. I want something to do. Plus, I want to help Joe out with the bills. I also want to save. There's one place I want to visit before I leave this world."

"Where's that?" Karen asked.

"I want to visit Jerusalem."

"Wow!" Karen said, "That would be nice. I would love to go with you. Now that's a place worth going to. You think Joe would mind you going to another country without him?"

"Who said I was going to go without him? I would love for him to go with me. We just have to save and save."

"I'll tell you what, Michelle, why not us four: you, Joe, Keith, and me? Yeah Michelle, let's start making plans for that trip."

"Deal," Michelle said back to her friend.

"Karen, you are my family. I just want you to know that. You are not just my best friend, but you are my sister also."

"Yeah, I feel the same for you too, Michelle. JERUSALEM, here we come!" YELLED Karen. "Oh, Michelle, I'm excited already. Just to be where Jesus and His disciples and all the prophets walked!"

"Oh my goodness, I know, Karen. I know." answered Michelle. "You know, Karen, when I look at this world, it makes me so sad at times. I see women cursing like sailors, children cursing and disrespecting their elders and parents, men and young boys lusting after the flesh and women also lusting. It's such chaos in this world. Sometimes, when I go into prayer, I cry for this world."

"Michelle, listen to me," Karen spoke. "All we can do is pray for people, walk with our Lord, and live according to His law for He loves us all. He hates the sin."

Michelle turned and looked at Karen with a wide grin, "Listen to you, girl!" Michelle said. "I'm proud of you. You have been studying your Word and listening with your heart. I'm happy for you, Karen, that you are walking with God."

~Little Girl~

Little Girl stepped off the bus in Virginia. She was so nervous that her hands were shaking. She remembered before she left that she spoke with her Aunt Sue, giving her the arrival time of the bus and what she should would be wearing. Her Aunt Sue also told Little Girl she would be wearing a blue hat.

Little Girl walked into the terminal. It was two o'clock in the afternoon and she was tired from sitting so long. Then out of the crowd, she heard a voice calling, "LITTLE GIRL! LITTLE GIRL!" Little Girl turned and saw a tall beautiful brown skinned woman standing right there.

"Oh, dear Lord, look at you! You are a young woman! Come here and give your Aunt Sue a hug!"

Little Girl did not like to be hugged; it was too close of body contact for her but she didn't want her Aunt to feel some kind of way so she let her aunt give her a tight hug and a kiss on the cheek. When she looked at her aunt, her Aunt Sue was crying.

"I'm sorry, baby," Aunt Sue said. "It's just so wonderful to see you. Oh, come let's walk over and get your bags and head to the house. Everyone is there waiting to meet you."

Aunt Sue and Little Girl retrieved the luggage, headed to the parking lot, and into Aunt Sue's car. Aunt Sue began talking a mile a minute.

"So, Little Girl, are you excited about meeting your family?"

"Yes, I am," answered Little Girl. "I'm just a little nervous; that's all."

"You should be twenty soon. Is that correct?" her Aunt asked.

"Yes, in about a month, August the 18th to be exact," Little Girl spoke.

"Well, here we are," Aunt Sue said as she pulled into a long driveway.

Little Girl looked out the window from the car. There stood a lot of people on the porch and walking in and out the house. She also heard someone yell, "THEY'RE HERE, EVERYONE!!!"

Aunt Sue got out and opened Little Girl's door. "Come on, honey! This is your family. Your flesh and blood family."

Little Girl stood outside the car frozen in her steps then a young girl with long silky hair walked up to her and just hugged her.

"Hi, I'm your baby sister, Debbie."

Then, a younger boy also walked over to her and just said, "Hi, I'm your brother, Kevin."

Little Girl smiled and began to cry. Her tears began falling fast and hard. Aunt Sue rushed over and put her arm around her.

"There, there honey! You come with me."

She took Little Girl, passed everyone, and walked her straight into the house, up the stairs, and into a very large bedroom.

"This will be your room. I will have your sister and brother bring you your things and I want you to wash up and change into something comfortable."

Fifteen minutes went by when Little Girl heard the sound of footsteps on the stairs. (The stairs had no carpet).

"Can we come in? It's your sister and brother, Debbie and Kevin."

"Please come in," answered back Little Girl.

The three sat on the bed and began talking. Debbie asked a ton of questions while Kevin talked about his football games and his friends. An hour and half had gone by.

"Let's go down and meet the rest of our family," Kevin suggested.

"Alright, but I am nervous. Do you think they will like me?" Little Girl asked.

"They better!" Debbie answered. "I know Kevin and I like you already."

Little Girl looked at her younger sister and asked. How old are you?"

"Oh, she's fifteen," Kevin blurted out.

"Shup up, stupid! She asked me, not you. I'm fifteen," Debbie said calmly turning back and looking at her big sister (Little Girl).

"And how old are you, Kevin?"

"Oh, he's just fourteen."

"Am not," Kevin yelled back at Debbie. "I am fourteen and a half. Our birthdays are coming up in two weeks?"

"Will you be here for them?" Debbie asked anxiously.

"I hope so," Little Girl responded back. "Now, let's go downstairs so I can meet everyone else," she said to her younger siblings.

~Michelle and Karen~

"So, what kind of work are you interested in doing, Michelle?"

"I don't know, Karen. Maybe something light, that isn't so stressful. You have any ideas?"

"Why not work at a retirement home? You like feeding people, so why not see if you can get a position in dietary? You know, working in the kitchen and serving room trays. I know someone who runs a retirement place. He's the director. He and I went to college together. I could put in a word for you, but you would still have to fill out all the paper work," Karen said to Michelle.

"Oh, would you, Karen? I would truly be so grateful and appreciative if you did that."

"Very well then, I will call him first thing in the morning," Karen said smiling back at her friend, Michelle. "Now can we order our subs?"

"Yeah, I guess we can," Michelle said.

After ordering their sandwiches, the women decided to eat there instead of driving home to eat.

"Come on, let's sit at the table near the window," Karen suggested.

As they sat and ate their subs, Karen said, "Michelle, let me ask you a question."

"Sure Karen, what is it?"

"Do you think you are healthy enough to go to work?"

"Sure Karen, I do. I am not claiming any sickness."

"Michelle, it's been only a few weeks since your surgery and how is Joe going to feel about you going to work?"

"Karen, my husband will stand behind me on most of the decisions I make. I believe he will agree with this. I mean, it will get me out the house and it won't hurt to have some extra income coming in with these bills we are trying to pay off."

"Okay sweetie, if you say so. I was just concerned, that's all. I want you to be happy, Michelle, really I do."

"Now, can you tell me a little more of the story of Little Girl? Since she went home to meet her family, did they all accept her?"

"Karen, most of them did. I mean her grandmother loved her so much and so did her Aunt Sue, her siblings, and most of her cousins, but you know there's always a few in the crowd that carry negative attitudes."

Karen let out a laugh. "Yeah, I had a few of them on my job I resigned from.

"So, how long did she stay there?"

Michelle smiled at her friend. "Little Girl stayed in Virginia a few years.

In fact, she met a young man there she liked. He was about three to five years older than her, though. He also didn't live in the city part of Virginia. He lived more in the mountain part, in a small town. If I can remember, it was called Orangetown."

"Orangetown!" Karen repeated the name.

"Yeah, it was a nice peaceful place. No hustle and bustle of so many people going here and there. You knew your neighbors who lived either up the road or down the road. There was a church that sat up the road. Most of the people in the town attended that church. Karen, it was a nice place, according to what Little Girl said."

Karen listened to every word Michelle was saying. "When was the last time you spoke with Little Girl?" Karen asked.

"Dag, Karen! Do you have to always put up your nosey radar every time I tell you this story?" Michelle said while laughing at her friend.

"Whatever, Michelle! I want to know so just tell me."

"Okay, Karen. I will tell you… NOT!" Michelle said bursting out in a loud laugh.

"Whatever!" Just tell me what else happened! Did she find the love her heart ached and longed for through her own family?"

"Karen, she didn't. I think she had so much stuff inside that she didn't know how to accept or really know what real love was. I can say she liked and enjoyed Virginia. She had made a few friends, but she would buy friends. She would do that by agreeing with whatever they said even if in her heart she didn't believe in what they said or did.

"There was a time when she started taking speed. She had taken so much that when she came down off of them, she crashed so hard, she admitted herself into the mental hospital for depression. Her younger sister, Debbie, walked with her early in the morning to the hospital and Debbie would go and see her every day. Debbie had become her best friend at that time. The two sisters would sit and talk until the sun rose in the morning, smoking cigarettes together. Debbie would stretch out across the living room floor and tell stories about their real mother. Some were very disturbing to Little Girl.

"Kevin, her brother, would go to the movies with her. Kevin was doing his own thing like most boys at that age."

"Michelle, where was her Aunt Sue all this time?" Karen asked

"She no longer lived with her Aunt. By now, Little Girl was living with her grandmother with her sister, Debbie, and her brother, Kevin, who lived on the steep hill.

"Little Girl felt a sense of freedom within herself. She just didn't realize she needed to find a job. Her family wasn't going to just watch her run up and down the hill every day and do nothing with her life. So, she signed up for a summer job that her Aunt Sue helped her get.

"She got a job with the Sheriff's Department sorting personnel and property taxes. The pay wasn't much but it was exciting for her."

"So, did Little Girl decide to live there for good?" Karen asked.

"Nope! I think Little Girl felt like she didn't belong there. I mean, she would watch her family sit around and talk about things that they had done together, things that happened years ago. Everyone would laugh about the things in the past or even argue over who was right about this or that, and all Little Girl could do was smile and maybe laugh at something that she thought was funny to her but still, she had not found whatever kind of love she was looking for."

"Well, I don't understand," Karen said to Michelle while still chewing on her sandwich. "If Little Girl so desperately wanted to meet her family, didn't she realize that they had a past that did not include her?"

"I don't think so, Karen.

"Look, let's head out of here and I'll tell you the rest when we get back to the house. I'm sure Joe and Keith are wondering how long it will be before we return."

Both ladies headed to the car and began driving home. As they reached the driveway, to their surprise Joe and Keith were still sitting in the same spot they left them at.

Michelle exited the car and walked over to her husband.

"Joe, I'm tired," she said. "I don't feel very well."

Joe then jumped to his feet, grabbed his wife's hand, and walked her into her bedroom.

"What's wrong?" he asked.

"I don't know Joe!" Michelle said as she sat on the edge of her bed. "I think I just need to take my medicine and maybe rest for a while."

Joe helped his wife take off her shoes and clothes and put on her night clothes. Then, he covered her up and closed the door behind him. Joe then walked out to the porch where Keith and Karen were sitting and talking.

"What happened to her?" Joe asked Karen as he returned to the seat he had been sitting.

"I don't know," Karen said to him. "She didn't tell me she wasn't feeling well. We were just sitting and talking about the story of Little Girl then she wanted to come home."

"Karen, I think you two need to give that story a rest for a while."

"Joe, she wasn't upset or crying when she was telling the story this time."

"Karen, what is it? I just don't understand you and this story. Why are you so interested in this story?"

"Let me tell you something. I think I have already said this to you. I strongly believe Michelle is talking about herself and she has held all this in for so long and is ready to let it out."

"Karen, I love you honey so much," Keith said to her, "but please be quiet now."

"KEITH!!" Karen yelled putting both hands on her hip. "Well, I'll just go inside and check in on Michelle if that's okay with you both."

"Oh no you don't," Joe said. "You stay yourself out here with us.

"Now talk to me about this marriage Keith has been telling me about. I think you two should go away and get married, come back, and we all go on a nice vacation. How does that sound?"

Karen looked at Joe and waved her hand in the air. "Really Joe! What marriage? And what do you think your wife will have to say about that? You know she would want to be there!"

"Karen, I think if she knows you are happy, she will be happy for you. Plus, I don't want to put too much on her."

"Joe, I'm not getting married tomorrow, you know. Keith and I need to plan. Right Keith?" Karen asked, looking Keith straight in his eyes with the hope he said, *no* to making plans.

Keith stood up, walked over to Karen, took her hand, and said, "Karen, I want to marry you tomorrow, sweetheart." Then he took out a very large diamond and slipped it on her finger. Karen suddenly jumped up, wrapped her arms around Keith, and let out such a scream. She screamed so loud Michelle came running to the front door asking "What's wrong? What happened?"

"Nothing honey," Joe answered his wife. "It's just that Keith and Karen are going to be married tomorrow." Michelle let out a scream of her own, threw open the screen door, and ran up to Keith, bypassing Karen, giving Keith a big hug.

"I am so happy, Keith. I'm so happy Karen has a man of God!" Then, she turned to Karen, snatched her arm, and dragged her into the house.

"Well, Keith," Joe looked at him, "welcome truly to this nutty but loving family, man. Now those two, I'm gonna tell you! All I can say is

Watch Out! They are thick together, okay!"

"Gotcha!" Keith said back. "Come on, Joe. Ride with me to the restaurant. I need to check in and see what's happening."

"Alright, I need to stretch my legs anyway," Joe said with a yawn and a long stretch of his arms while standing up.

Family

There are times we may disagree.

Will someone wash the dishes?

Clean up this room!

Stop fussing with one another!

I want... Please, can you buy me...

You hit your brother!

You hid your sister's dolls!

You don't like what mama cooked!

Mama burnt the dinner!

Daddy's working late.

You don't want to get up for school.

Do we have to go to the dentist, daddy?

Mommy, my stomach hurts.

Where's your father?

He's fixing the car.

Did someone feed and walk the dog?

Where's your mother?

She went shopping.

Time to go to church.

Mama's praying.

Mamas' reading the bible.

Mama's telling grandchild the story of Jesus.

Daddy's praying.

Mama and daddy are praying again.

Mama and daddy are praying and thanking God

For our family....

Family does not always have to be blood related. Family is a group of people who come together that share one another's love from within. They can be a blood-related brother, sister, mother, father, grandchildren. A spiritual family birthed from those walking with God, teaching one another about God's law, His glory, praising God, holding one another up in times of trouble, and praying together.

What does Jesus say about family?

Ephesians 5:21, "For this reason, I bow my knees before the Father, from whom every family in heaven and on earth is named."

Psalm 133:1, "A song of ascents. Of David. Behold, how good and pleasant it is when brothers dwell in unity."

1 John 4:7, "Beloved, let us love one another, for love is from God, and whoever loves has been born of God and knows God."

John 17:21, "That they may all be one, just as you Father, are in me, and I in you, that they also may be in us, so that the world may believe that you have sent me."

Author's Own Thoughts:

Embrace your family with love, the love that comes from your heart where our Lord lives. Family does not always have to be blood. Some have no blood relatives in their lives. Reach out, embrace, and become a family to those in need of love, of god's love, for that is where true love comes from. Thank our Lord every day for being a Father to all. Amen in Jesus name

10

A MAZE

~Little Girl~

Little Girl sat on her grandmother's porch waiting for her guy friend to show up and take her to his cousin's house. Lately, she's been visiting with him and a few other people her age. She noticed something about herself. She was falling for this guy. He had such a mild and gentle tone in his voice.

"LITTLE GIRL!!! LITTLE GIRL!!!" quickly her thoughts were interrupted with her grandmother's tiny little voice. "Come here, child," she heard next. "There is someone on the phone who wants to speak with you."

"Okay, grandma. I'm coming," she answered back.

Little Girl went into the living room and picked up the phone. "Hello," she said into it.

"Hello, Little Girl," the voice spoke back, "this is your mother." Little Girl froze. She couldn't sit or speak. "Hello," said the voice again. Still Little Girl said nothing. "Are you there?" came the voice once again.

"Yes, I'm here," Little Girl heard the words coming from her own mouth but felt like it was coming from someone else.

"Hi, I'm your mother. It's good to hear your voice. How are you doing?"

"I'm fine," answered Little Girl.

"You don't know what to say and that's okay," said the woman who just sent Little Girl into mental shock. The woman's voice sounded sophisticated. "I'm calling to ask if you would like to come and live with me here in Arizona? You think about it for a while and I will call mama back. We have so much catching up to do and I know you want to ask a lot of questions. So, remember mama loves you, okay?" Then, the woman hung up.

Little Girl sat on the couch. Who was this woman who just called and said she was her real mother? Who was this woman who wasn't saying much about anything and wanted her to come live with her and had the nerve to say, *I love you*? Little Girl just sat wondering... How does she look? Why didn't her mother talk more to her? Why didn't the woman ask more questions about Little Girl's life? What was her full name? Question after question filled Little Girl's mind.

Little Girl called to her grandmother. "Grandma, can I talk to you?"

"Sure, baby I'm coming."

Little Girl's grandmother came in and sat in her favorite chair, crossing her hands and placing them on her lap. Looking at her granddaughter, before Little Girl could speak, she said, "I know that was your mother. Did she talk long with you?"

"No," Little Girl answered back. "She wants me to come and live with her. Grandma, I don't know her. I want to go and then, I don't want to go. I'm scared to go."

"Child, let me say something. That is my daughter and I love her. She is also your mother. Maybe it's time you two meet."

"Grandma, should I go? Please tell me if I should go."

"I can't do that, baby. This is a choice you have to make on your own. Pray about it, okay, baby. Baby, you can always come back home here, alright."

As Grandma and Little Girl talked, there was a knock on the door. Little Girl rose and went to the door. It was the guy friend she was waiting on.

"Hi," she said. "Be back later, Grandma," she yelled over her shoulder.

"Alright, baby, be safe," her grandmother answered back.

"Are you okay?" her guy friend asked while they walked to his car.

"Yeah! Why do you ask?" she answered.

"You look a little upset."

"I'm fine."

"So, you want to go to my cousin's house or to the movies?" her friend asked.

"I think I'd rather go to the movies."

~Michelle and Karen~

"Michelle, why didn't you tell me you weren't feeling well at the restaurant?"

"Karen, because you would have made a big deal out of it. I was just a little tired, that's all."

"OOOOHHH, MICHELLE, you're lying! Girl, you should be aaasshhhaammmeeedd of yourself, lying to your best friend."

"Karen, be quiet about how I am feeling and let's talk about your marriage tomorrow. I'm excited and happy for you. Now, you can spend your time taking care of Keith instead of worrying about me all the time. And I am not lying about how I was feeling, I was tired."

"Whatever," Karen said while smiling with love in her heart at her best friend.

"Okay, let's change the subject. Getting back to me and getting married tomorrow. Girl, I do not have a thing to wear and I don't know what to wear. What color should I wear?"

"Karen, sweetie, wear what you want. Come on, let's go and look in my closet."

"Hey, isn't that your house phone ringing?" Karen asked Michelle.

"Yeah, I guess it is."

Michelle walked into her bedroom and picked up the phone.

"Hello," she whispered.

"Hey sis! How are you?" she said into the phone.

Karen walked into the bedroom and started looking into Michelle's clothes closet while Michelle talked with her sister on the phone.

"Hey sis! Yeah! I'm doing good. You know, I won't complain. My Lord has me covered. I was talking with Karen who by the way, you won't believe this, is getting married tomorrow! Yep! That's what I said, tomorrow."

Karen turned around, looked at Michelle, and whispered, "Ask your sister which colors I should wear."

"How do you know this is my sister?" Michelle whispered back to Karen.

"Because I'm nosey when it comes to you!" laughed Karen.

Michelle went back talking with her sister, ignoring anything Karen had to say.

"So, how's everything with baby sis going?"

Michelle heard her middle sister, Angie, respond on the other end of the phone with, "She's not doing so well. She just got back out the hospital, but Reggie is there with her. He decided to take a week off from work and stay with her since her nurse only comes once a week."

"Dag Angie!" Michelle said as she reached for her Bible and placed it on her lap.

Karen turned from the closet and looked over at Michelle and whispered, "What's wrong?" Michelle placed her fingers against her lips to motion Karen to be quiet.

"So, what are the doctors saying?" Michelle asked her sister.

"They say there's nothing else that can be done. Only to make her comfortable and continue to keep giving her medications," Michelle's sister answered back.

"What do you think, Angie?"

"Michelle, I think we need to make it down there soon."

"Yeah, you're right," Michelle answered back. "I'm going to start making arrangements. Let me talk with Joe and see what a good time for us would be to drive.

"If you come down here, Angie, we both can drive together. This way Joe wouldn't have to take off from work."

"That sounds like a plan," Angie said. "Let me check out a few things with school and work then we can see what's up."

"Okay," Michelle said.

"Tell Karen I said congrats on her wedding and I will talk to you later."

"Okay then, love you too," Michelle responded and hung the phone up.

"Everything okay?" Karen asked as she sat on the bed where she had thrown a few items of clothing from Michelle's closet while Michelle was talking on the phone.

Michelle turned towards Karen and simply said, "I give everything and all things to our Lord, Jesus Christ. Whatever God's will is, it will be done."

~Little Girl~

Little Girl's guy friend dropped her off back at her grandmother's house after the movies. *He's really nice*, she thought to herself. As she entered the house, her younger sister was sitting, reading a book. Her younger brother, Kevin, was watching wrestling on the TV.

"Hey, where's grandma?" Little Girl asked her sister, Debbie.

"She's over Aunt Sue's," answered Kevin. "Grandma left your dinner in the oven. Grandma said Mama called and spoke with you. Are you going to live with her?" Kevin asked, not taking his eyes off the TV.

"I don't know yet. I have to give it some thought," Little Girl answered while removing her dinner from the oven. She wasn't hungry. She and her guy friend went out to eat after the movie, but she didn't want to waste her grandmother's food. Sitting on the couch next to Debbie, she began to eat.

"Debbie, tell me more about our mother?"

"I don't know anything else to tell you," Debbie responded as she picked her head up from the book she was so engulfed in. "I'm glad I'm here with grandma."

"What about you, Kevin?" Little Girl asked her brother.

Kevin just shrugged his shoulders. "She's our mother," was all he said.

Little Girl stopped asking, finished her dinner and then walked onto the front porch. *I don't know which way to go*, she thought to herself. *Every time I try something different, I bump into a wall. What do I do?* She found herself talking aloud.

Grandma told me to pray. I don't know how to pray. She continued thinking to herself. *Why would God want me anyway?* So, she pushed that thought away. Looking down the hill, she saw car lights heading up the hill in her direction. *Must be Aunt Sue bringing grandma home,* she thought. She kept her eyes on the car lights until the car was in front of the small house.

"Hello, Grandma! Hello, Aunt Sue!"

"Hi, baby!" Aunt Sue said walking her mother (grandma) into the house. In a few minutes, Aunt Sue was back outside, finding a chair, and sitting next to Little Girl. "So, I hear my sister, your mother, asked you to come and live with her. Are you thinking about going?"

"Aunt Sue, can I have one of your cigarettes?"

Aunt Sue handed Little Girl a cigarette. "Aunt Sue, I think I will go to Arizona. I don't know if I will stay."

"Well, if you don't stay, you can always come back here. So, when do you plan on leaving?"

"Aunt Sue, I would like to leave this weekend."

"Well, Little Girl, you had better get to calling your mother now and let your grandmother know your plans."

~Michelle, Karen, Angie, Joe and Keith~

Michelle stood by her sister, Angie, as they both viewed their younger sister's body.

"Angie, why? Why did I wait so long to make my yearly visit to see her? Now it's too late. I know this is God's will. Our place here on earth is only temporary and then we're gone."

"Come on Michelle, everyone is waiting for us. We are all gathering together at the restaurant down the street from here."

"You go on, Angie. I'll be there in a minute."

"You want me to send Karen in here with you?"

"No, let her stay out there with Joe and Keith."

"Okay sis," Angie gave her oldest sister a hug. "Don't be too long okay?"

"I won't, Ang," Michelle said in a whisper while wiping the tears from her eyes.

Michelle just stood there looking down at her youngest sister.

"Sweetie," she whispered to her. "You are no longer in any pain. God says there will be no more pain. No more tears. No more hurt. I see the smile on your face. I'm going to tell you goodbye for now, but I will see you in His glory in heaven. I'm missing you already. I love you so very much. I thank our Lord for blessing me with a sister like you."

Michelle then gave her sister a kiss on the forehead, turned around, and headed alone outside to where the others were waiting on her. Her thoughts began to race. *When will the time be right to tell Karen the truth? I feel so alone. I know You're up there, God, and You're with me always. I just feel alone right now. I don't understand this feeling. It's a familiar feeling that has risen in me.*

Michelle walked outside and walked up to Joe.

"Joe, I want to go back to the hotel room and lay down. I want to be alone. Is that alright with you?"

"Sure, Michelle," Joe said to his wife. "Come on, let's go."

"Michelle?" Karen whispered her name then took Michelle's hand and squeezed it. "I'm so sorry, sweetie. Keith and I will go with everyone else to the restaurant. Joe, you will meet us there? Wont you?"

"Yeah, I'll be there shortly."

"Did you want to tell Angie and everyone else you won't be going with them?" Joe asked his wife.

"No, Joe. I just want to leave now."

Joe and his wife, Michelle, rode back to the hotel in silence. Michelle's thoughts were on pain. The pain she was presently feeling and yet there is a peace within her. *God,* she started talking to the Lord in her spirit, *I don't understand this pain. I feel peace and strength, yet I feel like I'm in a maze. I can't seem to find my way out. My children are saddened by their aunt's passing. My husband is staying strong as usual. I just can't find where I am inside right now.* As Michelle thoughts continued, Joe pulled up to the hotel. As they entered into the hotel room, he helped his wife change into something comfortable and slowly pulled the blankets up on her. Then, he sat down on the bed beside her.

"Michelle, what's really going on, honey? For a while I've noticed you aren't really yourself. I know you and Karen are friends, the best of friends, but you're not telling even her what's really going on."

Looking at her husband with tears falling from her face. She just answered with, "I love you so much, Joe."

"I love you, too," Joe said. And for the very first time while looking into his wife's eyes he saw the face of a little girl.

Maze of Confusion

I turn to the left... Wrong way.

I turn to the right.. Go back.

Abba, Father, my Lord, my God,

Lead me on...lead me the way You want,

For my ways are the wrong ways...

So, I pray to You, Lord,

Put a lamp at my feet and a light in my path;

Fire by night,

Cloud by day,

Then I'll know I'm going the right way.

Confusion: A lack of clearness or distinctness. Bewilderment. The state of being confused.

What does Jesus say about confusion?

1 Corinthians 14:33, "For God is not the author of confusion, but of peace.

The enemy tries to weaken or hinder by getting us confused or doubleminded.

James 1:8, "A double minded man is unstable in all his ways."

James 3:16, "For where envying and strife is, there is confusion and every evil work."

Psalm 71:1, "In thee, O, Lord, do I put my trust: let me never be put to confusion."

11

STRENGTH

Little Girl stepped off the train carrying only a small traveling bag. Her plans were not to stay long in Arizona. Looking around and feeling the Arizona heat, she took off the wind breaker she was wearing. *Now,* she whispered to herself, *where is my mother?*

Little Girl felt a soft tap on her shoulder. Turning around she saw a beautiful brown skinned woman about five feet three inches. *She's gorgeous,* she thought to herself.

"Hi, Little Girl! I'm your mother!" Then she gave Little Girl a hug. Little Girl's body tensed up as her mother embraced her with a hug. After the few-second hug. Mother asked, "Is this the only bag you have?"

"Yes, it's the only one," Little Girl said back.

"Well, come! My car is parked over there." Mother pointed to the right. "So, Little Girl, look at you! You are all grown up!" she spoke as both walked towards where the car was parked. "Are you excited about meeting me, finally?"

Little Girl looked straight ahead and responded with, "Yes, and no, then I don't know. I just don't know. I don't know what to call you. I don't know how I feel about you yet."

"Well, I can understand that. Okay, here we are!"

"This is your car?" Little Girl said with a smile. "Wow! It's a convertible and it's purple! Wow!" she said again.

"Can you drive, Little Girl?" Mother asked.

"No, I always took the train or bus. *I didn't have the luxury of cars,*" Little Girl answered in a sarcastic tone.

Mother, noticing the tone of voice, ignored Little Girl's response and continued with, "Well, I'm going to have to teach you how to drive."

After placing Little Girl's bag in the back seat, they drove off.

"You don't talk much," Mother said while steering the car into a driveway after driving for thirty minutes. "We are here, my daughter," Mother spoke. "Come on, I want to introduce you to your oldest brother, Steve, and your brother, Marcus."

Little Girl felt excited. Looking at the house, she noticed it was average size with a bed of flowers running down the walkway and a few large cactus plants sitting on both sides of the front entrance.

Opening the front door, Mother yelled. "Boys!! Your sister is here."

Standing in the foyer, Little Girl started getting nervous. *What if they think I'm funny looking or not smart? What do I say to them?* she asked herself.

"Come here." Mother reached out and grabbed Little Girl's hand and guided her into the living room. "What is taking those boys so long? I'll be right back," Mother said. Little Girl just smiled, then turned and walked to the picture window and looked out.

While standing and gazing out of the window, Little Girl suddenly felt a soft tap on her shoulder. Turning to see who it was, there in front of her stood two men, one young man and one older man.

"Hey sis! Glad to meet you!" The younger one reached and gave her a hug. He hugged her so tight and long that the other smiled and made a joke. "You're skinny and cute!" Little Girl looked into her brother, Marcus', eyes. His eyes showed pain and loss. Her other brother, Steve, she just didn't know.

"So, Little Girl, you are what, twenty years old now?"

"Yes," she said back, "and how old are you, Steve?" she asked.

"I'm just a year older than you. Marcus is two years younger than you. So, are you here to stay or just visiting us?"

"I don't know yet," she said back.

"Well, follow me. I'm going to show you around the house and to the room you will be staying in."

"Where's Mother?" Little Girl asked as she followed both of her brothers down a long hallway.

"Oh, Mother's probably on the phone inviting her best friend, Kim, over to meet you or making plans for her trip to Mexico," Marcus answered.

"I just got here. Why is she planning to leave?"

"She planned this for a while now. Plus, she wasn't sure if you would come."

"But I did come, Marcus! Couldn't she just reschedule her trip for a later time?"

"Little Girl, you will get to know our Mother. That's all I can say right now.

"This is your room," Steve pointed towards a beautiful bedroom.

Little Girl entered into the room and look around. The room was painted white with yellow border running around the top the wall. A small chair sat in the corner. The dresser stood on the other side of the room which was white. And there was the nightstand which held a small lamp and beside it was a Bible. Little Girl thought to herself, *Everyone has a Bible. Why?*

"Okay, let's show her the back yard," Marcus said with excitement in his voice. So, the siblings walked through the kitchen and out the back door.

"This is nice," Little Girl smiled and said. "I like this. It's large and it has a gazebo. Oh, my goodness look! There's a water fountain." She walked over to it. "It has goldfish swimming in it. Do you guys come out here a lot?"

"Nope," said Marcus. "I'm the only one that spends a lot of time out here. Steve and Mother are hardly home. Plus, this is the third place we have lived in six months."

"Mother doesn't own this?" she asked.

Both brothers laughed. "Nope, she is renting this place from a friend of hers. She keeps saying she is going to buy a big house. I guess it's going to take some time."

~Joe~

Joe sat at the edge of the bed and watched his wife sleep. His spirit hurt for the woman lying there. He loved his wife so much. He remembered the day they met; how beautiful she was.

Joe began to pray to God. "Father, whatever is happening to my wife, please don't let her hurt anymore. She has been through so much in her life. Only You and only You can help me. God, I know I'm not like my wife. I don't talk to You all the time but by just watching her study Your word and listening to her when she thinks I don't, I learned so much about You. God, my wife loves You more than anything or anybody. Nothing comes before You with her, not even me or our children. So, please, she told me that You are the Creator of all creation and that through Your Son, Jesus Christ, who died and was risen our sins and our forgiveness. So, God I want to say I repent of my sins and truly ask for atonement for my sins. She once told me it isn't about me. It's about You, Your purpose, and will for me in my life. I don't know much. I can't even recite a scripture from Your book, the Bible. I just know that You love me and my wife. I don't know about this favor she talks about, but I see You must have favor on her because of all the battles she has been through and she is still here. She said to me one day that if I ask anything in Jesus' name, You will bless me. So, I am truly begging You in Your son's name who You sent down here. In Jesus' name, please heal whatever is ailing my wife. Comfort her from the loss of her baby sister in Jesus' name. Help me to be also a comfort to her in Jesus' name. I don't know Your plans for my wife. All I know is God, she is a good girl, and just between You and I, God, I don't think she has let totally go of some past hurts. God, I'm a grown man and right now I feel like a little child talking to his father. My wife told me that one must humble themselves before You. Is this why I feel like this?

"Father, I ask You to please give me strength, or as my wife always prays, anoint me with spiritual strength. Renew my mind, my heart, and spirit. Make me whole in You. Put a lamp at my feet and a light in my path like she would pray. God, she told me, we are all sinners saved by Your grace and mercy. Have mercy on me right now. She always says You're an awesome God. She told me once that Yeshua is Your Son's name, also. I want right now, Lord, what You gave her. I want to feel that peace also. I know she isn't perfect God. She can still at times get angry to the point where she feels like hitting but she doesn't. She cries instead. She says her flesh is battling with her spirit when she gets like that. Everything she says about You is Your word, right out of the Bible. She says that Your word said it's okay to get angry but sin not.

"I remember one day, I had gotten so mad at this young man for being rude to a lady and I could hear her words in my head, *What would Jesus do?* So, I handled the situation in a calm way. Jesus, You know her inside and out. She's said in Your word also that it reads, *We all were fearfully and wonderful made.* Lord, I pray all this to You in Jesus' name. I say Amen."

Joe stood up and noticed that he had tears flowing from his eyes like a running stream. He walked into the bathroom, looked into the mirror, and saw himself looking back at him. Joe then let out such a cry of release, that his legs went weak. He fell to his knees with his face bowed down towards the floor. It was then he felt this soft hand on his shoulder. Without getting up or picking up his head, he said in a soft whisper, "Michelle, honey, go back and lay down. I'm okay." But his wife said nothing. Joe picked his head up and turned around to speak again to his wife. She must have gone back to bed. He rose from the floor and peeked into the bedroom. Michelle was sound asleep in the same position she was laying in thirty minutes ago. Joe went back into the bathroom and looked around. Sitting on the corner of the tub, he whispered, "You heard me, God. Thank You from the very depths of my spirit. You are the truth. You heard my cry. You listened to my prayer. Me, God, someone who doesn't even read Your word, someone who doesn't take the time. You still heard me. You came and touched me. Wow, my Father, You love me too. This is what my wife meant when she said in Your word that it reads, *Come as you are. Confess your sins and open your hearts to receive Him."* Joe walked back to his wife sleeping and laid next to her. And he, too, fell asleep.

~Suzy, Angel, Alice, and Thomas~

Michelle's children sat with the rest of their relatives along with Karen and Keith at the restaurant.

"Hey Thomas!" Suzy whispered to her brother who was sitting next to her. "I want to go and see mama."

"Me too!" Alice said, trying to whisper also. "I want to go see mama also."

Angel said, "I wanna go see my Nana."

"Yeah, let's go."

"You think we should tell Karen?" Alice asked.

"No!" Thomas replied. All three of Michelle's children and her granddaughter who was now twelve years of age, got up from the table and without a word to any of their relatives, walked out of the restaurant.

"You wanna drive, Thomas?"

"Yeah, I'll drive."

"No, let me drive! Alice yelled. "You can drive when we start heading home."

"I'll let you drive for a while. Don't go racing again," Thomas said to his younger sister.

"Mommy?" Angel said asked, looking at her mother, Alice, and taking her hand. "What's wrong with Nana?" Alice held her daughter's hand and spoke in a low voice.

"Nana's sad because her sister died."

"I know that. I mean, she doesn't look happy too much anymore. No, I mean something is different about Nana. Mama! Mama! Did you hear me?"

"Yeah, Angel, I hear you."

"Can I buy Nana something?

"What do you want to buy Nana?"

"I don't know," Angel said. "Maybe a rose. Just one rose. I want to buy Nana a purple rose."

Alice looked down at her daughter while they all continued to walk to the car. "Dag, Thomas! How far did you park the car?" Alice yelled.

"It's not far," Thomas answered his sister, "so stop complaining."

"I'm not complaining; I have on heels and my feet are hurting."

"Mommy, I wanna buy Nana a flower, a purple flower."

"Okay, Angel." Suzy answered back. "Thomas, before we go to the hotel room, stop at the store so Angel can buy mama a flower."

"What store?" he said back to his sister.

"I don't know, Thomas! Find a Walmart."

So, after about five minutes of walking, the children finally reached the car. Off they drove in search of a purple flower for Angel to give her Nana.

Driving about twenty minutes, "Hey, there's a Walmart!" Suzy yelled.

Pulling up into the parking lot and parking, Angel jumped out the car with Alice right behind her.

"Hey, wait for me!" Suzy hollered at her daughter. "Thomas, are you coming?"

"Nah, I'll wait here but hurry up."

Thomas sat in the car. His thoughts were on his mother. Thomas loved his mother so much. He wished he could tell her everything that was going on in his life. He just thought his mother was just a little too sensitive about certain things. He, too, wondered what lately was going on with his mother. His father, Joe, hasn't told him or his sister anything lately. His dad always tells them everything that goes on with their mother. Thomas felt a weird feeling come over him that felt peaceful. *That's weird*, he thought. He thought to himself, *I wish my mother believed just how much I love her. I think she thinks I don't listen when she speaks or pay her any attention. Mama, if you only knew I value you so much. You are a one of a kind, mother. My friends say you are so down to earth. I forgive you, mama, for your past, being addicted to drugs and the things that happened.* Thomas' eyes began to well up with tears. "Mama, I love you," he said out loud.

"Hey, what's wrong with you, Thomas?" Suzy said as she, Angel, and Alice entered the car with one purple flower.

"We couldn't find a purple rose, Uncle Thomas!" Angel said to her uncle.

"I told her they don't have purple roses!" Alice said back.

"You did not, and I don't care; it's for my Nana!"

"Whatever!" Alice responded. "I think it's pretty anyway, okay!" Alice said while putting her arm around her niece.

Thomas started the car and drove off, headed towards the hotel where their mother and father were. After driving for a minute and parking once again, the children all got out of the car and walked to the hotel room.

Angel knocked hard on the door.

The door opened and there stood the daddy, Joe. "What are you all doing here? Why aren't you at the restaurant?"

"We wanted to see Mama," Suzy said.

"She's lying down, but awake."

Michelle looked over towards the door and saw her children. Seeing them brought such joy to her spirit.

"NANA! NANA! Look what I brought you!" Angel walked over to her Nana and handed her a purple flower. She knew purple was her Nana's favorite color.

"Thank you, my little Ladybug." Then her children all piled themselves on her bed.

"How are you feeling, mama?" Thomas asked.

"Oh, I'm blessed; can't complain. I'm saddened about my sister, but I have a peace within me knowing she's not in pain or struggling anymore."

"Told you she was going to say that," Alice said. "She always says she's blessed."

"That's because I am, Alice. Look around. I have a beautiful husband who loves and cares so much for me. I have three children who love me and a granddaughter who loves and cares for me also. I'm blessed, sweetie. What was it you once posted, Thomas, on your phone? *We may not be perfect, but we're perfect for one another.* You were so right," Michelle said. "Now where's Karen and Keith and my sister, Angie?"

"We left them with the rest of the family at the restaurant. We wanted to come and check on you, mama," Thomas said.

"Yeah," the rest of children spoke in agreement.

"Why, thank you all. Did anyone bring their mother anything to eat? I am so hungry now."

"There's an Arby's and Hardee's right down the street," Alice said. "I can drive there if you want. Can I Papa? Can I drive?"

Joe looked at his her with a soft smile on his face and kindly said, "No, sweetie! Suzy, you drive, okay?"

"What do you want mama?"

"I don't know yet. Let me think. I know what I want from Hardee's, a strawberry milkshake."

"Mama, that's your favorite shake. Why?" asked Alice.

"Never you mind, that's what I want. From Arby's, I want a turkey sandwich with everything on it. Joe, what do you want?"

"I'll have the same except for the strawberry shake; make mine vanilla. Now off you all go. Please don't be long," Joe asked his children.

"I'm going to stay here with my Nana," Angel said. "Nana, can I get in the bed with you?"

"Off course you can, sweetie."

Angel got in the bed and sat next to her Nana.

"Nana, can I ask you a question?"

"Sure. What's on your mind?"

"Why does Jesus let people die?"

"Come here closer to Nana." Angel laid her head on Nana's lap. "Sweetie, God loves us all. We are not meant to live here on earth forever. We are supposed to be preparing ourselves for the Kingdom of God. This is just temporary, in other words. We are just passing through, but while we are here, we must be obedient to God's words."

"Nana, is that why you read the Bible a lot and help people and pray a lot?"

"Yes, I love my Jesus, Angel."

"Me too, Nana. Nana?"

"Yes Angel."

"Can I take a nap with you?"

"Girl, go to sleep!" Joe's voice came from across the room with a soft laughter in his words.

"Papa, are you going to take a nap?"

"No, I am not. I am waiting for your mother and them to return so I can go back to the restaurant."

"You're leaving, Joe? Michelle asked.

"Yes honey, I think I need to go and let your sister, Angie, Karen, and Keith and the rest of your family know you are doing fine, that you're just resting."

"Okay, sweetie. I have the children here now. You don't have to wait for them to come back. You might as well leave now."

Joe walked over and gave his wife a kiss. "Honey, you have such inner strength, more than I think you even know," and headed out the door.

~Little Girl~

Little Girl walked around the yard with Marcus, looking at the flowers.

"Marcus, can I ask you a question?"

"Sure, what's up sis!"

"Are you happy here?"

"I'm here; that's all I want to say about that."

"Is Mother a nice person?"

"Little Girl, you are going to decide that on your own."

"She's very pretty, Marcus, and fancy. She seems high quality. You know what I mean?"

"Yeah, that she is, sis. I'm ready to go back in the house. You can stay out here if you want."

"Nah, I'm going with you."

Mother was standing at the door when the two headed inside the house.

"So, how do you like it so far, Little Girl?" Mother asked.

"It's very pretty. I also like the room I'll be staying in."

"That makes me happy," Mother said to her daughter. "Come darling, let's find something to eat or we can order out and have them deliver the food. What is it you like to eat?"

"I want a strawberry milkshake and a cheeseburger with fries."

"Oh, no, no, darling! You have to expand your mind. Try something you haven't been exposed to. How about some oysters, crab legs, or filet mignon?"

"Filet who?" Little girl asked.

Mother giggled. "It's steak, darling. Come on, I'm going to take you out to a very nice restaurant. You go put on your finest clothes."

"Are Marcus and Steve coming also?"

"Yes," answered Mother.

Little Girl went into her room to find something she might be able to wear. *These jeans might do. Now, to find a shirt.* Little Girl found a red tie die shirt. After showering and dressing, Little Girl walked into the living room where her two brothers and mother were waiting. She looked at her brothers who were dressed in slacks and sharply pressed shirts Mother was dressed in a dinner dress that was so beautiful with stunning shoes. When they looked at Little Girl, their mouths opened except for Marcus. He just smiled and took his sister's hand.

"Come on sis, you look great."

"Don't you have any dinner clothes?" Mother asked her.

Little Girl felt anger rise up inside herself. "No, I don't! Didn't have anyone to buy or teach me what to wear for going out to fancy restaurants."

"Let's go everyone," Mother said, once again ignoring Little Girl's sarcasm.

Arriving at the restaurant after confirming their reservation, they were seated and handed menus.

"Now, Little Girl, I want you to look at the menu. Notice there are no fries or hamburgers or even shakes. What is it you would like to try?" Mother asked.

Pointing to something on the menu, Little Girl asked, "What is this?"

Marcus looked on, "Thats..."

"Marcus, let her try to pronounce it herself," Mother said.

So Little Girl tried. "Scargoat, no, I mean exsgoat."

Marcus whispered in her ear, "It's *escargot*."

"What's that?" she asked him.

"That's snails."

"Ugh! I don't want that."

Mother put down her menu. "Little Girl, she said, "how old are you now, twenty right? You will be twenty-one in a few months. It's past time that you start learning about the finer things in life. I will order for you."

So, Mother ordered filet mignon and shrimp for Little Girl.

"She will also have a small glass of the house red wine," she told the waitress.

Little Girl thought to herself, *I don't want any wine*, but decided on not saying anything.

"You don't have to drink it," Steve said to her.

"Yes, she does! Just a sip," mother responded.

They all sat, eating in silence and when they were through, Mother excused herself and went to use the pay phone. When she returned, she smiled and asked, "Everyone ready to leave? I have to go out tonight and I need to go shopping and get myself ready. Marcus and Steve, I expect you two to look after your sister."

"Mother, she is not a baby," Marcus said.

"Just do as I wish. You can see she doesn't know much. You can see just by the way she dresses. It's not your fault, dear. I don't believe you're strong enough or smart enough yet to survive in the proper setting. Don't worry, Mother will teach you how. I watched when you ate your salad. You used the wrong fork."

Little Girl felt hurt behind those words. *How dare she think I can't take care of myself?* Those old feelings that were stashed in Little Girl's file in her mind came to surface. *So, she thinks I'm dumb, too.*

On the ride home, Little Girl said not a word. She just sat there feeling inadequate. Once arriving home, Little Girl said she was going to take a nap and went into her room. There alone she started to cry. *What's wrong with me?* she asked herself. She then turned her head in the direction of the table next to the bed. She turned on the light and without noticing what she was doing, picked up the Bible and started to read the words of Jesus.

Little Girl felt a protection for the first time in her life and with that, she made her mind up that this was not the place she was going live. She decided to go back to her grandmother and see the young man. She hadn't realized it then, but she fell in love with him.

~Michelle and Her Children~

"We're back!" shouted Michelle's children as they entered the room with their mother's food.

"Here's your shake, mama." Suzy handed her mother the food. "Angel fell asleep?"

"Yup, she sure did. She and I had a little talk about Jesus."

"Mama, I'm going to use the bathroom. I brought my clothes to change into," Suzy said.

"Go on, sweetie. Look in my bag, there you will find some towels, soap, and toothpaste."

"That's okay, mama. I bought my own."

Thomas and Alice sat on the other bed. Alice fell asleep while Thomas scrolled through his phone and ate his food. (Thomas was a vegetarian.) Michelle sat there smiling. Next to God, Jesus, and the Holy Spirit, she loved her children and husband. She then whispered, "I'm going to miss you so much, baby sister."

Suzy started her shower and began to pray. "God, mama doesn't think I pray, but You know I pray, maybe not often. I know I need to read my Bible more. God, You have protected this family through so much. Thank You, God, for my family. We are truly a family. I love my family." Suzy continued to talk to Jesus while in the shower.

"Jesus, does mama feel alone in this family? Does she feel like an outsider? We used to have Family Day. Even Angel wants Family Day back. What am I and Thomas doing that's so important that we can't put a day aside for family? Jesus, please, I ask You for the strength that You bless mama with for me also. Mama always tells us she not only loves us but likes us also. I think my mama is specially made from You. She's different from a lot of other mothers. Mama can be nosey about me and Thomas. God, I guess to her it's not really being nosey, it's being a mother who's concerned about her children and just wanting them to be safe and happy.

"We all know she wants us to go to church with her. Why don't we go? Lord, when I really think about what mama asks of us, it really isn't much. Wow God! Mama is really cool. I am blessed to have mama, daddy, my sister, and brother, and my special Angel, my daughter. God, why do people do this? Get caught up in all the stuff around them and not look at the blessings You have given us.

God, mama's been sick so many times, but this seems different. I don't know what's going on. My Auntie is dead now, her baby sister. I look at mama; I don't want You to take her anytime soon, God. God, it's like I feel something inside of me that I cannot explain the feeling. It's not a bad or disturbing feeling. Just don't know.. I know it's an unfamiliar feeling. God, You have changed mama. Mama has come a long way when she gave her life over to You. Thank You again, Jesus for loving mama and daddy and this, my family in Jesus name.

"Hey Suzy, did you drown?" It was Thomas waiting to use the bathroom. "Girl! I need to get in there."

"I'm getting out, Thomas," yelled Suzy.

Suzy walked out the bathroom ten minutes later.

"Dag girl, what took you so long?" asked Thomas while laughing and rushing into the bathroom.

"How are you feeling, mama?" Suzy asked while walking over and sitting on the side of her mothers' bed.

"I'm good, sweetie. You have a glow on your face and your eyes are red. Have you been crying, Suzy?"

"I'm okay, mama. Mama, when will we be headed back home?"

"Maybe tomorrow."

Looking down, Suzy noticed her mother only drank the strawberry shake but didn't eat the rest of her food.

"MAMA! Why didn't you eat? Thought you were hungry."

"I'm going to eat, just got full off the shake.

"So, Suzy how's business?"

"Mama, I've started designing leather bracelets and selling them."

"Wow, that sounds good, Suzy. How's that coming along?"

"I've made over two thousand dollars so far in just two weeks. They are selling fast, mama."

"Suzy, you are so gifted. I'm so proud of you. Make me one with Jesus' name on it. Can you do that?"

"Sure, mama."

In the middle of Michelle and Suzy talking, there was a knock on the door.

"I'll get it!" yelled Alice.

"I thought you were sleep," Suzy said.

"Nah, I was just laying here thinking about stuff."

Alice flew off the bed and darted towards the door. Opening the door, there was Michelle's sister, Angie, Joe, Karen, Keith and Michelle's cousins were also entering the room.

"Hey sis!" Angie said as she walked over towards Michelle. "How are you feeling? I bought you something to eat," handing Michelle a chicken salad and a large bottle of water. Michelle's cousins came over and gave her a hug. These were Michelle's favorite cousins out of her entire family.

Everyone gathered around in the room, finding anywhere to sit. Michelle and her sister sat talking while Karen talked with Michelle's cousins. Thomas, who made it out the bathroom, talked with Keith about his restaurant business and Joe sat laughing with Alice and Angel who finally woke up from her nap.

"Angie, I'm going to close my eyes now. I'm tired," Michelle said to her sister with a smile gleaming from her eyes.

Michelle looked around the room, closed her eyes, and let go. Michelle was surrounded by family and friends. The strength that was in that room was through God, Himself.

"But they that wait upon the Lord shall renew their strength; they shall mount up with wings as eagles; they shall run, and not be weary; and they shall walk, and not faint," Isaiah 40:31.

Joe retired from his job and spent most of his time relaxing with his new grandbaby and children and reading his Bible. Joe talks to his wife every night after praying.

Michelle's children became successful in their businesses and spend most of their spare time with their father, Joe.

Karen and Keith opened a young girls' center in memory of Michelle, something she always wanted. The center was named Christian Center for Little Girls.

Karen began a search on the details of Little Girl's truth.......... ????

ABOUT THE AUTHOR

Tracie M. Brown is a woman, raised in the foster care system, who has been through so many battles in her life. She battled the loss of her youngest sister and has overcome drug addiction through her faith in God. Based on a true story, this book gives details of her life and the real hard core struggle in today's world. It tells how "GOD" has changed things around in her life for the good of which she is still experiencing in her life today.

"I CAN DO ALL THINGS THROUGH CHRIST WHO STRENGTHENS ME," - Philippians 4:1.

Made in the USA
Columbia, SC
22 January 2024

29828661R00165